Praise for Kendel Lynn's Elliott Lisbon Mysteries

WHACK JOB

"Elli Lisbon is proving herself to be the most lovable OCD PI since Adrian Monk."

– Maddy Hunter,
Agatha-Nominated Author of the Passport to Peril Series

"A must-read mystery with a sassy sleuth, a Wonderland of quirky characters, and a fabulous island setting that will keep you turning pages."

– Riley Adams,
Author of the Memphis Barbecue Mysteries

"A great second entry in this delightfully amusing cozy mystery series...The mystery is well-conceived and keeps readers' attention until Elli can solve the case."

– *Fresh Fiction*

BOARD STIFF

"A solid and satisfying mystery, yes indeed, and the fabulous and funny Elliott Lisbon is a true gem! Engaging, clever and genuinely delightful."

– Hank Phillippi Ryan,
Agatha, Anthony and Macavity Award-Winning Author

"Kendel Lynn captures the flavor of the South, right down to the delightfully quirky characters in this clever new mystery series. Elli Lisbon is the Stephanie Plum of the South!"

– Krista Davis,
New York Times Bestselling Author of the Domestic Diva Mysteries

"A sparkling new voice in traditional mystery."
— CJ Lyons,
New York Times Bestselling Author

"A cross between an educated, upper class Stephanie Plum and a less neurotic Monk. Put this on your list for a great vacation read."
— Lynn Farris,
National Mystery Review Examiner at Examiner.com

"Packed with humor, romance, danger and adventure, this is a good mystery full of plot twists and turns, with red herrings a plenty and an ending that I found both surprising and satisfying."
— *Cozy Mystery Book Reviews*

"A mystery full of humor and the mannerisms unique to the South that combine into a fun-filled ride."
— *Kings River Life* Magazine

OTHER PEOPLE'S BAGGAGE

"A cozy triple-scoop that tastes divine...the pleasantly contrasting novellas make it easy to finish off a story in one sitting."
— *Library Journal*

"Lost luggage has never been this fun! With well-drawn characters, *Other People's Baggage* is your first class ticket to three fast-paced adventures full of mystery, murder, and magic."
— Elizabeth Craig,
Author of the Southern Quilting Series

"Kendel Lynn's *Switch Back* [*Other People's Baggage*] is a clever, entertaining mystery with small town flavor and Texas flair!"
— Debra Webb,
USA Today Bestselling Author

WHACK JOB

The Elliott Lisbon Mystery Series
by Kendel Lynn

<u>Novels</u>

BOARD STIFF (#1)
WHACK JOB (#2)
SWAN DIVE (#3)
(April 2015)

<u>Novellas</u>

SWITCH BACK
(in OTHER PEOPLE'S BAGGAGE)

AN ELLIOTT LISBON MYSTERY

WHACK JOB

Kendel Lynn

HENERY PRESS

WHACK JOB
An Elliott Lisbon Mystery
Part of the Henery Press Mystery Collection

First Edition
Trade paperback edition | May 2014

Henery Press
www.henerypress.com

ISBN-13: 978-1-940976-12-9

Printed in the United States of America

For Mom

ACKNOWLEDGMENTS

I'm a girl blessed with love and encouragement and support, and I'm so very grateful.

Thank you to Hank Phillippi Ryan, Mary Daheim, Elizabeth Craig, and Maddy Hunter.

Thank you to my Sisters in Crime Guppies and to all the chickens in the Hen House. Whether swimming in the pond or playing in the coop, you make this all possible.

Thank you to Art Molinares, for reminding me daily about the dream, and to Diane Vallere, a better friend I could not ask for.

ONE

A guy walks into a bar with a satchel full of cash in one hand and a banana in the other. He approaches a man sitting at a corner table and asks, what will you give me for this banana? The man looks him over and says, how about this? He pulls out a gun and shoots banana guy point blank.

Unfortunately, there's no punch line. I know this because I was halfway through a corned beef on marble rye when the banana guy crashed into me. It took one second for the shooter to leap over the table, another second to grab the satchel, and two more to make it out the front door.

Chairs slammed into the hardwood floor and plates broke as diners hit the deck, even though the shooter was long gone. I struggled to get up from the sticky floor where I'd landed, and the long strap of my hipster handbag had tangled around my legs.

The guy with the banana was older than me by about ten years, but tall and solid muscle. Weighed a buck eighty easy and was now crushing the life out of my right arm.

I wiggled and kicked and finally twisted free while two ladies took turns screaming for someone to call 911. I grabbed a lunch napkin and frantically searched for the man's wound. My hands moved from his chest to his neck to his arms.

"My arm—it's my arm!" he hollered at me only an inch and a half from my face.

I recognized him. Gilbert Goodsen, local insurance agent and sometime donor to the Ballantyne Foundation, the warmest billion-dollar charitable organization in all the South where I served as director.

I pressed into Gilbert's right arm, high near the shoulder, using the balled up napkin. Only the napkin wasn't the thick fancy white kind; it was an old-fashioned dish towel. Its rustic nature may have blended with the bar's décor, but it soaked up blood faster than a sheet of Kleenex.

"Help! That hurts!" He tried to sit up. "Wait. Where'd he go? That wiley bastard stole my fifty g."

"Fifty g? Gilbert, are you crazy?"

What kind of fool carries around fifty thousand in cash? I accidentally squeezed harder and he screamed, so I pressed his wound harder, pushing him into the floor. It made the bleeding better, but his bellowing worse. I decided I could live with the bellowing but he couldn't live with the bleeding, so I pushed with everything I had.

"*Stop*! Oh good God in heaven, woman, what are you doing? You're killing me!" He smacked at me with his other arm.

The restaurant patrons crowded close, their feet crunching on the broken plates scattered on the floor. Sirens blared in the distance. The steady ebb and flow of sound recognizable to anyone in any town in any place. It couldn't have been more than six or seven minutes since the man in the baseball cap fired his gun and fled. The napkin in my hand squished with blood. I started to shake. Wooziness hit me. I was now kneeling on Jell-O legs.

"Ambulance on the way, Elli," Tug Jenson said. As barkeep, head chef, and owner, Tug put the Tug in Tugboat Slim's. He knelt down with a large towel in his hand. "Let me."

He took over compressing the wound and I tried to stand. The room tilted a bit to the left, then to the right. I glanced down at my palms, slick with blood. They smelled tinny, and a little sweet and salty. The backs of my hands were coated in Russian dressing, a cup of which I'd ordered with my sandwich. It may be a while before I eat corned beef.

I held my hands up like a surgeon headed to an operating suite and fast-walked straight to the ladies' room. With a butt-smack to the door, I rushed the two feet inside. One pedestal sink, two small stalls made of faded wood, and a large oval mirror. Barely a step up from a campground restroom, but it was clean and had a full soap dispenser. I used the inner edge of my forearm to turn on the water, then used the outer edge to depress the soap lever, pushing until at least an entire cup of thick liquid cleanser filled my palm.

Muffled sounds of emergency personnel filtered through the ladies' room door while I lathered up like a kid in a bubble bath. Except the bubbles were a muted shade of dark pink with red splotches. Some splashed onto my blouse. The image of the Gilbert's gashy wound where the bullet ripped the flesh stayed with me and my stomach sank. My whole body sank. I rested my forehead on the cool porcelain sink ledge. My knees shuddered and sweat pooled on my neck so fast, I feared a faint was in my future.

Someone knocked on the door.

I slowly turned my head to the left, squinting between my armpit and the basin. "In a minute."

The water still ran, dissipating most of the bubbles. I sighed and stood and grabbed a wad of paper towels and another massive blob of soap, then wiped the sink clean. With two big splashes of cold water on my face, I felt much better.

But I looked like shit. A mix of Russian Dressing—aka mayo and ketchup—managed to stain the top of my cotton voile blouse and both knees of my khaki capris. And from the strong tangy smell, I'm fairly certain I had a handful of pickles stuck someplace. I desperately needed hand-sanitizer. Or maybe all over body sanitizer. But my little lifesaver bottle was in my handbag way back near my splattered lunch.

The knock returned. With another long sigh, I tossed the last of the paper towels in the bin and whipped open the door, coming face to face with Lieutenant Nick Ransom.

He leaned against the plank wood wall opposite the door. "Hiding out?"

I took two blinks to gather myself, then stood tall. Confident, composed, fully unruffled. "Just a pit stop. Drank lots of Pepsi with lunch."

He nodded and plucked a bread and butter pickle from my hair. "You're looking good. Up for a few questions, or do you need a moment to put your head between your knees?"

Nick Ransom and I met twenty years earlier in a college forensics class. One where I slid to the floor in a dead faint during a crime scene slide show. He found my slight aversion to guts and gore amusing in light of my desire to fight crime and/or evil.

"I'm fine, Ransom. Ask away." I stalked across the short bar decorated in typical style befitting a joint named Tug Boat Slim's. Oars and nets on the walls. A giant clamshell. A large starfish. An enormous marlin which may or may not have been purchased off eBay.

I spotted my handbag on the floor, somehow unblemished, next to Gilbert on a gurney. I picked it up just as a paramedic jabbed an IV needle into Gilbert's arm.

Whoa. I spun around and slipped on a bloody napkin wadded on the floor. Now I had blood on my sneaker. I pointed to the side door. "Quieter outside," I choked out.

The fresh sea air saved my life. Or at least saved what little lunch I ate. Breathe in. Breathe out. Breathe in. Breathe out. Once I hit the back patio, I kicked off my Vans and pulled a bottle of hand-sani from inside my hipster. It wouldn't save my shoes, but it would help with my sanity.

Tug Boat Slim's is a local bar on the far north end of Sea Pine Island. It fronted a short harbor on the Intracoastal Waterway at the foot of the bridge to mainland South Carolina. It also sat behind the only combo RV, trailer, and boat resort on the island. Fisher's Landing Trailer Park and Yacht Club. As I sat on a long bench near the railing, I could see a faded turquoise single wide to my left and a shiny bright sailboat to my right.

"Please tell me how exactly you're involved in this shooting," Ransom said.

"Totally not involved," I said. "Just eating my lunch like everyone else."

"At the shooter's table? Do you mind telling me his name?"

"Not at his table. The table next to his. I faced the window and he faced the bar. So I guess we sort of sat across from each other. But I certainly didn't know him."

I actually only glanced up at the guy briefly when I sat down. I'm a big fan of privacy and have no problem eating alone. I just threw my hipster handbag over the side of the chair, slapped my notebook on the table, and studied the menu. "He wore a black t-shirt and a dark baseball cap. Not sure what it said, maybe a Cubs logo. I didn't see his face."

Ransom jotted down my meager tidbits of information while I spoke. He looked good. He looked great. All taut and sexy and dashing. Like a Harvey Specter, only he carried a badge instead of a briefcase. Our past was a bit speckled, Ransom and me. We didn't just meet in college, we dated. It was hot, heavy and heart-pounding. Until he left one night without notice and came back twenty years later. He took the Lieutenant's position at the Sea Pine Police Station some four months earlier. We'd gotten along pretty well considering he nearly got me killed less than a month after he arrived.

The warm breeze from the harbor blew scents of briny oysters and saltwater, along with the sweet, late-blooming jasmine growing beneath the deck.

"How was Columbia?" I asked.

The state police built a new training facility and had asked Ransom to teach a class on advanced hand-to-hand combat. I glanced at his hands. The last time we were this close, they were up my dress. That was the night before he left. A call from dispatch interrupted our make-out session and we hadn't spoken since. Like I said, our past is a bit speckled.

He noticed me looking and my face flushed pink. "Miss me?

Did you even try to stay out of trouble while I was gone?"

"No trouble," I said. "I'm telling you, Ransom, the island is quiet. That last incident was just a fluke."

"Incident, huh? You were smack in the middle of a murder. And now this shooting? It's just a coincidence you're here?"

"Absolutely. How would I know Gilbert would get shot and robbed before he joined me for lunch?"

His jaw tightened and he stared at me for a full minute. "Tell me, Lisbon. Now."

I shrugged. "Gilbert Goodsen asked me to meet for lunch. He got shot before he sat down."

Ransom stared some more.

I tried to stare him down, but my fifteen years working at a charity were no match for his twenty in the FBI. Besides, it's not like lunch was a secret.

"Gilbert wants the vacant seat on the Ballantyne Board." A spot opened up four months earlier in May with the untimely death of another board member, and as director of the charitable Ballantyne Foundation, it was my job to compile a list of replacement candidates. "I guess he's hoping I'll put him on the short list, but his soon to be ex-wife also wanted on, and with a divorce pending, not likely, but I agreed to meet for a quick lunch. I was taking notes for a different meeting I'm now late for back at the Big House, when I heard Gilbert ask the guy something weird about a banana."

"A banana?"

"Yes, a banana. Like, what will you give me for this banana? Then the guy in the cap shot Gilbert, grabbed his bag of money, and took off. Though I didn't realize it was Gilbert until after he slammed into me. I admit I may have glanced over when Gilbert mentioned the banana." I didn't admit I eavesdropped purely out of habit, but judging by the way Ransom was looking at me, he'd already figured that part out.

"That's it?"

"See? No involvement."

The ambulance team wheeled Gilbert out the back door and across the patio. His screaming had finally stopped, but he was still pale. They slowed as they approached us.

"I'll be by later this afternoon," Ransom said to Gilbert, who nodded vaguely in response.

Corporal Lillie Parker, the closest person I had to a friend on the force, and who I must have missed seeing inside earlier, waved to us both while the paramedics adjusted and checked and did paramedic type things with needles and bags and other scary medical implements.

Ransom tucked his notebook and pen back into his suit jacket pocket, never taking his eyes from mine. "Listen to me on this. Do not. I repeat, *do not* get involved in this investigation. Just because Gilbert Goodsen is a friend of the Ballantynes, does not make this your business or part of your PI pursuit. Do you understand me?"

I smiled. Sort of. With squinty eyes and scrunched up lips. I nodded and stood and watched Gilbert get wheeled down the ramp toward the waiting ambulance.

"Say the words," Ransom said. "Out loud."

"I will not investigate this shooting. Happy?"

He looked skeptical. When he stood, he towered over me by at least six inches. "Stay out of trouble, Lisbon."

I wiggled my fingers in a wave and walked back into the restaurant. Several officers were still interviewing witnesses, including Tug Jenson. I figured I owed him at least twenty bucks for lunch and at least a gallon of hand soap, so I pointed to my handbag and mouthed I'd be back later to settle.

I ditched my sneakers in a metal barrel trash can, then took the deck stairs—the same ones the shooter took when he escaped with Gilbert's fifty G's—to the side parking lot and hopped into my almost new blue Mini Coop convertible.

Lola Carmichael passed me on her way to the Fisher's Landing office. She lifted her arm in a wave and her plastic bracelets clacked and rattled.

I smiled back and made a mental note to stop by later. As

resident manager and activity director, Lola may have seen the shooter. I stashed my hipster beneath my seat and slipped on a pair of flip-flops I kept in the car for beach emergencies, then called the Big House.

"Hey, Carla. Listen, start the meeting without me. I'm headed to the hospital to talk to Gilbert Goodsen. Seems a guy shot him this morning and stole a satchel filled with cash and I want to know why."

TWO

Sea Pine Island is shaped like a shoe. Or a foot. Or perhaps more accurately a foot wearing an unattractive ankle boot. The bridge to mainland South Carolina hooked on at the ankle and the Harborside lighthouse decorated the big toe. I was headed to Island Memorial Hospital, snuggled in around the heel area, from Tug Boat's up near the ankle—all connected by Cabana Boulevard. I contemplated Gilbert Goodsen's shooting while I drove, the glorious September sunshine easing some of my tension. A mild cold front blanketing the entire eastern United States lowered both our temperature and humidity. Still warm by most standards at eighty-two, but a perfect Labor Day weekend to me. I loved to drive with the top down, but can't for most of the summer. With a natural wave in my dark red hair, too much humidity exposure and I resembled Shaun White in his wild-man glory days. Might work on the snowboarding circuit, but not on the fundraising circuit.

I turned onto the winding drive to Memorial Hospital, then parked the Mini beneath a sprawling oak and debated my options. Emergency visitors generally use the Emergency entrance. Which entails walking through a germy lobby, explaining oneself to the admissions clerk, then waiting a ridiculously long time for permission to enter the secure area. Or one could enter through the automatic doors in the ambulance bay with complete disregard to the posted Authorized Personnel Only sign.

With a quick step across the tiny lot, I hustled to the bay and through the doors, wearing a slightly panicked look on my face. Part worry, part shock: an aggrieved relative searching for a recent emergent situation. I glanced at the large white board posted on the wall midway down the hall. Spotted "Goodsen 12" written in sloppy black marker and kept on walking.

The rooms were conveniently laid out in sequential order. I found Goodsen's room just around the corner. Though "room" may be overstating. It had two solid walls and two curtain walls, one of which covered the entrance. Curtain 12 stood open.

"What have you done now?" a doctor said to Gilbert as I entered. The doctor wore a long white doctor's coat with Island Memorial stitched in blue above the left breast pocket. His name badge said Dr. Carl Locke and the accompanying picture must have been taken fifteen years earlier. Short gray hair now thinning on top; defined jaw line now giving way to gravity.

Gilbert noticed me in the doorway and waved away the doctor. "Hey, Elliott. Meet the doc, here. Worried about me, but I'm fine. I'm a trooper. Don't worry."

Dr. Locke nodded at me and left, with one last worried look over his shoulder. Gilbert's right arm was haphazardly bandaged from bicep to shoulder, as if the medic let Gilbert wrap it himself, one-armed, lying down in the back of a speeding bus. An IV ran up his left arm, and he still wore his bloody and ripped clothes from lunch. A purple plaid button-down and blue seersucker Bermudas. A thin white blanket covered his feet.

"Are you alright?" I asked Gilbert. "The doctor didn't look too happy."

"Not bad considering you tried to kill me." He pointed at a bent fork on the roller tray next to his bed. "I must've fell on that when I went down. Every time you pushed my arm down, you rammed it in deeper."

"I'm sorry, Gilbert, but I didn't want you to bleed to death. Though that explains why you were screeching like a woman in labor."

"The bullet seared right through my arm, almost missed me altogether. I bobbed and weaved at the right time. Got to be faster than a gunslinger to bust a cap in me." Gilbert scooted up and adjusted his IV tube, then pulled the blanket over his knees, exposing his mismatched socks. One blue, one brown.

A young nurse wearing pink scrubs and a teddy bear pin popped in. "Can I get you anything, sir? Ma'am? Cup of ice chips, water, coffee? Magazine?"

Gilbert glanced up, and tried to grimace out a smile. He ran his hand through his thinning black hair and nearly knocked the IV stand over. "No, no. I'm fine. Well, not fine. I went down in a hail of bullets in a bar fight today. Took a piece of lead in my arm."

"Some ice chips, then?" she asked.

"We're good for now," I said with a smile. "It was actually more of a severe fork injury."

I slid the curtain shut behind her. "So talk to me, Gil. Who shot you and why?"

"This is just a misunderstanding about a boat. What I really need your help with is with my wife," he said. "I know you help folks out on the side, you know, us loyal Ballantyne supporters, with investigations and string-pulling and favors."

No doubt he was referring to the discreet inquires I sometimes handled for Ballantyne Foundation patrons. My director duties for the largest charitable organization in the South sometimes extended beyond paperwork and party planning. I helped with minor issues like a pilfered Pomeranian or a questionable houseguest. Not gunshot wounds or grand larceny. I was working toward my PI license and still needed over five thousand hours. So really, every little bit helped.

I nodded at his mismatched socks, then his wounded arm. "Is this about the divorce?" As long as I'd known them, Jaime'd held the threat of divorce over Gilbert's head like Wile E. Coyote wielding an ACME anvil.

"No, of course not. It's not related."

"You meet me to talk about the divorce, then some guy shoots you and steals a satchel full of cash, and it's not related? Come on, Gil, how is Jaime involved?"

"She's not. She wouldn't shoot me. Or get a guy to shoot me. She may be high-strung, but she's not violent. Really. That often. There was the one incident with the garden hose, but that was an accident. Mostly. I only asked you to meet at Tug's because I had some quick business there, and figured we'd talk over lunch after. Killing two birds."

This was going to be convoluted. I sighed and sat, perching on the edge of a squat stool on wheels. I crossed my legs and noticed my stained pants and the faint stench coming from them. I rolled the stool across the chipped linoleum floor to the wall-mounted hand-sani dispenser and helped myself to a squirt.

"What kind of business deal did you arrange in a bar?" I asked.

"It was a down payment on a new boat. A gorgeous fifty-foot ocean trawler listed in the *Islander Post*. How was I supposed to know the guy would rob me?"

"He had you bring cash to a bar? Does that sound legitimate to you?"

"Tug's is a public place. A little overcrowded today, probably why the guy was so nervous. The banana was my idea. You know, so I wouldn't walk up to just anybody with a bag of cash."

"Shouldn't he have held the banana, so you'd know who to walk up to?"

"It works either way. Like I said, it was a public place and a good plan."

"Of course. You do realize you chose the closest restaurant to the bridge? Only one minute to reach Cabana Boulevard, then thirty seconds to the rest of the United States."

I could almost see a little light click on above his head, and he paled a shade, started fidgeting.

Now I'm definitely going to talk to Lola at the manager's office, I thought.

"Okay, okay. I made a mistake, and now I'm the one with the

bullet hole. Can we please get back to Jaime before these pain meds knock me out? They're taking me to X-ray soon."

"You're right, I'm sorry. Go ahead."

He adjusted his thin blanket over his feet. "This is all discreet, right? Confidential?"

"Absolutely. Of course."

"Ed Ballantyne is considering me for the Ballantyne Board. For Leo's old spot."

At my raised eyebrows, he added, "I know, I know, Jaime wants on the list, too. So I asked Ed to help me keep the divorce civil. Jaime's being unreasonable. I need someone to negotiate a small matter. She wants something from you, to be on the board, so she'll be friendly. I'm in sales, I know what I'm doing."

I glanced at his arm. "Uh-huh."

"She kicked me out of the house. My house! I'm living on the *Tiger Shark* now, which is why I'm shopping for a new boat. I need to upgrade if this goes on much longer. And the way she's playing it, it'll be months."

"I'm not a lawyer or a marriage counselor. I'm afraid I can't really help with this." Especially with my recent track record with relationships. Okay, my complete lifelong track record if you must know all of my business. Never married, never engaged. Never even co-habitated. Though I once babysat a fish for a whole month.

I stood to leave and carefully wheeled the stool back into the corner.

"Wait, Elli. Just listen. Jaime took something of mine, something personal, and I want it back. A Fabergé egg. A real one, not a miniature. Turquoise blue enamel with gold trim and a deep orange fire opal clasp. Jaime's mad because she thinks I'm hiding assets."

"Like fifty thousand dollars for a new boat?"

"You can cut the sarcasm, I'm wounded here."

"Just asking. Why not just list it as part of the divorce paperwork? She'll be forced to turn it over in the settlement."

"It's mine, not hers. A family heirloom. *My* family heirloom."

"Still, you should list it. That's my best advice. Let the lawyers work it out."

He fidgeted with the blanket again. It was thinner than a dryer sheet and couldn't have been doing much more than making him itch. "Well, I can't prove I own it. It's not insured."

"Not insured? So you mean stolen?"

His face turned tomato red and his tone turned indignant. "It's been in my family since 1902. Given to my great-grandmother as a gift upon the birth of her daughter, my grandmother. They left Russia when the war began at the turn of the century. It's not like they declared the egg at the border. Jaime knows it's priceless to me, so she's blackmailing me."

"*Are* you hiding assets?"

"Of course not. How can you even ask?"

I rolled my eyes, then leaned against the back wall. Even though I wasn't considering Gilbert for the vacant Ballantyne board seat, Mr. Ballantyne might be. And believe it or not, Mr. Ballantyne outranked me. Besides, Jaime was on my short list of candidates, and as eccentric as our board members may be, extortion wasn't a practice we particularly admired.

"I'll talk to Jaime," I said. "See if she'll at least let you inside the house to retrieve it. Maybe switch the egg for something else. Like a swap."

"It's not in the house. She broke into my office and stashed it someplace. And she won't admit she did it, even though we both know she did."

My palms started to itch. "How can she blackmail you if she won't admit she has it?"

"No one else took the egg, no one even knows about it. She's just playing hardball. She's a tough noodle, that one."

"Uh-huh." Finding stolen trinkets and misplaced heirlooms was actually my strongest skill set at the Ballantyne. Not what one would expect from a charity director, but you'd be surprised how often it came up. And right now I really really needed a notch in the win column. Even I wasn't that impressed with the job I did last month. But how was I supposed to know you don't feed a goldfish every single day?

"And the egg and the shooting, they are completely unrelated?" Pleasing Nick Ransom was definitely not on the top of my list, but neither was kicking a hornet's nest with a bare foot. Angering one of Sea Pine's finest did not score points with my boss, the aforementioned Mr. Ballantyne. And I needed those boys in blue for my PI activities. The captain signed off on my actions. At least the ones I reported.

"Look, I already told you," Gilbert said. "This hoodlum ripped me off over a new trawler. Jaime's only involved because she's locked me out of the house and I can't live on my old boat. You're an investigator. I hear a really good one, too. Please get my egg back. It's important to me, so it's important to you. I'm good for the Ballantyne. Tons of wealthy clients. Wealthy clients equal wealthy donors. And vice versa."

I sighed. "Investigator in training."

"It'll be easy. Negotiate with Jaime. Tell her I'll give her half the value of the egg as an asset. That's twenty-five g."

I watched him for a minute. The earnest look on his face, his bandaged arm propped on the tray next to the bent fork I nearly jammed to the bone. His one blue sock peeking out from the blanket. I walked to the curtained doorway. "Twenty-five thousand? Aren't Fabergé eggs worth more, like millions?"

"It wasn't owned by Alexander the Great."

"I think that's the wrong Alexander. By like fifteen hundred years."

"I'm not a historian. You get my point," Gilbert said and adjusted the blanket.

"Do you have a picture of this egg?"

"Trust me, you see a blue egg with a fire opal and it's my family's. No one else in the whole state of South Carolina has a Fabergé egg."

The pretty in pink nurse popped in again. "Just checking. You ready for those ice chips now? Maybe another blanket? And later we can get ice cream."

"No ice chips," Gilbert said. "Though I think a double scoop of mint chip might help with the pain from this gaping gunshot wound."

She nodded and patted his foot, then left.

"What's with the nurse?" I asked. "She another reason Jaime's mad at you?"

"God no, what is she, twelve?"

Well, she's hanging around for some reason, I thought. Those bubble gum scrubs screamed pediatrics, not trauma.

A burly technician in gray scrubs walked through the curtain door. "Dude, heard you got forked." He expertly pushed away the roller tray, unhooked the IV bag from the tall hanger, and adjusted the height on the bed. "Time for X-ray. You feeling better? Those meds kicking in?"

Gilbert nodded, then looked at me. "Let's talk tomorrow, okay?"

I nodded back and left. My shoes squeaked on the shiny vinyl floor as I walked down the hall to the lobby exit. I smacked the big metal square on the wall to auto-open the doors and stepped into the sunshine.

Gilbert's story had definitely got me thinking. An insurance broker who doesn't insure a fifty thousand dollar Fabergé family heirloom? And why did both he and Jaime want on the Ballantyne board? Something stunk and I was all over it.

THREE

Island Memorial Hospital was located near the airport, the police station, and a short drive from Oyster Cove Plantation, a gated community housing both the Ballantyne Foundation Big House and my small beach cottage. I grew up in Michigan, but my parents summered in Summerton, just over the bridge from Sea Pine. Not in the same financial league as the billionaire Ballantynes, but Edward and Vivi Ballantyne were sweet and kind and generous and treated me like family, almost more than my parents did. After they died and left me the cottage, I joined the Foundation full time and loved every moment.

Well, almost.

With stained and stinky clothes, I decided to make a quick pit stop at home before going to the committee meeting. I sped down Spy Hop Lane and whipped into the driveway, a mere fifty feet from the sand's edge. My little street was quiet this time of day—most of the plantation landscaping crews had already come and gone—so the gentle roar of the ocean waves could be heard from the road.

Though my cottage had two bedrooms, it was really built for one occupant. Compact kitchen, living room, half-bath downstairs, and two bedrooms upstairs. A quick shower to wash out the pickle smell was in order, so I stripped down and hit the hot water. Some might say I'm obsessive about my routines. I prefer efficient. I was back downstairs in the Coop in thirty minutes flat. Showered and dressed in linen capris, a white ruffle tee, and bright orange ballet flats for a splash of color.

I drove the mile or so up the road to the Big House, which sits at the very top of Oyster Cove Plantation. The Big House resembled a miniature Biltmore Estate, only less museum and more farmhouse. An enormous flatbed truck, as large as a tractor trailer without walls, backed into the long drive when I arrived, its bed filled with a half-dozen whimsical topiaries tied down with ropes. A giraffe with a monkey on its back, an elephant mom with her baby's trunk hooked to her tail. Lawn art for the Wonderland Adventures Tea Party we were hosting next week.

Tod Hayes, Ballantyne Administrator, stuck his head out the door as I walked up the brick steps. He was trim and slim and neat and had helped me run the Foundation for the last ten years. "Finally, Elliott. You've got scoop and we want it."

"It has to wait. I'm late for the meeting and Jane's probably been here since breakfast."

"She would've if she could've, but the meeting hasn't even started yet. You aren't the only late arrival. Actually, I don't think anyone arrived on time."

I stashed my hipster in my office and grabbed a notebook and pen, then hurried to the parlor at the front of the house. Fresh peonies and sweet stargazer lilies sat center on the long maple boardroom table. Carla Otto, Ballantyne chef and resident mother hen, had laid out a spread fit for royalty on the side board. I nearly swooned. While I'm sure most would assume I'd've lost my appetite after the earlier Russian dressing and pickle debacle, that was hours ago.

I helped myself to a quick plate of the most scrumptious fried chicken and waffles, Carla's own recipe, topped with spiced pecan and honey glaze, and a tall glass of Pepsi before sitting at the table.

Tod sat to my right and Zibby Archibald sat to my left.

"Zibby, your hair is spectacular today," I said as she scooted into her seat.

Zibby Archibald defied the blue hair designation. She liked to dye her hair to match her mood or her outfit. Today's shade was sunburst orange. Like a magic marker.

"Thank you, dear. I found the most lovely suit for the Tea in poppy and pink stripes, goes so perfectly with my chintz." Her cup rattled as she set it down, and the fork she used to stir her coffee hit the tabletop. Closing in at eighty-eight, Zibby was the oldest member of the board, but definitely had the most character.

"May we start now?" Jane Walcott Hatting said from the head of the table. While Tod and I ran the Foundation, Jane ran the board. She wore a striking houndstooth blazer with bright Pucci scarf around her neck. "I simply cannot wait any longer. Now, we have yet to—"

"Hello, babies, I'm here!" Busy Hinds entered the room with a swoosh. A chic black feathered hat on her blonde head and a handbag large enough to tote a Great Dane on her arm. Busy wasn't on the Ballantyne board, but wanted to be, so she volunteered for every committee she could raise a hand for.

"My God, Biz, look at that leopard skirt," Tod said with so much awe dripping from his voice I thought he would melt. "Tell me it's Oscar."

"Yes! Oh my God, I scooped it up and wore it out. Isn't it bananas?" She wooshed over to the last two chairs at the end of the table and set down her entourage of handbags, shopping bags, and accessories. "Girls, I'm having a day. I almost didn't arrive. Had the dates mixed up by a week."

"We need to stay on topic," Jane said, completely unmoved by the leopard skirt. "The Wonderland is in five days and this tardiness is not helping anything."

The Wonderland Adventures Tea is the most whimsical and most complicated event the Ballantyne hosted every September. Benefitting the children's wing at Island Memorial and the Children's Hospital in nearby Savannah, every sick child well enough to attend brought their parents and their doctors to a delightful tea party befitting Alice and her friends.

"Yeah-yeah-yeah, I hear you," Busy said.

"How are we on tables? At last count, we're at two-fifty guests," I said. "The hand-painted tea sets arrived yesterday." The most adorable china pots with matching cups and saucers, specially commissioned for this year's event.

"I'm on it, sweetie," Busy said. "I've arranged the tables, linens, everything. Don't you worry about a thing."

"What time shall we be here on Monday, Elli, dear?" Zibby asked. She tucked a pink napkin under her chin and ate a spoonful of French butter. "I'm bringing my best chintz set. Did I tell you or was that at the board meeting?"

"We haven't had the board meeting, Zibby," Jane said. "Next week. After the Tea. When the Ballantynes return home."

"Speaking of the fabulous board, Janie, who's on the short list for the open seat?" Busy said. "I'm dying to know if I'm on there."

"No board business, this is not a board meeting. Which is for board members only." Jane set down her fountain pen and folded her hands on the tabletop. "Carla, I need the complete menu today, surprise or no surprise. Zibby, nine a.m. for the tea set drop off on Monday. Do not be late. Where is Deidre? Where is Whitney? Wait, where's Carla? And the rest of my committee?"

"It's Labor Day weekend, Janie," Busy said.

"You're the one who wanted to move the Tea up three weeks," I said.

"I didn't *want* to, Elliott. The Savannah Food Festival was moved to the week we wanted, then the Jazz Festival after that, then we're into October on the calendar. The Tea is always in September."

Unfortunately, most of the Tea committee was phoning it in. Literally. From various spots north of the Mason-Dixon line. Our most affluent residents tended to be the opposite of snow birds, living in the South but migrating north during the summer. Like Canadian Geese.

"Deidre's running behind," Carla said from the doorway. She hailed from Nashville, specialized in crawfish gumbo, and held her wild black curls back with a headband. "The Friends of the Library held a bake sale this morning and she had to man the cupcake table."

"Finally, Carla. Where have you been? We need more coffee."

"Carla, honey, do you love my idea or what?" Busy said. "Major ballistic, right?"

"Love it," Carla said. "Love love. I'm already on it."

"What idea? All ideas must be approved by me," Jane said. She flipped through her neat portfolio with the speed of an accountant two days before tax day. Her shiny straight bob fell forward as she really put her back into it. "What are you talking about?"

"It's a surprise," Busy said.

"Not from me, it isn't."

"Yes, Janie, even from you."

Jane's eyes narrowed to slits. "I don't like surprises."

She didn't like anything she couldn't control. And by the way her fingers gripped her Monte Blanc, I feared Busy was going to get a surprise of her own.

Carla ignored Jane and waved at me. "Mr. Ballantyne is on the line for you."

About the shooting, no doubt. A two thousand mile land mass and a five hour time difference was no match for an island filled with retirees with nothing to do but golf and gossip.

"Carla, can you take my spot? I won't be but a minute."

I gave her my best smile as I quickly gathered up my blank notebook and rushed to the door.

She patted my arm when I passed her. "Only because I'm supposed to be in the meeting anyway."

"Those chicken and waffle things were your best yet."

The door clicked shut behind me and I scurried to my office in the west wing of the first floor. A converted solarium filled with fresh flowers from the garden and windows to the ceiling. I tossed my notebook on the desk and picked up the handset.

"Mr. Ballantyne, how is Alaska?"

"Hello! Hello! Elliott! Can you hear me?" Mr. Ballantyne

shouted into the phone as if he was using a tin can on a string.

"Loud and clear, sir."

"The turtles are abundant! We've rescued three so far. And a leatherback, Elliott, right here in Cordova. The most beautiful creature I've ever seen."

Longtime advocates for the local loggerhead turtle population, the Ballantynes, Edward and his adorable wife Vivi, left for Alaska six weeks earlier. They accompanied a research team from Sea Pine Island intent on aiding a recent uptick in turtle migration in the Gulf of Alaska.

"Wonderful! I hope you're taking pictures. The *Islander Post* wants to do a special feature for the holidays."

"Vivi has taken so many, we may be shareholders with Kodak by now! How are things for the Wonderland Tea? I'm hearing great things from the hospital."

"On schedule. We're hammering out the final details now. The topiaries were being unloaded as I arrived."

"Yes, yes, seems you've had a busy morning so far. Spoke with Gilbert Goodsen a bit ago. Shameful to hear such crime on the island. But I do suppose one must be diligent when dealing with strangers, even those on our conversant community."

I shook my head as he spoke, remembering Gilbert taking a bag full of cash to a bar with a banana as a plan. Gilbert needed to have his head examined while he was at the hospital. Pop up to psych and see what's shakin'.

"Gilbert says you're enthusiastic to help him with Jaime. Getting started lickety split, he said. Is that right, my dear?"

I rankled at Gilbert using Mr. Ballantyne to push me. It'd only been an hour since I agreed to find the egg. "I'm already on it, Mr. Ballantyne. With Jaime's name on the short list, I was already scheduled to speak with her today, as a matter of fact."

I wasn't actually, so I grabbed my Rolodex as we spoke, flipping through the cards marked "G."

"Brilliant! Right up your alley! One last thing. The Labor Day Regatta is tomorrow and Vivi sponsored one of the junior yachts.

She's just blue over not being there to see her favorite little sport come in. You'll step in and take her place?"

"Absolutely, Mr. Ballantyne. I'm on the case. Both of them." I abandoned the Rolodex in favor of my calendar. Yes, an old-fashioned spiral-bound paper one with big boxes for each day of the month. I tried using a PDA, but all that thumb-typing and tiny print made my forty-year-old eyes hurt.

"We're headed south today to Kayak Island. We'll be home next week, Elli. Be well!"

"Be well, sir," I said, but he had clicked off. "Well, shit."

"Sounds like that went well," Tod said as he plopped into the seat across from my desk.

Carla sat in the other. The true heart and soul of the island. She placed a fresh plate of fried chicken and waffles in front of me. She'd added a pile of warm homemade potato chips topped with melted parmesan.

"You don't need to bribe me," I said with a mouthful of crispy pecan chicken. "I'll do whatever you want."

"Details, chicken, details," she said.

I quickly told them the short version of the shooting, skimming over my brief meltdown in the ladies' room. No need to bore them with every little detail.

"How did Gilbert ever get on the short list?" I asked.

I'm supposed to be the only one compiling candidate names, but the scuttlebutt over the vacant seat (and how it was vacated by Leo Hirschorn's murder four months ago, my biggest case as director-turned-PI to date) seemed to bring out the crazies from nooks and crannies. Which meant everyone on the Ballantyne payroll was currently fielding requests.

"Gil's insurance co-op sponsored the Loggerhead Research Team's trek to the last frontier. The very one Edward Ballantyne is on right now," Tod said. "Then he gets shot and needs your help, giving him lots of Ballantyne attention. Coincidence?"

"No such thing," I said. "The team left two months ago. How'd Gilbert know he'd get shot?"

"So Gilbert Goodsen knew his wife hired an assassin to kill him?"

We all three turned toward the familiar voice. Tate Keating, the *Islander Post*'s lead reporter. He leaned against the doorjamb with a combination of greedy excitement and tempered cynicism etched on his tan features. "'Wife Kills Husband for Ballantyne Seat.' Sunday's headline. Care to quote?"

"Gilbert isn't dead, Tate," I said. "He's barely wounded."

"I'll add 'almost' and 'suspected.' I let you off easy with the Hirschorn murder."

"Easy?" I scoffed. "'Board Stiff at the Big House Slaughterhouse' is not a headline I consider 'easy.'"

I grabbed my hipster from the bottom drawer of my desk. I needed to track down Jaime before Ransom squirreled her out of reach. With any luck, she'd confess to snatching Gilbert's treasured egg, hand it over, and I'd be done with the Goodsens before dinner. How's that for lickety split?

"And he wasn't shot over a seat on the board," I added on my way past him.

"He's on the short list," Tate said.

I whirled around. "How do you know who's on the short list?" I glanced at Carla and Tod.

Tod shrugged and Carla shook her head. I knew they'd never tell.

"My lips are sealed," Tate said. "Call me if you want to go on the record. Deadline's tomorrow at five." He waved at the three of us and waltzed across the foyer and out the front door.

"You're a little shit," I said. "Put that on the record."

FOUR

(Day #1: Friday Late Afternoon)

Gilbert and Jaime Goodsen lived in Sugar Hill Plantation, a sprawling gated community situated mid-island with a massive entrance off Cabana Boulevard. The security guard met my car as I slowed at the shack. He rambled out in full uniform, including a tan Smokey the Bear hat.

"I'm here for lunch at Molly's by the Sea," I lied.

Sugar Hill was a popular destination for temporary residents and visitors. With two resort hotels, six restaurants, three golf courses, tennis facilities and five miles of bike paths, there was something for everyone. Including me, who needed access to a resident's house without calling ahead. Any old restaurant would do.

He tucked the pass in my dash and I sped down Sugar Hill Drive toward the Atlantic Ocean. I'd only been to the Goodsen's once before, five years earlier for a meet and greet at their new house, and after only three wrong turns and one close call with a speeding golf cart, I parked the Mini in the Goodsen's circular driveway. Right behind a slick silver Mercedes McLaren Roadster. Nick Ransom. Our cars resembled a brief pictorial of the convertible food chain. Both sporty and spectacular, but one priced four-hundred and fifty thousand dollars more than the other. Guess which was which.

The brick pavers in the drive were slightly cracked and enough pine needles to mulch a golf course littered the drive. The house looked quiet, abandoned. The windows were dark, and the Goodsens favored a pair of front doors with glass insets and sidelights, so I could see the entire front of the house all the way through to the lagoon in the backyard.

"See anything interesting?" Ransom said from behind me.

He was leaning against the front of his car. Feet crossed at the ankles, hand on the hood. His silky shirt pulled tight across his broad chest. His cologne floated over. Sandalwood and ginger, with a hint of Cuban tobacco.

Where did he come from? I thought. He's a sneaky one, and I needed to remember that. I casually turned around and walked down the front steps. "Not looking, knocking. Doesn't seem like she's home."

"It's strange to see you here. Especially after we agreed just this morning you weren't going to get involved with the Goodsens."

"So you're saying Jaime is involved in the shooting?"

"You look good, Red," he said. "Your legs healed nicely."

I had a small run in with a fire back in May during that first murder investigation. Turned out killers didn't like to play nice, and both of my calves ended up in bandages.

Ransom's gaze lingered on my legs and I was happy I remembered to shave. And put on clean shoes.

I smiled. "If you're going to check out my body parts, you're going to have to answer my questions. Give and take, remember?"

He laughed and put his hands up. "Just being friendly. I'm the law enforcement officer here. I'm the one who asks the questions."

"Fine. Have it your way." I walked past him to the path along the side of the house. Slim brick pavers in a herringbone shape directed me to a door, then the back gate.

"Lisbon, this isn't a joke," Ransom said from behind me. "This shooting has nothing to do with you or the Ballantyne."

"I'm not here for the shooting, big shot. I'm here on a completely unrelated matter."

The side of the house looked as quiet as the front. I turned to go back and noticed a plastic tray next to the door. Half filled with water and half with a brush. For scrubbing your shoes. I smiled. "Anyway, I was just leaving."

He followed me to my car. "I like your new matchbox. You finally decided to part with the white one?"

After the discreet inquiry that turned into the incident which nearly cost me my life, I'd been rattled. So much so, that not once, but twice, I accidentally left the top down whilst working at the Big House, only to have major storms crop up and soak the interior. I took it as a sign of bad juju and traded it in for an almost new ice blue one. This time I got the turbo.

"I didn't think I'd love it as much as the white one, but I do. Even more." I checked my watch and opened the driver's side door. "Gotta run."

"What's this 'unrelated' matter you're handling?"

"Well, unlike you, I'm awfully cooperative, so I'll share. It's a marital dispute involving a Fabergé egg. I need to talk to Jaime. So, if you'll excuse me." I plopped into the seat and dug in my handbag for the key.

"You know where she is?"

"As a matter of fact, I do. Good luck with your shooting. I have a very valuable heirloom to track down. A priceless Fabergé, not so easy to find. There's the black market, international trade, smuggling rings..."

He leaned in close and studied my face. "It's an egg. I think even you can handle an egg. Now where's Mrs. Goodsen?"

"Only if you tell me what you know. And I can go with you."

"What happened to 'awfully cooperative?'"

"It's a rolling scale. Based on your cooperative sharing. So what do you think?"

He rocked back on his heels. "Nope."

"Okay, then. See you later."

I slowly fiddled with my purse as if getting settled. I found the key, pushed it into the slot, and revved the engine. I checked my mirrors, adjusted the rearview using micro movements.

He tapped on my shoulder. "Fine. But I'm driving."

Yes! I did a quick internal victory dance and parked the Mini on the street, then trotted over to his racer. He held the wing door for me as I slid into the snug seat. More Cuban tobacco and tanned leather. Memories flooded back and my skin began to tingle.

I pushed them aside. Business first. I needed Ransom to drive because we were headed to Haverhill Plantation. A residential encampment guarded by guards who took their positions seriously. As in no way I could talk my way past their united and armed front. But a man with a half-million dollar car and a shiny police badge could sail right through.

The engine hummed and purred as we rolled down Cabana Boulevard. "How do you know she's at Haverhill?" he asked after I told him our destination.

"You underestimate my investigative abilities too quickly. Always judging me by the way I handled bloody wounds and germy situations. I'm every bit as skilled and determined as you, Nick Ransom."

"Uh-huh. Then from one professional to another."

"The scraper tray by the side door. It's for cleaning your shoes after playing on clay courts. Jaime's very big in the tennis scene. She hosts our annual Wimbledon party at the Big House in June."

"Why play at Haverhill and not Sugar Hill where she lives?"

"They recruited her to their 4.0 division a couple years ago. Haverhill takes their tennis seriously."

He slowed at the gate and the uniformed guard looked like a soldier defending the palace gates. I think his gun was bigger than Ransom's. Literally, not a euphemism.

Ransom showed his credentials and the nice man wearing the nightstick and Glock issued a day pass. We followed the tree-lined road until it ended at Magnolia Drive. Large magnolias, crape myrtles and fat palms bermed both sides of the crossway. Homes across the street fronted a meandering waterway with over thirty-some acres of harbors winding around miniature residential islands.

I'd once visited a home in nearby Savannah. Very minimalist. Short, flat roof. Sleek, steel windows. Minor adornments. Modernist architecture.

These homes were the opposite of that. Over the top elegance with every possible ornate structural detail thrown in for good measure. Enormous columns, elaborate arches, oversized tile roofs, scrolling plaster niches, and a dozen other elements to make these estates feel at home as if perched on the Riviera.

We turned left and crossed two tiny bridges to reach the Haverhill Yacht Club, which also housed the Tennis Club and the Beach Club. Ransom pulled beneath the green awning of the porte cochere, parked the car, and showed his badge to the young man at the door. It's so much easier to get around with one of those things.

The foyer resembled a large European hotel with pink marble floors and Tiffany glass skylights. We passed the restaurant, ballroom, card rooms, and entrance to the east and west wings leading to the locker rooms and lounge facilities.

"Where should we start? This place is huge," Ransom said. He started down the west wing and I grabbed his arm.

"That badge only gets you through the door. No chance they'll let you roam uninvited. Follow me, hot shot."

I walked through the French doors to the outside patio. Café tables lined the long veranda. Women drank chilled cocktails and ate cheese from delicate plates while sitting in white Adirondack rockers overlooking a field of tennis courts.

I followed the path to the pro shop, adjacent to a pair of large tennis courts. Each had tall light posts and a short rack of benches. The stadium courts.

"Elliott, you finally taking lessons?" asked Jake, the resident tennis pro for Haverhill. He arranged a display of custom monogram tennis towels outside the pro shop door.

"The last time I played, Jake, you kindly asked me to leave the court for the safety of the spectators. Listen, is Jaime Goodsen around?"

"She's finishing up on court fifteen. Fall doubles started and they're going to States this year."

I thanked him and led Ransom along the brick path between courts. Tall chain-link fences covered in custom covers bordered each one. The soft thwacks as rackets smacked balls accompanied us to the back of the complex. Jaime Goodsen and her partner were shaking hands with their opponents across the net.

Jaime was petite with spiky dark hair gone mostly gray and an athletic body Anna Kournikova would envy. I pointed her out to Ransom right when Jaime saw us and walked over with her doubles partner, Alicia Birnbaum.

"Is he dead?" Jaime asked with wry interest. She spun her racket in her hand.

"Miserly bastard should be," Alicia said.

"Ladies," Ransom said with a nod and a quick flash of his badge. "I'm Lieutenant Ransom with the Sea Pine Police, and I think you know Elliott Lisbon."

I smiled sweetly.

"You realize those little plastic badges they hand out as souvenirs aren't real," Alicia said to me. She pulled off her visor and shook out her soft brown hair, then smiled up at Ransom. Another petite, athletic little dynamo. Man I hated sports. "But I bet yours is real," she added.

"Yes, very real, and no, Mr. Goodsen is not dead. Minor wound to his upper right arm. Should be out of the hospital tomorrow."

"That's a shame," Alicia said.

"Not a fan?" Ransom asked.

"He's put Jaime through years of embarrassment, about time someone shot the asshole."

"Are you confessing?" Ransom pulled out a slim notebook and started taking notes. "Or maybe an accomplice?"

"Hey, don't look at me for this," Jaime said. "I've been here the whole time. He frustrated the life out of me for twenty-seven years. He's not getting another minute of my time." She packed her racket into a soft bag with Babolat stitched on the side.

"I'm her alibi," Alicia said. "We've been playing all day, since this morning. Two different leagues."

"Look, I don't want him dead, just out of my life," Jaime added as she stuffed two white towels into the bag and stood. "And my house."

"I hear you, Jaime," I said, trying to get chummy. "Gil's definitely quirky."

Alicia stepped in front of Jaime. "Quirky? Why don't you skip on back to your Big House and let the grown-ups do the talking."

Jaime placed her hand on Alicia's arm. "Gilbert's a pain in the ass. An embarrassment, a letdown. I've waited and supported and spent two decades putting up with his hair-brained get-rich-any-minute ideas. I'm done. I did my best, now I'm out."

I was losing her and fast. She and Alicia grabbed their tennis bags, and Ransom put away his notebook.

"Do you know where his egg might be? He'll give you twenty-five thousand for it. Half the value," I said as I followed them to the edge of the path.

She turned around and laughed. "The whole half, huh? Listen, if you want to be some kind of negotiator, more power to you. I admire the Ballantyne and the work you do—"

Alicia scoffed so loud I thought she might choke.

"—but I don't want the egg or half the value, I want half the assets. Only what's mine. Tell him that."

I watched them walk down the path. Jaime may not have taken his egg, but she could've easily had him shot. And she couldn't have been playing here all day. The tennis staff waters the courts between twelve and two. Standard procedure for every clay court. Maybe she went to lunch? Or maybe she paid some trailer park transient to pop her husband.

"Your eyes are spinning like pinwheels. Don't get any ideas about my case," Ransom said.

I put up both my hands. "No ideas. Simply enjoying the sunshine."

"Mrs. Goodsen seemed friendly enough, but I think Alicia hates you."

"Alicia?" The two women disappeared behind the courts and I plopped onto a bench. Fresh jasmine wafted over from the tree line and I breathed in the sweet soothing scent. "Yes, well, we had a mild disagreement a few years ago and she never got over it."

Ransom joined me on the bench. "This I need to hear."

"Alicia Birnbaum was elected Chair of the Haverhill Ladies Association the same year, the same month, I was promoted to Director of the Ballantyne. We'd known each other for a while, no surprise with the island being so small. And I may have accidentally dated the same guy she was dating at one point. Accidentally," I repeated. "Not a competition."

Ransom sat back and crossed his legs. His eyes crinkled with merriment as if watching a particularly juicy episode of Jerry Springer.

"Anyway, the Ballantyne board decided to host an Irish Spring beer tasting fundraiser the weekend before St. Patrick's Day. You know Savannah boasts the second largest St. Paddy's Day parade in the nation?"

He nodded. "Go on."

I sighed. "Apparently, Alicia's association was also planning a similar event. Same idea, same weekend. Of course, I contacted her to let her know of the conflict. It's tough to host two events on the same weekend, there are only so many fundraising dollars to go around, not to mention the same exact theme.

"But she didn't budge. Said I was welcome to postpone my own event in light of their already large guest list. But Mr. Ballantyne loved the idea, and a pre-St. Patrick's Day Saturday night party pretty much narrows down the date to one night. So we carried on. Twenty micro-breweries and hobbyists set up tasting tables. Carla corralled ten local chefs into a corned-beef and cabbage cook-off. Two hundred guests and many tens of thousands of dollars later, Alicia's party cancelled."

"Sounds hardly memorable by your standards."

"I'm not finished. Alicia turned up in the Big House backyard Zen garden, half-naked and making out with my date. Raising holy hell and uninvited. We may frown on the half-naked part, but crashing is totally unacceptable."

"Did you throw her out?"

"God no. Vivi Ballantyne would be mortified if we threw someone out. Yet we can't allow crashers or every party would be overrun. It's a delicate balance. That's where I really shine."

He raised his brow. "Ah yes, I've witnessed your delicate touch. Like a bomb squad sergeant with a pair of tweezers and a flashlight. Let's see, there was the food fight, the swimming pool incident, the handbag melee, the sidewalk tantrum…"

"Relax. Do you want to hear this or not?"

He grinned a big shiteater and patted me on the back. "Please."

"Forget it," I said and stood. "I can see my talents are unappreciated. You'd be smart to remember your underestimations of me haven't turned out so well for you in the past."

I stalked down the path toward the clubhouse and his shiny sports machine. I may have acted miffed, but I was relieved not to have to finish my story. It ended with a bucket of green beer thrown at my head and a green cupcake jammed down my blouse.

I planned on keeping a very close eye on Alicia Birnbaum.

FIVE

(Day #1: Friday Evening)

I longed to go home and tuck in for the three day weekend, but I still needed to pay Tug for my earlier lunch. If he happened to mention details from the shooting, well, I couldn't stop him. I wasn't purposely setting out to nose around the investigation, but come on, some guy almost shot me. Or would've if he wasn't aiming straight at Gilbert.

I drove down Cabana to Washburn Lane, a short dead end street right before the Palmetto Bridge. I wasn't halfway down before the street got crowded. Cars were parked on both dirt shoulders all the way to the water's edge. I squeezed into the drive to Fisher's Landing, and putt-putted the Mini around to the little lot which housed the trailer park's entertainment complex: a squat park office with a miniature laundry mat slash game room, one tennis court, a swimming pool with a bbq pit, and Tug Boat Slim's restaurant, located above the office.

The upside to having a car no larger than a go cart: the ability to park anywhere. I wiggled into a small area, half on the grass, half on the sidewalk. The line to Tug's started at the base of the steps, wound through the bar, and ended on the back patio, where I found Tug setting up additional tables and plastic chairs.

"Hey Elli, you didn't have to come back," he said.

"I owe you twenty bucks."

Tug rushed across the back deck and grabbed a stack of tablecloths. "Keep your money. I should pay you. We haven't been this busy since we opened ten years ago."

"Word travels fast." I grabbed a handful of napkin-wrapped silverware setups and placed them on the tables.

"Oh yeah. A guy from the *Islander Post* came by, took a ton of pictures. He said he's running a full page in Sunday's paper."

Tate Keating gets around. His story would dominate the *Post*'s front page and probably half the inside. I made a mental note to call him in the morning with a quote.

I arranged a pair of setups on a two-seater table near the deck's railing. "Did you recognize the guy who shot Gilbert Goodsen? Maybe he's been in before?"

"Nah. Not really. I'd been in the kitchen most of the morning. We signed up for a booth at the regatta tomorrow. We're preparing our famous shrimp and grits. The shooter? He's a guy in a cap to me. We get a dozen of them a week."

I helped him layout the last additional table. "I hear you. Look, I better let you go. Even the marina is filled. Your take-out delivery guy may need roller skates." Every slip was taken. Folks spilled out from the decks to the docks, eating, drinking, celebrating. Except one boat in the prime center spot. The *Tiger Shark*.

"Isn't that Gilbert Goodsen's boat?"

"Yeah. I let him take my slip. I went to the hospital to see how he was doing, we got to talking. My boat's already in Key West, my winter dock. So I thought it's the least I can do, let the guy take this slip for a while." Tug gave a nod goodbye, then started seating guests.

I trotted down the back steps to the dock. The smoky smells of beef on the grill made my stomach growl in the most unladylike way, but I had one quick stop to make before I could head home for take-out.

I followed the dirt path that stretched from the office to the main road of the trailer section of Fisher's Landing Trailer Park and Yacht Club. Down two spots to number three. Lola Carmichael sat out front of a long silver Airstream circa 1952. Actually, everything about Lola was circa 1952. She wore her dyed black hair in a beehive, a pair of rhinestone reading glasses, and more Bakelite accessories than a dime store jewelry department.

She was painting her nails when I walked up. Actually, I think she may have been gluing them on. "Hey Sugar, I need two shakes to finish this pinkie. This little sucker's been giving me trouble for a half hour now."

I sank into the aluminum beach chair next to her table. The stringent scents of nail glue and polish remover nearly made my eyes water.

Lola held her hand two feet from her face and squinted her eyes. "Perfect. Or perfect for now. Party at Tug's and I'm puttin' on the glitz. Can I getcha a cocktail? I made a fresh batch of Singapore Slings."

"Thanks, Lola, but I can only stay a sec. Just wondering about the shooting up at Tug's earlier. You hear about the guy in the cap?"

"Honey, all I've heard today is about that kid in the cap. I think it's Bobby, over in the last row, closest to the highway. But what do I know? I never saw him, or anything, up at Tug's today."

"Seriously? The guy lives here?"

She waved her hand, letting the air dry her shiny red nails. "Sure sounds like him. Scruffy beard, always wearing that Cubs cap. I haven't seen him today, though."

I scrambled for my notebook out of my hipster. "What's the guy's name? Bobby?"

"Bobby Smith. But don't worry about writing that down. I've got more 'Smiths' in this park than a Smith family reunion." She carefully sipped what I assumed to be a Singapore Sling and leaned back in her bright yellow aluminum chair. "He rented one of my transient trailers, a beater for flopping. Paid six months in advance three months ago."

I jotted it all down whether I needed to or not. I'd probably hear a version of this story fifteen times before Monday. But nice to hear it from the source first.

Her phone rang. A turquoise princess model sitting on the table with a mile of phone line hooked up from inside the trailer.

She picked up the line and I stood. "Uh-huh... yeah, sure, uh-huh... two shakes, sweetie," she said, then hung up.

"Coin machine's jammed again," she said. "Don't know what those kids do in there."

"Think it'd be okay if I take a peek at Bobby's trailer? Just a drive by?"

"Sure, honey, you go on. It's the pink single at the end of row five. Can't miss it. Has a giant flamingo in the front yard next to the parking pad."

I decided to drive my car rather than walk. Even though I hadn't ridden my bike in a week, I didn't feel the need to make up for it with a walk through a trailer park at dinner time. The line at Tug's had barely moved since I'd last seen it, and a couple in a golf cart were pleased as punch to take my illegal sidewalk spot as soon as I backed out.

Five minutes and two turns later, I rolled down the bumpy asphalt road known as Row Five. A mix of motor homes and trailers dotted the small street, with plenty of empty spaces in between. A pair of fuzzy poodles lazed under a palm near the end of the block. They watched me park in front of the pink flamingo. Highway sounds floated over a worn wooden fence. I couldn't see Cabana Boulevard through the brush, but based on my wobbly sense of direction, it had to be about a hundred feet back through the pine scrub.

Pretty deserted at this end. Only the poodle house two pads to the north, no one across the way for at least six pads. No car in the carport. The trailer itself was a faded Pepto pink with awning poles, but no awning. Three rickety metal steps led to a front door without a screen.

I walked around the side, confident the place was vacant. Not much to see. Overgrown brush, wildflowers gone to seed, abandoned cinder blocks probably once used to hold up a car or part of the house. My stomach began to growl again so I decided dinner was much more important than wandering in the scrub around an old trailer.

I made a note about Bobby and his pink flophouse next to a big star reminding myself to call Corporal Parker in the morning. I may not have discovered anything helpful, but maybe the police did.

SIX

(Day #2: Saturday Morning)

I woke early Saturday and ate breakfast on my deck. Cereal and Pepsi, with my notebook for company. The sun was warm as morning joggers took to the sand for their daily burst of exercise, their soft rhythmic steps mixed with the low tide rumble as I tried to find rhythm in the egg case.

Jaime didn't seem too concerned about Gilbert's missing egg, or even his gunshot wound. Though I guess no one should look inside somebody else's marriage. No way Gilbert told me the whole truth on the Fabergé egg. I always thought those things were worth millions, not a measly fifty grand. And I say measly in the context of a valuable Russian artifact, not my own finances. Both of the Goodsens wanted on the Ballantyne Board, and it didn't seem right to help one rip off the other. Even if I didn't know who was ripping off whom.

I dialed the Sea Pine Police station and Corporal Parker picked up on the second ring.

"If I pinkie swear I'm not at all interested in the shooting of Gilbert Goodsen, will you tell me if the shooter lived in the pink trailer at the back of Fisher's Landing?"

"Nope. Not even if you cross your heart," she said. "I've already been lectured by the Lieutenant this morning and have no plans for another round when he finds out I'm talking to you."

"Parker, we're friends. Besides, I'm not kidding about my complete disinterest in the shooting. I'm calling for an entirely different reason. This is an official Ballantyne discreet inquiry. And it counts toward my PI hours, so totally in the clear with the Lieutenant." I scribbled a quick note about Ransom being bossy. "Have you had any reports of a stolen Fabergé egg recently? Or ever?"

"A Fabergé egg? Like from Russia?"

"Yes, exactly. I'm trying to mediate a minor marital property dispute and I want to make sure the egg I'm looking for isn't stolen property. Or somebody else's stolen property, anyway." Ransom would pop out a peanut if I got involved in some kind of robbery ring. Not that I cared what he thought.

The sound of rapid finger taps filtered through the phone. "Nothing reported in South Carolina, but I can expand the search nationwide. May take a few days."

"Thanks, Parker."

"Sure. And Elliott, stay out of trouble. I'm sure this involves Gilbert Goodsen. If you stumble into the shooting investigation, even by accident, the Lieutenant will not be happy."

I nodded to myself and clicked off. He might not be happy, but no sense worrying about that now. Our paths would cross and connect from time to time, and this was one of those times.

Next I called the hospital, but Gilbert had checked himself out the night before. I washed my dish and grabbed my hipster handbag.

Ransom's sleek roadster wasn't in the driveway next door, a cottage he purchased when he moved to the island. I think he had plans to build a big house on the beach with all the money he made from selling his social media stocks early on. Serving as the Lieutenant was his retirement plan.

I zipped out of the Oyster Cove gate with the top down and a hat on my head, heading south on Cabana Boulevard. Traffic was heavier than normal, but it was the last weekend of the official season. Visitors and residents had flooded the island for the final two events: an oyster tasting festival at the Coastal Seaquarium (which I was not attending, as I don't eat seafood, especially the slimy raw kind) and a regatta later that afternoon (which I was attending at Mr. Ballantyne's request).

But I wasn't sure if the cars on the boulevard had slowed due to crowded traffic or because of the clothes that littered the streets. A mass of shirts and pants, ripped and burned, had been strewn in the oaks from mid-island to the traffic circle at Harborside, like a crop duster passed over head spilling laundry rather than pesticide.

I ran over a pair of running shoes and green socks as I turned onto Ocean Boulevard near the busiest beach on Sea Pine. I wound around a long drive to a parking lot in the back of a boxy three-story building. Two minutes later, I found the door marked Goodsen Insurance and walked inside.

A receptionist in her mid-twenties greeted me. Mary-Louise Springer as stated on a plastic nameplate at the edge of the desk. "May I help you?" She wore her long hair flat-iron straight and her eyes were red from crying. "I'm afraid we're not really open today."

I smiled and held out my hand. "I'm Elliott Lisbon with the Ballantyne Foundation. Is Gilbert in?"

"You cheating bastard," a man's voice boomed from the closed door behind Mary-Louise and she jumped. "You can't do this!" he yelled, then coughed and hacked for a solid ten seconds.

"Maybe you could come back on Monday, when we're open," Mary-Louise said. Her hands shook slightly as she fidgeted with a pen.

I didn't budge.

The closed door swung open and two people emerged: a tall woman with her right hand wrapped around the thin wrist of a tiny old man. Like stick figure thin. "Come on, Dad, this isn't helping," she said softly.

He coughed and shuffled toward the door, his daughter more of a crutch than a guide.

"Listen, Peter, honest. I'd help if I could, but I can't," Gilbert said, following them to the door. His arm was in a white sling with a blue sleeve.

They didn't look back or respond. Simply opened the door and shuffled out.

"Take care, Mr. Whitaker," Mary-Louise whispered.

Gilbert ran his good hand through his hair. It stuck up on end as if it hadn't been washed in three days. He still wore the same plaid shirt and seersucker shorts from the day before, but his socks were missing and he looked a little dazed. "I can't give him what he wants. I honestly can't."

Gilbert noticed me standing there and brightened. "Did you find the egg? I told you Jaime liked you."

"Why aren't you in the hospital? You don't look so good."

"I'm not staying there like a sitting duck."

"The shooter already stole your money, right? Is that what you're thinking? Why would he come back?" I put my hands on my hips in my most intimidating posture. "What's going on, Gilbert? Who is Bobby and why did he shoot you?"

"Bobby?" Gilbert grabbed my shoulder so fast, Mary-Louise yelped as if she'd been the one grabbed. "You know who shot me? Where is he? At the police station? How do I get it all back?"

"Calm down, Gilbert, I don't know who Bobby is," I said and wiggled out of his one-handed grasp. "Just a name I heard over at Fisher's Landing. Might be nothing, might be everything. But if I'm going to help, I'm going to need the whole story."

"What story? So you didn't get the money? What about the egg? Did you talk to Jaime? Tell her I'd give her half the value? It's all the cash I have now. Twenty-five g."

"She was unimpressed." I nodded toward the entrance. "And that? What did they want from you that you can't give them?"

He looked over at the door, then back at me, deflating as the adrenaline surge from my Bobby revelation quickly seeped away.

"Oh, right, the Whitakers. His life insurance. He wants the payout back."

At my confused look, he actually smiled. Not a thousand-watter or anything, but enough to bring his light back. "Viaticals. Come in my office. Come, come."

Mary-Louise looked relieved when Gilbert's spirit returned and she busied herself at her desk.

Gilbert's office was about double the size of the outer reception area. Big oak desk in the center, two worn but sophisticated leather visitor chairs opposite. The carpet was metal gray and the walls were covered in man memorabilia. Pictures of Gilbert from his football days at Clemson. His old jersey, number eighty-three. A faded orange pennant with 1980 stitched in felt. Newspaper articles from the sports section. A photo of Gilbert and friends on his boat, the *Tiger Shark*. Fishing trophies and large reel mounted above his credenza.

"Sit, sit," he said and gestured to one of the side chairs. He sat in the other. "Have you ever heard of viaticals?"

"Never."

He smiled and clapped his hands. "Well, I've cornered the market for all of South Carolina. I'm looking at expanding to Georgia next year. Great stuff. When a guy buys life insurance, it's usually for his family. An inheritance. But what if he wanted to use it for himself? Take a trip around the world or something, fulfill a lifelong dream? He's paid the bill his whole life for a payout he'll never see. Now he has an option."

"Viaticals?"

"Yes! I simply buy his life insurance policy from him so he can enjoy his last days in luxury. He can spend the money on his family, while he's still alive to use it."

"For a fraction of the value, I'm assuming," I said.

He waved me away. "A big fraction. It's all fair. And legal. I give them a reduced payout now, they make me the beneficiary. It's a win-win."

"Mr. Whitaker didn't act like a winner when he was here."

"Yes, that's an unfortunate situation. Peter Whitaker is dying. Fast. His family wants another payout from the life insurance so he can try a new treatment. But I don't have the policy anymore. It's complicated. We pay a fair amount, then flip the policy to an investor's group. The deal is already done."

"Was that his daughter?"

"Yeah, Kat Whitaker. A quiet gal. Spent the last three years of her life taking care of her dad," he said, then leaned forward. "They were happy with the deal when they took it. Honest. They paid his medical bills and the first experimental treatment. And it worked, too. For a while..." He drifted off, then cleared his throat. "But anyway, you're here to help me with the Fabergé egg."

I made a mental note to talk to Mr. Ballantyne about the viaticals. Not sure if undercutting life insurance payouts was in line with a charitable foundation. "So the egg was stolen from here? May I see your safe?"

"Okay, well, here's the thing," he said and scooted out of his chair. He walked around to the front of the credenza along the side of the office. "I don't have a safe, per se. More like a locked cabinet."

He opened a low door on the left side and pulled out a felt lined leather tray. Several collectibles sat on top. A white porcelain box with a pink rose on the lid. A set of nesting dolls, un-nested. A silver spoon. Twin enamel thimbles. "This is all that's left of my family's Russian heritage. The beautiful turquoise Fabergé egg was the most valuable and sentimental."

"And you kept it here because..."

"Because I knew Jaime would swipe it as soon as I left the house. Blackmail me for more money. And she did. I'm pretty quick. Got to get up early to beat me and all that."

"Of all the things in your house, you only took this tray? I've seen your house, Gilbert. You have lots of valuable things."

He coughed and stuck the tray back in the cabinet. "I may have stashed a few other items, but nothing as valuable as this. And this is the only one she's taken. So far."

I checked out the lock on the cabinet. Barely take a bobby pin to pop it. And that's assuming he even locked it. It certainly wasn't locked now–before or after he pulled out the tray.

"You know, Elliott. Jaime is being unreasonable. She won't even let me near the house. She promised to deliver my clothes, so

I could wear something clean, and she lied about that, too. Special delivery, my ass. Pardon my French."

Uh-oh. He may have underestimated her anger. "Do you, by chance, have an extensive collection of Clemson sweatshirts?"

"Yes. Why?"

"I think they're over on Ocean Boulevard."

"What do you mean 'on' Ocean Boulevard?"

"Um, well. In the trees. The median. The bushes."

"Son of a biscuit." He whipped around his desk and tore out of the office, catching the doorjamb with his elbow in a loud thump. "Lock up, Mary-Louise. I may not be back."

"You're looking better," I said to Mary-Louise and sat in the chair next to hers. "Have a rough morning?"

Her fingers shook and she dropped her pen on the floor. She laughed. "I'm so totally freaked out." She bent to grab the pen, then almost fell out of her chair. "Over Jaime. You know the secretary always gets blamed in the divorce."

"And there's the thief with the gun."

She went pale. "Yes. And him, too. Maybe Gilbert's not so crazy."

"You think Gilbert's crazy?"

She busied herself shuffling papers from one pile on her desk to another. "Well, paranoid for sure. I love him to death, he's the sweetest boss and friend, do anything for a client," she said and sighed. "But he's been down this road before. Now he tells me he's getting hang-ups all the time, thinks someone's following him. He's been sneaking over to the library, like five times last week. Gilbert hates to read, but needed the phone bill to get a library card. Who does that?"

Someone trying to research in private, I thought. Find information on your own computer and it's traceable. Go to the library and it's anonymous.

"What can you tell me about this Fabergé egg?"

She pulled out a slim file from the cabinet behind her. "Been in the Goodsen family forever. I think Gilbert finally wanted to get insurance because of the divorce. He was so worried Jaime would take it. He got an appraisal, but she snatched the egg before he could insure it." She tapped the file, but didn't open it.

I waited for her to continue, but she didn't. Just kept tapping the file.

"Simple enough," I said, then coughed. "Sorry. Do you think I could get a glass of water before I go?"

Mary-Louise smiled for the first time since I entered the office. "Sure, sure. Here, one second." She hopped up and walked through a doorway on the other side of the office. Presumably a copy/coffee room.

I quickly flipped open the file. A ticket from a pawn broker. Some scribbles, notes, "estimated value of $60,000." Another appraisal beneath it, from a different firm. Antiques dealer on the island. More scribbles, notes. "Estimated value of $150,000."

I heard the click of her heels getting louder, so I slapped the folder shut and jumped to my feet. "Thank you, perfect," I said and took the Styrofoam cup. I gulped it down in two enormous swallows.

She followed me to the door, anxious for me to leave.

"Does Jaime have keys to this office?" I asked.

"Yes, yes she does. And she knows the alarm code. It had to be her, we're the only ones who know it."

I stared at the square number pad next to the door. The ink on the eight key looked nearly rubbed clean off. I looked back to Gilbert's office with the bright orange altar for Clemson football. "1980, a big #83. The code has to be eight-oh-eight-three. Or maybe eight-three-eight-oh, right?"

Her hand flew to her mouth. "How did you know?"

I patted her arm. "I'm a trained professional." And people are predictable. It took me less than thirty-seconds to figure that sucker out, and I'm seriously not all that trained. Or all that professional.

Once inside my car, I wrote down the two names of the appraisers from the file before I forgot. Huge discrepancies in their estimated values, along with their respective establishments. Why go to a pawn broker for a Fabergé? A call to Sotheby's seems more likely. Which meant a trip to both for me.

SEVEN

(Day #2: Saturday Evening)

I drove the five miles home along Cabana Boulevard admiring the tenacity of Jaime Goodsen. While it must totally suck to have your clothes ripped and burned and scattered along the main thoroughfare, Jaime really put it all out there. And I mean all. Shirts, shoes, socks, underpants. Not an armload or suitcase full, but an entire wardrobe.

So why take a single egg?

The afternoon sun was sinking lower in the sky when I returned to my cottage. I wasted no time lounging around, even though the sofa and my Tivo tempted me. My close friend Sigrid Bassi was meeting me at the regatta at six and she promised not to go in without me. After a leisurely but regimented shower, I dressed in my most dashing sailing attire: white shorty pants, navy and white striped sweater set, and dark red sneakers. I plopped a straw boater on my head, switched everything into a matching straw handbag, and headed to the boatyard.

The annual Labor Day Regatta brought out sailors from all over South Carolina. Hosted by the Bay Harbor Yacht Club in Pelican Bay Plantation, local residents sponsored their favorite vessels and junior yachtsmen while a dozen restaurants provided tables of food and drink.

The line to enter the Pelican Bay gatehouse had cars stacked in a strip nearly to the bridge, so I patiently waited my turn. Ironically, directly across the highway was Washburn Lane, the road that led directly to Fisher's Landing and Tug Boat Slim's, scene of yesterday's shooting. I stared at Washburn Lane pretty intently, but nothing jumped out, so I took the gate pass when it was my turn and followed the car line toward the Yacht Club.

Pelican Bay is probably the loveliest plantation on the island. Narrow streets accented with low brick curbs and a grove of oaks draped in Spanish moss. White plantation homes with tall black shutters, columns, and breezy front porches with swings and wooden ceiling fans. So very Southern, one expected to see Scarlett fiddle-dee-dee-ing on the front steps.

Sid stood by the entrance to the club. Tall enough to feel at home on the women's Olympic volleyball team with a tan to match, Sid's athleticism served her well as one of the top realtors on the island. She never ran out of energy whether to show a house, attend an event, or make a deal.

We walked through the clubhouse to the rear deck where the party was rocking. Colorful lanterns were strung from pillar to post ten feet high and a beach band rocked the dock.

"Cocktails or appetizers first?" Sid asked. She wore her long brown hair pulled back in a vintage Hermes scarf with a sailing motif.

"Definitely cocktails," I said as my gaze stopped on a gorgeous looker stepping onto the dock. Matty Gannon. Rugged and sweet, with soft brown hair and matching soft brown eyes.

Matty and I met on a blind date almost two years earlier. I adored him immediately. Everything about him. His laugh, his laid back manner, and surprisingly, for a planner like me, his spontaneous nature. Then his brother crashed our date. Somehow things slipped from affection to friendship before our dessert forks hit the table, and they never slipped back. Until Matty made a move at the beginning of this summer, but apparently I suck at dating.

"Now you going to tell me how you ran Matty Gannon out of town?" Sid asked me.

I watched Matty walk across the faded wood slatboard deck.

He tied a rope from a white sailboat around a metal cleat. His strong legs looked damp from a recent splash, his arms tanned from a summer in the sun. His brown hair windblown.

Sid elbowed me. "Okay, sweetie, close up your jaw and tell me the story."

A waiter swung by with a tray of mai tais and we scooped up two.

"I didn't actually run him out of town. We were on a date. Well, just finishing it, really. It was going swimmingly. Then I may have mentioned to Matty I was having fun dating two men at once. And maybe something about making out with Ransom two nights earlier." I took a deep sip of my fruity libation. "The night deteriorated from there."

"Why would you say all that?"

"I don't know. Soon I was babbling about rounding bases and crap. I don't think I can handle two men at once."

"At least not those two."

I clinked her glass. "Amen, sister."

Sid and I stepped across the deck, closer to Matty's brother's boat. Matty saw me and waved, and we met in the middle of the dance floor.

"Hey, Matty," I said. "You look good. I mean, it's good to see you."

He laughed low and I tingled. "Good to see you, too. Been awhile."

After our date debacle, Matty left two days later for Maine. Took his brother's boat, the *Fire Escape*, up the coast while his brother, wife, and new baby flew up to spend the summer with their parents. That was the first of June.

"The entire summer. I haven't seen you since, well, okay, then, it was—" Sid elbowed me to stop and I took a swig of mai tai. "So how was Maine?"

"Beautiful," he said. "Spent a lot of time sailing, working on the boats, enjoying the family time."

Remembering him holding the sweet newborn made my heart

catch, and I heard a faint tick from the tiniest of biological clocks. A light breeze picked up his cologne, a salty sexy blend of seawater, grapefruit and sage. "Can we do lunch, Matty?" I blurted. "It'd be nice to catch up. Tell me about your trip and you and things."

He watched me, all warm brown eyes and dreamy long lashes.

My palms started to burn, and I felt a patch of heat start to creep up my neck at the thought of him turning me down. He'd never turned me down before.

"Tomorrow's Sunday, but with school starting, I've got a pretty busy day on campus. Both days, really. With the holiday."

I quickly waved him away to cover my embarrassment. "Oh, sure, of course. No big deal. Another time."

"I still have to eat. Might be nice to escape campus for an hour."

He was definitely making me work for it. "Can we meet at the Big House? It's the tea set drop-off for the Wonderland Adventures this week, so I'm trapped all day. But Carla can make us something by the pool."

"Sounds good. I'll see you at noon, then?"

A perky little blonde interrupted us. She bounced over to Matty and hugged him. Arms up around his neck and a kiss right on the lips.

Pretty in pink scrubs from the emergency room.

"Elliott, this is Elaine," Matty said. His arm was around her shoulders.

"Hi! I'm so excited to meet you," she said. "I mean, meet you for real this time. I'm Elaine, from the hospital. But you must call me El."

El? I'm El, I thought. El's my name and I obviously had it first since I'm a solid ten years older than her. Fine, maybe twelve years, whatever.

"You are just a hero to me," she bubbled. "A role model. Like an elder in a tribe."

"Okay, then." I belted back the rest of my mai tai and lifted my empty glass. "Think I'm ready for another drink. You, Sid?"

Matty smiled, all crooked and low. "Maybe y'all should have an appetizer or something."

"Definitely. I noticed the spread Tug Boat Slim's put out way, way, way on the other side of the deck." I nodded at Elaine to say goodbye and Sid grabbed my elbow.

"*Elliott!*"

I whirled around and saw Gilbert Goodsen rushing through the crowd.

"Oh, good Lord," I whispered.

He was wearing a lime green tee with a dozen burn holes and only one short sleeve. His yellow linen shorts were stained with blue splotches. The pockets stuck out on both sides.

"She stole my boat! *My boat!*" He yelled so loud, nearly every head turned to watch. He grabbed my shoulder with his good arm. "*She stole my boat!*"

I smiled at the lookyloos and gripped his arm, tugging it off my shoulder. "Gilbert, calm down."

"Oh my God, you're the man who got shot," Elaine said. She reached for his sling. "You shouldn't get this agitated. Is it the medication? Are you on medication?" She turned to me. "It's the medication. It can have severe side effects."

Gilbert nodded at me rapidly, like a bobble head on a roller coaster. "Elliott. Elliott. You have to help me. You said you'd help me. *Why won't you help me!*"

"You're *helping him*, helping him, like with the investigation?" Elaine perked. "How exciting! What are you doing? Tracking down the killer? Or his wife? I hear they're getting a divorce and she hired a hit man. Did you find the hit man?"

I glanced at Matty whose smile only deepened.

"No hit man," I said to Elaine, then gripped Gilbert's arm. "No hit man, right, Gilbert?"

He gripped my grip and we stood six inches apart. "You need to call that lieutenant. The one from the bar? He asked all about you, sounds like you're close. He can pull strings. You can pull strings. *Someone pull strings! Make him help us!*"

Matty's smile left the regatta.

I didn't see it leave, just felt it. I didn't have the nerve to look at him.

"Sounds like you have your hands full, Elli," he said. "I think we'll go try Tug's chowder now."

He led Elaine away, and I turned to Sid. "I don't know how this happens to me."

"I know, Sweetie. I'm going to mingle a bit, let you handle this."

I nodded and led Gilbert through the clubhouse to the benches out in front of the Yacht Club entrance.

"Why would Jaime steal your boat?" I asked after I called Sea Pine dispatch.

"Money. I think. She wants all my money," he said in a low voice. "I've worked. I've paid my dues. I'm getting a good roll now. Took a while, but I never gave up. I knew I could get there. Oh, man. The rest of my cash was on that boat. Everything."

"Don't you believe in banks?"

"Not in this economy." He started pacing the brick paver driveway, gesturing wildly with his good arm, letting his sling bounce against his chest. "She must've known all along, that's why she didn't want the twenty-five g, she wanted it all. Everything I had. I don't understand."

"It didn't occur to you that she knew you were hiding money and she'd figure out a way to get it back?"

He stopped pacing to stare at me just as two patrol cars pulled under the awning.

Corporal Lillie Parker stepped out of the first car. She was thin and lanky and graceful as a dancer on a stage. She'd been my ally at the police station after my old ally retired to Florida and stuck me with his replacement, Nick Ransom.

The other cop barreled out of the second car as if fired from a cannon. Built like a bulldog and ready for a fight. I'd never seen him before.

"Where's the lieutenant?" Gilbert pointed at the lead patrol car as if Ransom was hiding in the back seat.

"Off duty," Parker said. "What can we do for you, Mr. Goodsen?"

"My wife stole my house and I need it back."

I put my hand on Gilbert's sleeve. "His boat is missing. It's basically his house right now. Divorce."

"That why you're wearing that getup?" Officer Bulldog said.

"Who are you? You're not the lieutenant." Gilbert asked.

"Deputy Russell Prickle, that's who. I'm not dragging a lieutenant down here for a missing boat." He pulled out a thick notebook and flipped the pages until he reached the middle. "You got any proof your wife took your houseboat?"

"It's not a houseboat. Well, it's a house boat, just not a houseboat. It's a workhorse. But kind of small for a fulltime residence. Not that I need a fulltime residence. Jaime and I are in a rough patch. She took my egg so I'm sure she took the boat."

"An egg? You brought us down here for an egg?" Officer Prickle said.

"Another matter altogether. This is about the boat," I said and turned to Gilbert. "Tell him about the boat. Not the egg. I've got the egg."

"You've got the egg!" Gilbert grabbed me with his good arm. The one without a sleeve. "All this time I'm talking about the boat and you've got my egg?"

"No, not like that. I meant I've got it handled."

His dejected expression, sad eyes, and droopy frown, made me reach out and hug him. I walked him to the bench to sit down.

Gilbert told Officer Prickle the specifics on his boat: name, type, length, license number, while Prickle scratched down minimal notes.

"You can pick up the report from the station in three days, after the holiday weekend," Prickle said. "Take it to your insurance company. Give a copy to your attorney."

"When will I get it back? You think by tonight?"

"It's gone. Probably halfway to Bermuda now."

"What?" Gilbert jumped up so fast, his shorts ripped.

Parker stepped forward. "We'll notify the Coast Guard and Harbor Patrol. But honestly, we only have one officer on boat patrol for the entire county. Includes the docks, harbors, and miles of coastline. Nearly impossible to locate a stolen vessel once it's out to sea. Unless your wife brings it back."

"Thanks, Parker," I said.

She nodded and they left.

"Is it insured?" I asked.

He sighed and shook his head.

"Let me guess, another heirloom smuggled out of Russia?"

Gilbert sank down onto the long park bench and put his head in his good hand.

EIGHT

(Day #2: Saturday Night)

He looked worse than dejected. He was torn, burned, injured, and homeless.

"You still have your credit cards and bank accounts, right?"

He nodded slightly.

"Go check into a hotel. Buy some clothes. Just one outfit and a pair of matching shoes." I searched for a clean spot on his shirt so I could pat his back. I settled for a not quite burned patch on his shoulder.

"I'm going home, to my house," he said. "Where I should've been all along."

"No, Gilbert. Please. Stay away from Jaime. You'll only make things worse. I promise, I'll talk to her. I'm doing everything I can. Can you call me in a gate pass?"

"She's not even there. I checked. She's gone. The house is empty. She went away for the weekend. She does that now. Me time, personal time, a yoga retreat."

"Still, get me a pass and stay away from the house. You'll only make things worse. Try the Tidewater Inn. Enjoy a quiet dinner and get some sleep."

"Fine. But Elliott, please find my egg." He shuffled to his feet, then out into the lot.

I watched him drive away, then I went back through the clubhouse to the rear dock. The party was really hopping now. Most of the boats had returned, and the regatta officially moved from a sailing party to a dock party. I quickly found the boat Vivi Ballantyne had sponsored. After introducing myself to the crew, and congratulating them on their sail, I left them to celebrate.

I spotted Matty and Elaine on the far side of the dance floor. Well, at least I spotted Matty. His head was a good foot above the crowd. He looked happy. Without me.

"Here, sweetie, you need a cocktail," Sid said and handed me a fresh mai tai.

I took a sip and handed it back. "I can't stay. I need to wrangle Jaime Goodsen before Gilbert gets checked into the loony bin. You'll be okay if I go?"

She smiled at a handsome man walking over to us. Dark skin, dark eyes, impeccably dressed. Milo Hickey. Local financier and underground poker game host. I know this because Sid and I crashed a game last May. All in the name of investigation. "I think I'll manage. Call me tomorrow. I'll be at the hospital all day."

In addition to working real estate seven days a week, Sid also served on the Island Memorial Hospital board. But her board was more tame than my Ballantyne board.

The indigo sky boasted streaks of deep pink as I zipped down Cabana Boulevard toward Sugar Hill Plantation. I needed to get over to Jaime's, hoping she was now home, and beg her to work things out.

The gate guard handed me a pass after I gave him my name and destination. It expired on Tuesday, in three days. Gilbert's not so subtle way of telling me to hurry.

I wound around the development to the Goodsen's house on Brambleberry Lane. The house was dark. So was the street. Quiet, deserted, off-season. I drove around the first half of the circular drive, parking right in front of the steps. I tucked my hipster beneath the seat and my phone into my front pants pocket, then got out. The driveway was still covered in mounds of pine straw as if the house was heading for foreclosure.

No one answered my repeated door bell ringing, so I peeked through the front door. I'm not sure it's really considered peeking, since the entire thing was made of glass. The back patio lights shone through all the way to the front door, bathing the interior in faded light.

Gilbert may have understated the nature of his visit earlier. The place was a disaster. I decided to walk around to the back to get a better look, but I only made it to the side door. It stood open. I casually looked over my shoulder, but no one was around. The house directly next door was as dark as the Goodsen's. Not even a stray dog bark to warn the neighborhood of my presence.

I stepped inside. Might as well check out the damage, since I was pretty sure I'd be the one who'd have to mediate the clean up. Nothing looked broken, just strewn haphazardly everywhere. Dishtowels, pots, pans, silverware. I tiptoed through the kitchen to the living room. Same scene. Cabinet doors open, CDs and DVDs on the carpet, knick knacks thrown on the upturned sofa cushions. Did Gilbert think she hid the egg beneath a cushion?

"Come on, Gilbert. Seriously? It'd break if you sat on it," I yelled to the empty room. No one answered. Thank God or I would've totally freaked out.

I eyeballed the staircase, then the door to the master bedroom. Which I deduced using my exemplary detective skills. A massive four-poster bed was visible through the open doorway. The linens dumped in a heap, the mattress tilted caddywhompus.

I edged inside, hoping he didn't do anything drastic to escalate their contention. A quick peek to the bathroom revealed the same as the rest of the house: open drawers, the contents scattered on the floor. The vanity top looked untouched. Guess you can't hide a Fabergé in a tiny pot of eye cream. And really nice eye cream, too. The thousand-dollar-a-jar kind. Actually, she had a fine array of face products. A twang of jealousy hit me. Ever since the doctor used the phrase "a woman of a certain age" when discussing my vitamin situation, I've been studying wrinkle creams like a law student studying for the bar.

I flipped on the closet light. I expected it to be pristine, nearly empty, since Gilbert's entire wardrobe decorated the streets of Sea Pine. But I was wrong. Jaime had kept the best pieces for herself. Decent suits, with coordinating dress shirts, destroyed. And it looked like she took great pleasure in it. Each shirt sliced to threads, almost literally. Threads dangled by the hundred dozen. Colorful stickers decorated boxes, some sized to fit shirts, others looked to fit ties, were smashed in the corner. A wastebasket overflowed with burned shirtsleeves and what were probably once silk ties. A can of spray paint lay on its side next to a crumpled suit on the floor. The suit was a cringe-inducing shade of blue/green, somewhere between the *Miami Vice* logo and a Furby.

If their separation were arson, I'm guessing this was the flashpoint. The place where Jaime exploded, sending flames racing across their marriage.

It was as if they wanted a *War of the Roses*. She kicked him out and dumped his clothes all over town. He ripped apart her house, she stole his boat. I did not want to know what came next. If the egg meant that much to Gilbert, it would not be pleasant.

"Oh, Gilbert, you're not getting it back," I said. "Not in one piece, anyway."

The lights blinked out.

Someone slammed into me.

I crashed into the wall, face first, then collapsed to my knees.

"*Where is she*?" a man screamed. He was behind me. On top of me. Pulling my hair back.

I tried to scream, but nothing came out. I bit back panic in large gulps. It was dark and he was heavy. He wrenched my shoulder until I laid flat on my back. His knees pinned my arms to the carpet.

I flailed my hands, but they barely moved. They started to feel tingly.

"*Where is she*?" he repeated with hot breath. Rage radiated from his everything. His fingers dug deep into my neck. Real panic finally sank in.

"Off...you..." I choked. I coughed and whispered as he screamed into my face.

I started to buck, desperately trying to knock him off. His fingers only dug deeper.

"No...stop..."

And he did.

He grabbed my hair by the handful and whispered directly into my ear. "You get her back here or you'll pay."

Then he was gone. I couldn't stop coughing and choking. Tears slid down my cheeks. I grabbed my phone from my pocket.

"What's your emergency?" a tiny voice said.

I must have dialed, though I couldn't remember. "Hello? Help?"

I heard distant thumping. I scrambled deeper into the closet, and in a whisper, sputtered out the Goodsen's address. I searched the floor in the dark for a weapon. I wrapped my hands around the discarded paint can and hoped to hell the nozzle wasn't pointed at my own face.

My hands shook and tears continued down my cheeks. Mostly from the earlier choking, but my reaction angered me. I was cowering in the closet like a sorority sister in a horror movie, scared and helpless and alone.

A door slammed and I scurried back until I hit the wall. So much for angry and brave. The door whipped open and a flashlight shone straight into my face.

"*In here*," a man yelled. "I'm Officer Prickle with Sea Pine Police. Who are you?"

"Elli..." I started to stay. I cleared my throat and said in a scratchy voice, "Elliott Lisbon. I called dispatch."

The light switch flipped on and I saw Corporal Parker.

"Elli!" She helped me to my feet. "Are you ok?" She spoke into the handset attached to her shoulder. "Is medical on scene?"

"One minute out."

"Is this your house?" Officer Prickle asked me.

"No," I rasped out. "Gilbert and Jaime Goodsen."

We walked through the bedroom and out into the living room. We stopped near the side door.

"Do you have permission to be in the house?" Office Prickle asked. He stood about a foot from me. A scowl on his face, which I could plainly see now that every single light in the house was on.

"Um, well, I needed to talk to Jaime," I stuttered out.

"Place your hands on your head and turn around," he said.

"What?" Parker asked. "Russell, it's Elliott. She's the victim."

"Yes, I'm the victim."

"She's also an intruder. She could've easily tossed this place." He grabbed my arms, roughly I might add, and handcuffed my wrists behind my back. "Let's go."

He dragged me out the front steps to the waiting ambulance.

"Hey, I have permission to be here," I said and tried to walk tall, but my arms hurt, my neck was throbbing, and I was pissed. And teary.

He let Parker remove the cuffs so I could sit on the gurney, but then he handcuffed me to the rail. As if I might hop off and run like the wind, an escapee in a 1940's cops and robbers movie. As if my Mini wasn't parked ten feet away.

The medic checked for injuries. He asked questions and I answered, mostly about the attack and where the man touched me. Parker took notes while Prickle glared, ready to pounce should I make a run for it.

I snapped my arm close to my body when I saw the medic with an IV bag. He gently pulled my arm toward him and started tapping on my hand.

I yanked it back. "Nope."

"I need to start an IV, ma'am." He reached for my arm and I tried to slap his hand away, but my wrist was still shackled to the gurney rail and I nearly yanked my hand clean off. "Shit. That hurt. Stop already."

"I haven't started. Let me have your arm back."

"Are you refusing medical treatment?" Prickle said. "I'll take you in right now if you want to skip the hospital."

"I'm refusing to let this man jab me with the needle." As soon as I said the word needle, I got lightheaded. He tapped my hand again and I gritted my teeth. "Listen to me. *No* IV for shit's sake. Can't you just hand over some extra-strength Advil and a band-aid?"

"What a surprise seeing you here, Elliott," Ransom said from behind me. His words pleasant, his tone friendly. His musky cologne floated over me all heady and divine. After swooning over Matty earlier, and now Nick, I was beginning to believe smell was my strongest sense.

I admired Nick's beautiful tan suit and elegant blue shirt before I saw the look on his face.

"Hey, Nick. I didn't know you were here." I looked pointedly at Parker, silently asking, *what gives*? I wasn't worried about Prickle and his handcuffs, but no way I wanted to face Nick Ransom.

"Care to start at the beginning?" he asked.

"Care to uncuff me?" I rattled my wrist against the rail. *This boob thinks I'm an intruder,* I added silently to myself.

He nodded to Prickle who did not look happy, but complied anyway.

I rubbed my wrist dramatically and hopped off the gurney. "Can we walk a bit? I need some air." And away from the needles and creepy supplies and medicinal smells in the back of the ambulance. Definitely my strongest sense.

"Elliott Lisbon," he said through clenched teeth. "If your neck wasn't already wrung, I'd wring it myself. What the hell are you doing here?"

I kept walking, even when I hit the street. I told him about Gilbert at the regatta, the stolen boat, and the open side door. "I didn't see the guy's face, but I felt his anger. Desperation, jealousy. Whoever he is, he wants Jaime back in a bad way. My guess is she came home to this mess and decided to take Gilbert's boat. Probably sailing it to Charleston right now, to hide out for the weekend or a yoga retreat. I guess she does that now. But didn't tell her boyfriend, who probably saw Gilbert here earlier, and now he thinks they're off reconciling."

"Do you remember all the way back to yesterday? I ordered you to stay away from this shooting."

"Ordered me? You can't order me."

"Yes. Ordered you. This is a criminal investigation. You are not a criminal investigator. Now you are breaking and entering, obstructing, contaminating evidence..."

"Stop. I'm an investigator in training, and you know it. Gilbert gave me permission to be here. Just because Jaime isn't here, doesn't mean I can't be." I fudged a little, but I knew I could get Gilbert to back me up. I just needed to call him before Ransom did. "What evidence did I contaminate exactly? This is a domestic dispute gone senseless and you know it."

"How's your egg hunt? Seems like it's taking an awfully long time to find an egg."

"Don't call it an egg hunt. And it's barely been two days. One day. A day and a half. I'm working on it and you're holding me up. Am I free to go?"

He grabbed my arm and stopped me, towering over me. His silky shirt stretched across his chest like a canvas but I refused to admire the art. He leaned in close, so close his dark blue eyes were mere inches from my own. Which meant our lips may have been even closer.

"I'm letting you go. But let's not repeat past mistakes. Deal?"

I wasn't sure if he was talking about us or the case, and I didn't want to ask. He released my arm and I walked back to the Mini.

Well, tonight sucked. The Goodsens had dragged me into a hurricane of hate and revenge, Matty had moved on, and I think Ransom just dumped me. And I totally forgot to eat dinner.

NINE

(Day #3: Sunday Morning)

Sunday morning started earlier than usual. Meaning I actually set my alarm and crawled out from under before nine a.m. I felt sludgy and lost and wanted to get organized. I needed progress on the egg investigation and I had the feeling I was missing something huge. Yes, getting strangled was a large clue.

I sat on the patio with a bowl of cereal and a fresh notebook and wrote down the story as I saw it. Jaime Goodsen gets tired of waiting for her husband to become successful, at least to the level she expected. Determined to seek vengeance for the years she wasted on him, she throws Gilbert out of the house, steals his heirloom egg, burns and scatters his entire wardrobe, takes up with a new man (possibly more successful, definitely more dangerous), then hijacks Gilbert's boat to leave him homeless after Gilbert ransacks her house. Now neither has a place to live.

As for Gilbert, he got shot and all he cared about was the damn egg. Not the artwork, watches, jewelry, cash, investments, clothes or even his boat. Sure he was distressed over it, but the last thing he said was "find my egg" not "find my boat."

I called Gilbert, then Jaime. Neither answered, so I left messages all over town: cell phones, home phones, office phones. Next I dialed Sid at Memorial Hospital, hoping to catch her between board meetings.

"What can you tell me about Nurse Elaine?" I asked when she picked up.

Sid laughed, but ignored the question. "How you doing, sweetie? Everything work out last night after you left the regatta?"

I touched the collar of my crewneck tee. I'd worn it to hide the bruises, a loose ring of red and blue marks just above my collarbone. Like a necklace.

"Oh, I'm good. But I'm getting nowhere fast. What about you? The regatta work out for you?"

She laughed. "Milo and I nearly shut the place down, then held our own regatta. Turns out he owns a lovely sixty-two foot Princess. Sleek and fast, just like Milo. Now why do you want to know about Nurse Elaine?"

"I don't like her. She was hanging around Gilbert when we were in the hospital. And last night she was interested in him again."

"And Matty, I noticed." The sound of her fingers tapping on a keyboard drifted through the phone. "Looks like she's been here about six months. No complaints, works in peds. She talks too much and is ridiculously bouncy."

"It says that?"

"No, but I thought it would make you feel better."

"It does, actually. I'm going to keep my eye on that one," I said. "Now I'm off to collect the finest tea sets the ladies of Sea Pine have to offer, then my lunch with Matty."

"Have fun, sweetie. And try not to mention Nick Ransom this time."

"His name will not pass these lips, I promise," I said and hung up.

Today was official tea set drop-off day for the Wonderland Adventures at the Ballantyne Big House. While we commissioned whimsical hand-painted tea sets for the children and their parents, all of the Ballantyne donors brought their own. Some choose their finest place setting, while others spend the year traversing antique shops and auctions, seeking out the most unique set they can find to win the Particularly Peculiar Pot Prize.

I arrived at the Big House shortly after nine a.m., barely

fifteen minutes late. But it's not as if I punched a time clock or anything, so there was no one to notice. I whipped open the front door and nearly slammed into Tod.

"Where have you been?" He stood with his hands on his slim hips. "You didn't confirm the set up for today, did you?"

I peeked around him. The large foyer yawned behind us. A beautiful hand-stitched rug covered the thick plank floors and matching oversized Queen Anne wing chairs graced the alcove near the wide center staircase. But no people, no tables, no boxes.

I heard distant clinking sounds from the kitchen. At least Carla was there.

"Didn't Busy confirm? I swear she said that at the meeting."

"The one you attended for ten minutes?"

"Yes, that one." I walked around him toward my office, scoping out the halls, the parlor, the foyer. Nope, still deserted.

"Well, Busy got her dates mixed up and confirmed everything for next week. The tables, the tents, the crews. And not just today, Elliott. For Wednesday. The Big Day."

I threw my handbag in the bottom drawer of my desk and grabbed the phone directory, quickly flipping to Sandpiper Party Rentals. "Look, I'll just call up Rusty, he'll help us out."

"Not on a holiday weekend he won't. The Oyster Fest is still going on, plus the last day of the regatta is tomorrow. You are supposed to confirm Busy's confirmations. You know she's a busy Busy this time of year."

"You're hysterical. I'm busy, too, you know."

"Uh-huh. With the egg hunt? How busy can you possibly be?"

"Never mind me, busy Busy is a criminal attorney, she doesn't have a 'this time of year.' And shouldn't she have assistants to confirm?"

"They did. For next week," Tod said.

The Sandpiper's office phone rolled straight to voicemail, so I left a message, then dialed up Rusty's cell. He answered on the fourth ring.

"Rusty, it's Elliott Lisbon at the Ballantyne. How have you

been?" I put it on speaker so Tod could follow along.

"Just working the Oyster Fest over here, then heading to Savannah 'fore dark. I hear you got a date mixed up." His voice boomed like a truck driver on a CB radio.

"I did indeed. Can you help a girl out? The Wonderland is Wednesday and we need set ups today."

"Well, now, little Elli, I'm afraid we've got the Ghost Tour Jamboree this week. Got everything tied up. Not a chair to be had. With the Jazz Festival coming and the psychic's convention, gonna be a bear to get local. Everyone's busy."

I rubbed my hand over my eyes. "I see that. Thanks, anyway, Rusty."

"Sure thing. We'll see you for the Palm & Fig."

I clicked off the phone and Tod dramatically slumped into the chair across from mine. "You better figure out how you're going to explain to Edward you had to cancel the Wonderland Adventures. First time in fifteen years."

"Calm down, Tod. Rusty is but one rental place. There must be dozens we've used."

"Well, you better do something. The ladies will be arriving with tea sets in about fifteen minutes and we've no place to put them. I'll go clear a spot on the table in the parlor, but it won't hold many."

I flipped through the directory looking for rental companies. Apparently we've not used dozens. More like two. It also seemed Sea Pine Island wasn't teeming with set up crews for big events. I called the only other place on the island, but same result. No can do.

After seventeen phone calls to every party rental from Savannah to Jacksonville to Atlanta to Charleston with nearly every shop closed for the holiday, I started to worry. We could probably live without tents. The forecast predicted sunny skies for the rest of the week, and there were plenty of trees for shade. But we could not live without tables and chairs for two-fifty guests plus children.

I put my forehead on the cool wood surface of my desk. It was my bright idea to stop using our own major supplies for parties some five years ago. Too much work, expense, personnel, storage. Easier to just hire a crew to come in, set up, take down.

I couldn't believe the rental shops who did answer didn't have a single crew available. I'd even tried reaching out to contacts of contacts, hoping to get some strings pulled, but I only got sympathy. And two requests for invitations to the Tea. I had one last resort so-desperate-it-might-actually-kill-me-to-make-the-call contact, but I wasn't there yet.

"Three ladies just arrived with settings, Elli," Tod said from the doorway, his normally neat brown hair slightly tussled. "With coordinating teapots and sugar/creamer sets. And their own silver. Shall I crush their dreams and tell them you're canceling? Or perhaps you're planning to switch to a picnic with paper plates. We can spread bath towels on the back lawn and ask the guests to bring folding chairs."

"Don't panic. I'm on it. Just make do. I'll be out in a minute."

I waited for him to leave, then I groaned out loud and slowly dialed the phone.

"Hey Nick, how's it going?"

"Hello, Red. To what do I owe this surprise? Did Prickle arrest you again?"

"Funny. Can't I just call you, to you know, say hi?"

"Hi."

I don't know why he had to make this so difficult for me. "So how are things? Work, your parents?"

He laughed. "Work? My parents? Either you're very bad at flirting or you want something. And while your flirting is often painful to watch, you must need something. So spit it out, I'm on a case."

"Is Mimi still active in the Charleston fundraising community?" Mimi being Mimi Ransom, his mother. She and her husband were a longstanding Charlestonian couple who enjoyed their horses, their careers, and their status.

"Are you in need of an invitation?"

"Tables. Apparently Busy Hinds mixed up the dates for the Wonderland with the party rentals and we're without tables, chairs, and tents. It's for Wednesday afternoon and I desperately need a crew."

"I figured desperate worked into this if you're asking me. I can make a call, but no promises."

"Thank you, Nick. I appreciate it."

"Sure, Red. I love it when you owe me. I'll let you know when I'm ready to be repaid," he said and hung up.

My stomach betrayed me and did a little flip. Traitor. If my lips started to tingle, I'm calling him right back to cancel and going straight to the picnic scenario.

The phone rang before I could imagine what a hundred checkered tablecloths would look like spread out on the grass. Thank God. I have no idea how to tell Carla to prepare crumpets best served with dirt.

"Elli! Hello, my dear!" Mr. Ballantyne shouted into the phone.

"Oh, hello, sir," I shouted back, slightly disappointed it wasn't Ransom on the other end of the line.

"How is my Tea? Are the teapots arriving as we speak?"

"Indeed they are. We are right on schedule. Running smoothly, no glitches so far. Knock on wood." I rapped on my desktop so hard I bruised two knuckles. At this point, if I was going to use superstition to get me through, I needed a salt shaker, a four-leaf clover, and a horseshoe.

"Good news! And the minor discord between Gilbert Goodsen and his lovely wife? I expect you've been able to mend the fence?" Wind whistled into the phone, as if he were standing on the wing of an airplane.

"Almost, sir. It's a tricky one, but I hope to wrap it today. How are the turtles?"

"We're sailing across the gulf. Full speed. Destination: Hawkins Island. The sea is giving us her dandiest performance, my dear. We're nearly soaked through! Vivi sends hugs!"

And with that, he was gone.

"*Elliott!*" Tod's shout reverberated through the Big House.

I tapped my knuckles against my desk one more time and scooted out to the foyer.

"Don't shout, Tod. I'm right here."

He carried a full tea service in his hands and had a pink straw hat on his head. One with a yellow polka dot ribbon on the brim and a flower the size of a soccer ball pinned to the front.

"I'm heading to the attic right now," I said and tried my very best not to laugh.

With almost fifteen thousand square feet in the Big House, you'd think there would be plenty of storage. Not the case. Every room is a reflection of Southern style and elegant furnishings, ready to be enjoyed at a moment's notice. Beautifully painted, lovingly adorned. No boxes of knick knacks shoved into a corner or discarded accessories placed out of sight and out of mind. And no surface large enough to hold hundreds of tea cups in one place.

But the attic above the third floor housed an assortment of accoutrements. Odds and ends collected over the years. I used the back staircase near the solarium and hiked up three massive flights of steps to reach the attic door.

The stale heat hit me like a smack upside my head. Hot and dry. And dusty. I couldn't remember the last time I'd been forced to drag something out of here. Maybe two years ago when I needed a pinball machine for a retirement brunch?

The ceiling was low, and heavy wood beams crisscrossed above my head. I avoided looking up. I did not want to encounter any hidden creatures. Better to assume there weren't any. I dug deep into my front pocket and clutched my hand-sani in one hand while I poked around with the other.

Cardboard boxes in varying sizes and shapes were neatly marked and scattered around the raw plank floor. A trunk of circus supplies, a bin of oversized metal letters, a pair of mannequins dressed as court jesters, an old wagon wheel. In the way back, beneath a tarp coated in something I did not want to know about, I found a short stack of portable tables.

I yanked the tarp away so nothing squirmy could jump out at me, and ended up spraying the entire area with a year's worth of dust. My face felt gritty and I slathered on more hand-sani. I was more sticky than clean, but I swear I could hear Tod shouting my name all the way up there.

The tables were only four feet long and a little awkward to carry, so I half-slid, half-wobbled them over to an old service elevator. I broke my thumbnail and ripped my pants and I felt wispy cobwebs in my hair.

The elevator was creaky and tight and smelled like dirt, which is why I hadn't ridden up in it to begin with. Once I had five tables piled into the tiny compartment, I hit the "down" button and jumped out. No way I was riding in that thing.

I trudged down the three massive flights of steps, walked through the solarium to the storage pantry in the kitchen.

"Good Lord, woman, look at you. Do I need to call 911?" Carla said. She was bustling around the commercial kitchen in a spotless white chef's coat, her name embroidered on the front in pink script.

"That bad? Wait. Don't tell me, I'm pretending I'm clean as a rubber duck in a bathtub." The elevator binged and the doors slid open. "Can you hold this? I'm going to get Tod to help me carry these."

She looked at me as if I had said I was going to ask Tod to marry me. "Good luck with that."

Turned out I needed more than luck. Tod was juggling two donors who were insisting on explaining the lengthy heritage of their tea sets. He looked less happy than I was.

After twenty-five minutes of trudging, dragging, washing, and wiping, the tables were finally lined up in the foyer. We may not have anything to sit on at the party, but at least the tea sets could be properly checked in and accounted for. I decided to worry about Wednesday later.

Women started arriving in waves. I'd barely set one teapot

down, when another was thrust into my hands. I nearly dropped three saucers and rattled at least a dozen more. Who exactly was entrusting me with a hundred and fifty sets of heirloom china?

Jane Walcott Hatting marched across the marble foyer in a perfectly pressed linen suit with Busy Hinds strolling behind. "Well, I don't care about your tragic pet carrier mishap, Busy," Jane said. "You should have figured out a way to free your PDA from within its locked doors. It's made of cloth. Next time try scissors."

"Oh, Janie, you're adorable," Busy said. She waggled her fingers in my direction. "See, looks like everything's fine. The tables are here, just like they should be."

I smiled at Busy, confident I was leaving deep dust lines in the creases of my face. "A small delay. No worries."

"I'm still waiting for you to tell me what you and Carla are planning," Jane said to Busy. "I insist that I be kept in the loop."

"It's a surprise, darling! It's batty and you'll love it." Busy whirled away in the swirl of her flouncy cape. "Why, Zibby, this set is bonkers. Wherever did you find such a delicious chintz?"

"One of a kind," Zibby said. Her orange hair did indeed coordinate perfectly with the pattern on the tea cup. It helped that she'd pinned a poppy to the top of her head. "A quaint pawn parlor up in Charleston. Except they had two. A pair. But the other was marked sold, to a London collector, so I immediately bought this one."

Zibby handed me her tea set; first the cup and saucer, then the teapot. She wobbled out with a wave and a blown kiss.

"Jane, do you have a second?" I asked before she could march into the parlor.

"Not now, Elliott. I'm trying to get this place organized. You may not have bothered to shower for today's drop off, but I've been preparing for a week."

I bit back the lengthy explanation in favor of diplomacy. "I'm wondering about a Fabergé egg you may have in your shop. I think I saw it last spring."

"It's not a 'shop,' it's a gallery. And a Fabergé is way out of your league. Stick to matchbooks, or shot glasses, or whatever it is you collect."

I gripped Zibby's teapot handle so tight, my bruised knuckle actually hurt. "Not for me, Jane. Gilbert Goo—well, it's a private matter and I'm hoping you can answer some questions. Maybe this afternoon?"

"Make an appointment with my secretary. I think I have room next month." She clicked off without even looking at me.

I could have slapped her. I wasn't paying attention and missed the table when I went to set the teapot down and dropped it right on the floor. In case you were wondering, bone china using gravity to travel straight into a marble floor results in said bone china cracking into several pieces. Like the spout detaching from the mainframe.

Oh. My. God. I watched it happen in horrifying slow motion, Zibby's words of "one of a kind" echoing in my head like a soundtrack to this disaster.

I didn't know what to do. The foyer was empty. The pieces lay in three big chunks on the floor. I heard footsteps clicking on the marble floor and quickly picked up the dismembered pot.

"Chicken, you've got your hands full today," Carla said to me. "Tug called. He found Gilbert Goodsen's boat. I didn't even know it was missing, but he says it doesn't look so good."

I lifted my hands and showed her the broken teapot.

"Any chance it arrived that way?" Carla asked.

"Zibby Archibald's one of a kind. She's been bragging about it for a week. Dyed her hair orange to match the poppy print."

She clucked at me and shook her head. "Who in the world entrusted you with heirloom china?"

I tucked them into a cupboard in the hutch behind me. "I asked myself that very same thing. What about Gilbert's boat?"

"Tug tried to get Gilbert, but no answer. Thought he'd call you, you'd know how to reach Gilbert. It's back in its slip at Fisher's Landing, but he said the boat's in bad shape."

I squirted my hand-sani on my palms and tried to wash up my face. "I'm going to run over there really quick. Please find Tod and have him finish this. And tell him to be careful. These suckers are fragile."

I called Tug as I drove out of the lot. He said he put up an orange cone on the dock to keep folks away. I glanced at my watch. Plenty of time to run over to the boat, make sure it wouldn't sink, find Gilbert, report it to the police, then make it back to the Big House for my lunch with Matty.

Only in my dreams.

TEN

(Day #3: Sunday Late Morning)

Tug was not exaggerating when he said the boat was in bad shape. I've seen wrecked cars at the junk yard look better than that boat. Vandalized, spray-painted, demolished. The mast looked to have been sawed in two. How it made it into the slip, I have no idea. But Gilbert was going to freak. I dialed his number, but it rolled straight to voicemail. I asked him to call, but didn't explain why. Though I did use the words "urgent" and "please."

The lunch crowd on Tug's back deck watched me step around the bright orange cone on the dock and onto the battered sailboat. Someone, I'm guessing one Jaime Goodsen, had spray-painted a dozen unladylike epithets in dripping blue/green paint, the same garish shade from her closet, from the bow, across the deck, over the captain's chair. Each one bawdier than the next. One or two of those derogatory names I'd never even heard of.

And something stunk. Pungent and sour. Something foul like eggs that had long gone over to the other side. I soon found what when I accidentally kicked a large bucket of dead fish and splashed half a pail of smelly liquid on my left shoe. I gagged as I nearly slipped in the slime.

"Shit shit shit. What the hell were you thinking?" I muttered. I squished forward, and my skin started to crawl. "So freakin' *rude*. And petty."

I tiptoed to the stairway leading to the lower deck and debated whether to climb down into the darkened cabin. On one hand, it's not my boat, so why do I need to be the one to traipse through the trash? On the other, Gilbert will be a twisty worried mess and want me to do it instead of him, and I was already halfway there with fish shit on my shoe.

Remarkably, the smell wasn't so bad downstairs, but I grumbled anyway. So far, nothing broken to snap and crackle beneath my squishy shoe. I felt for a light switch, eventually finding a small lamp to flick on. Maybe Jaime used up all her anger upstairs where the whole world could see it.

Or maybe she was dead on the floor with a bullet hole in her head and blood in her hair.

Jaime Goodsen's lifeless eyes stared up at me, almost pleading at me. Her expression was frozen, eyes wide with terror, her arm stretched toward the door, as if trying to warn me.

"Oh my God," I choked out. I stumbled backward until I hit a cabinet. "I'm sorry, I'm sorry, I'm sorry," I whispered over and over, unable to stop.

Something thumped and I ran.

Up the stairs, onto the deck, and straight into the bucket of dead fish. This time I fell. I flew across the deck face first, sliding through slime and guts, screaming my head off. Something splashed my face. I slapped my lips closed and tucked into a ball until I rolled to stop.

"Elliott!" Tug's voice bellowed over the crowd.

I heard the pounding of his footsteps as he barreled down the pier to the side of the boat.

"Are you okay? Can you move?"

I stood up so fast I nearly passed out. With shaking hands, I waved him off. "Don't come on the boat, Tug. Just call dispatch. Or 911. Or whatever. Just get them here now."

He reached for the rail and I ran forward. "*No!* Crime scene. Honest, please, please call them." I lowered my voice. "Jaime Goodsen is dead down below."

"Oh, man." He staggered back and reached for his phone.

I pulled out my hand-sani. My hands were shaking so badly, I bobbled the bottle and almost dropped it twice. I flicked the lid and squirted. Nothing came out.

"No no no no no no." Panic drove bile into my throat and I was sweating like a pig in July. I squeezed and shook and pleaded until a single lonely blob plopped into my palm. I'd used it all up in the attic earlier at the Big House and hadn't even noticed.

"They are on their way, Elli," Tug hollered up from the deck.

I wobbled over to the side and he helped me down from the boat. The lunch crowd had moved from the deck to the dock, held back by a single orange parking cone.

"Can you...um, can you..." I cleared my throat.

"Go clean up, Elli. I'll stand guard."

I kicked off my shoes right there on the wood planks and fast-walked barefoot through the crowd. They stood back out of respect. Or maybe it was the smell.

Once inside the tiny lavatory, I used my elbow to unload enough soap to wash a car. I scrubbed my face, arms, and hands until they stung, then rinsed. After I dried off with a scratchy brown paper towel, I rested my forehead on the basin edge.

Wasn't I just here, doing this same thing? I thought. First Gilbert, now Jaime.

"Oh, man. Gilbert." How was I going to tell him? Now's he's really going to freak out. Jaime attacked and dead on his boat. Did he kill her? What about her boyfriend who attacked me at Jaime's house? Is this why she wasn't home? My God, it could've been me.

I was about to fully indulge in a breakdown when someone pounded on the bathroom door. Think me silly, but I recognized the pounding.

I tilted my head back and took a deep breath, then swung open the door.

"Hi, Nick. We simply must stop meeting like this."

"What the hell is wrong with you?"

I pushed the hair off my face and felt fish juice. "Oh this? I fell into a small bucket of fish. It'll wash out."

"Not the fish smell part, Lisbon. The going aboard a stolen

boat that's been obviously vandalized part. The destroying a crime scene part. The interfering in an active investigation part."

"It was just a missing boat, Ransom. Why would I call you?"

It was hot and tight in the doorway and the sour smell of me was making me queasy. I pushed past him, through the dining room and out the back door into the fresh air. I breathed out, not even realizing I was holding my breath.

"Lisbon, we're not done."

"No one in the department was even looking for the *Tiger Shark*. Deputy Prickle made a point of letting us know that."

"Us?"

"Yes, us. Me and Gilbert Goodsen when we reported it last night." I leaned against the rail and watched the activity on the assaulted boat. "Talk to Prickle. Or Parker, she was there, too. And, Lieutenant Investigator Nick Ransom, I mentioned the boat to you at Gilbert's house, after the attack. You didn't say to keep you in the loop. On the boat."

Half a dozen evidence technicians with heavy cases and a handful of medical personnel buzzed on and around the boat. Dr. Harry Fleet, the county medical examiner, a large black man with a natural scowl and cranky disposition, slowly clambered across the deck.

"Start at the beginning," Ransom said. He pulled his notebook from his sport coat and leaned against the rail next to me.

"The shooting at Tug's bar? The attack at Jaime's house?"

"The murder on Goodsen's boat."

I explained how I tiptoed gently around the boat deck, extremely mindful of the damage, careful not to touch anything, and how I inexplicably happened upon Jaime down below.

"And how did you happen to end up dipped in fish guts?"

"Minor mishap on the deck with a bucket. Anyone would've crashed into it. It was very hard to see."

He nodded and took notes while I spoke. "And Gilbert Goodsen? Why are you here and not him? Something to do with your egg hunt?"

Shit. I'd forgotten to even look for the egg on the boat.

Harry Fleet and a team of assistants lifted a black body bag from the boat, then secured it to a gurney on the dock.

"Tug couldn't reach Gilbert, so he called me. He knows I'm helping Gilbert with a few things, and didn't want the boat sitting out here in this condition. I was going to call Parker after I looked around."

He snapped his notebook shut as my phone rang.

I checked the caller ID. Gilbert Goodsen.

"Hey Gilbert," I said and Ransom shook his head once. "I've been trying to get a hold of you all morning. Can we meet?"

"Did you find the egg?"

"Not yet."

"Well, I've got my hands tied up right now. Business is starting to cook, had appointments all day. I'm headed to Memorial Hospital from Charleston. A client died last night and the family asked me to come, should be there in about an hour."

"Perfect. I mean, not about the client dying, that's terrible and definitely not perfect." Ransom's brow started to rise. "Listen, I'm close by, so I'll just meet you, okay?"

"Sure, Elli. I'm hoping for good news. I think things are turning my way. Except for my late client. And my divorce. But I know you'll knock some sense into Jaime and get this worked out."

He clicked off and I turned to Ransom. "He'll be at Memorial in sixty."

Ransom slowly took in the guts in my hair and my dirty clothes. His brow raised at my torn and stained capris. "All this from one bucket of fish?"

I went to brush away the dust, but stopped myself. No way I wanted my hands to touch my pants in the state they were in. "Not exactly. I spent the morning at the Big House setting up the Wonderland Tea. Tea set drop-off day didn't go as planned."

"Uh-huh. Isn't tea just tea bags and cookies?"

"If I was five years old and inviting Hello Kitty and Mrs. Beasley."

"Mrs. who?"

"Never mind. Any chance you've heard from Mimi?"

"When I hear, you'll hear."

I glanced at my watch. It was well past twelve. "Are we done here? I'm late."

He tapped his notebook against the rail and studied me. "Yes," he finally said. "But I want to talk to Gilbert Goodsen before you do. Understood?"

I agreed and took off for the Mini parked on the sidewalk near the street. Matty was waiting for me at the Big House, Gilbert may have killed his wife, I'm the worst egg hunter in the state, Ransom thinks I'm a moron, and poor Jaime Goodsen was dead. And it was barely even lunchtime.

ELEVEN

(Day #3: Sunday Lunch)

After borrowing a handful of plastic garbage bags from Lola Carmichael in the Landings office, I covered the inside front half of the Mini and raced down Cabana Boulevard toward the Big House with the top down. I checked my watch. Nearly one p.m. An hour after I was supposed to meet Matty for lunch. I dialed him up, but it went straight to voicemail.

I flew through the Oyster Cove Plantation gate, down the road, and around the driveway, skidding to a stop in front of the wide steps to the front door. Matty's 1960s convertible Land Cruiser was parked in the side lot. He'd waited for me.

"Good God, woman, what have you done?" Carla said to me as I ran into the foyer. She studied my face, which had to be pale white and grimacing. "Do you need medical attention?" She started patting me, checking for injuries and sanity.

"Hand-sanitizer and Matty. In that order."

She pulled a miniature plastic jug from her apron pocket. I'd like to think she kept it there because she's also germ-conscious, but I know she kept it for what she dubbed "Elliott Emergencies." "Matty's on the back porch finishing lunch."

"He started without me?" I slathered hand-sani from my fingertips to my elbows, then added a layer to my face for good measure.

"Chicken, he finished without you. Don't you have a cell phone? I couldn't let the boy starve. He's on his lunch break. Lord knows what in the world you've been up to."

"I can't explain now, but it's a shocker."

"Well, it hasn't exactly been a Zen garden over here. Busy and I kicked Jane out of my kitchen and she's due to break down the door any minute."

I thanked her for the sani and scooted through the solarium and out the back door.

The Big House sits on over thirty-five rolling acres covered with magnolias, pines, crape myrtles and palm trees. A sparkling lap pool stretched across the patio, framed by chaise lounges and umbrella'd dining tables, one of which hosted Matty Gannon and Jane Walcott Hatting. Eating lunch. Together.

Laughing.

I took a deep, calming breath. The kind they teach you in yoga class. But instead of feeling calm, I breathed in a whole lot of stink and gagged in the most unladylike manner. Maybe Matty wouldn't notice the stench.

"Jesus, Elliott, you smell like the gutter," Jane said. She literally pinched her nose with one hand while she spoke, waving me away with the other. "What have you done now?"

Nearly the same thing Carla asked, but it sounded so rude coming from Jane. I straightened my back. "I hear wonderful things coming from the kitchen. These surprises are really going to knock your socks off, Jane. I've never heard such genius ideas."

She jumped to her feet. "They told *you*?"

I smiled and shrugged vaguely.

Matty placed his napkin next to his plate, then joined us on the other side of the table. "Jane, I should let you get back. I appreciate you joining me for lunch."

"The pleasure was all mine, Matty. I'll see you at the Tea, then?"

"See you then." He nodded to Jane and she walked away.

"I'm so so sorry, Matty. I got held up and called, but you didn't answer. And you had to eat lunch with Jane, I'm so sorry about that, too."

He took a small step back. "You okay, Elli? Looks like you've been swimming in a tub of chum."

"Something like that," I said and tried not to cringe at the word chum. "Someone vandalized Gilbert Goodsen's boat and I accidentally slipped into a bucket of disgusting. I would've showered, but I was already late to meet you."

"You're fine, Elli. But listen, I have to get back to campus. School starts Thursday and I'm tied up tomorrow, you know how crazy the preparations can be."

He walked across the brick patio toward the steps.

"Hey, Matty," I called and waited for him to turn to me. "Can't we go back to being best friends? I miss you."

He slowly smiled, low and handsome. "I miss you, too, El."

Tod bustled from the doors behind Matty. His neat button-down was partially untucked and had a smudge near the pocket. "Do you have any idea what I'm dealing with around here? I'm a mess and it's your fault."

I dramatically looked down over my outfit, then back at his. "I win."

"Well, win this. Detective Handsome is on the phone, demanding to speak to you immediately. Says you're late for your date. And Tate Keating called four times in the last hour saying almost the same thing." He glanced over at Matty and smiled. "Looks like she overbooked today." Then he turned on his heel and marched back through the doors.

"Not overbooked. Not dates. It's not like that, I swear."

"It's okay. I know you're complicated." He half-waved, barely lifting his palm in my direction. "You take care."

I stood rooted to the ground and watched him walk away. You take care? That's the exact thing Nick Ransom said to me when he waltzed out of my life twenty years ago. What's going on? Three months ago I had both men fawning over me, and now I had none. How did that happen?

My phone beeped.

Tod texting me: *Get on the phone already.*

I texted back: *So NOW you text. Thanks.*

My pleasure, he typed back.

After thirty seconds on the phone with Nick Ransom in which I explained to him I'd be at the hospital in less than twenty minutes, and he explained he was starting without me so let's meet in the morgue, I hopped into the Mini and sped home. I was not going to the hospital smelling like dead fish.

TWELVE

(Day #3: Sunday Afternoon)

After my detour for the fastest shower in the history of all those with OCD, I whipped into the hospital parking lot only to discover it full. Perfect. I abhor cruising up and down the aisles (all three of them) scouting for spaces. Such a waste of time. I finally wedged the Mini between a beat up old VW bug and an old Plymouth Fury.

Normally I might park over by the entrance to the Medical Examiner's office, an office building attached to the back side of the hospital. It resembled a rambling brick house more than an office, but I didn't want Gilbert Goodsen to freak if we walked out of the hospital together. Better to not have to walk down those cold, impersonal halls.

Sea Pine Memorial Hospital is actually quite small. The emergency entrance is on the south side, the medical office on the east, and the main entrance on the west. I scurried through the sliding doors, slapped on a visitor's sticker, and followed the maze of hallways to the morgue, located near a series of visitation rooms and a non-denominational meditation chapel.

"I can't do it anymore. Jesus, man, look at you," a man's voice said in the distance. It sounded tense, almost desperate.

I rounded the corner and saw Gilbert Goodsen talking with Dr. Locke, the doctor who was talking to Gil in the emergency room the day he got shot.

"Yes, Carl, look at me," Gilbert said. "I'm the one in the hot soup."

Gilbert reached out for Dr. Locke's lapel, but he brushed Gilbert off when he spotted me. "Get us out of this." He spun on his heel and hurried down the hall.

"Everything okay, Gilbert?" I asked.

Gilbert turned. Definitely not okay. His yellow and brown bowling shirt was mis-buttoned and stained; his long orange swim trunks hung down past his knees with strings dangling all the way to his shoes. Wingtips, no socks.

"You said to buy new clothes, so I did."

"I meant at a department store, not a thrift shop," I said, then immediately regretted it. Poor guy just found out his wife is dead and I'm picking on his lack of fashion sense. "I'm sorry, Gilbert. You look good, considering. We should go inside."

"Considering? Considering what? What did you find? Something happen to my egg?" He looked at me with such intensity, I actually took a step back. Then he looked around the hallway as if someone might be listening, but we were all alone.

"No, Gilbert. Well, not that I know of. I'm talking about why we're down here."

He pushed open the door behind him marked "Visitation Room Two" and dragged me inside. "Oh that. I'm here once a week."

The room was bathed in shades of tan and pale blue. Large seascapes painted with broad strokes hung on the walls. Floral chairs hugged low tables with strategically placed tissue boxes on top. Two families huddled together on opposite sides of the room. Gilbert sat with one. A couple, maybe in their late thirties. The woman wept and the man stared at the floor.

I recognized the other huddle, or at least the daughter of the older man from Gilbert's office. The Whitakers, I thought. A woman in blue scrubs sat next to the daughter and talked to her in a low voice, and another man, a brother or husband, maybe, sat on her other side.

I stood in the center of the room, equidistant between each set of grievers. I didn't know them or their loved ones, and didn't feel comfortable carving out my own spot to sit since I didn't know Jaime all that well, and I had the feeling Gilbert didn't yet know she was dead.

A nurse walked through the interior door and I spotted Ransom in the other room, just before the door swung shut. I muttered to Gilbert that I'd be right back and snuck through the door.

Ransom was gone, but it didn't take long to find him. I peeked through the autopsy suite and found him deep in conversation with Dr. Harry Fleet, the medical examiner. They stood at the far side of the room near a steel table. Wet, as if it had just been washed. I tried to hide the heebie jeebies that were crawling up my skin and marched forward.

"Don't tell me you're involved in this one," Harry barked. "You go on out of here before you start trouble."

I smiled one of my best charmers. "Now, Harry, I don't start trouble."

"You certainly manage to find it, though," Ransom said.

"You two carry on like I'm not even here."

Harry growled and Ransom stared at me. Neither said a word.

"You might as well let me eavesdrop a little," I said. "This is practically the Ballantyne Memorial Hospital and Jaime Goodsen was a well-respected, quite revered, really, member of the Foundation."

No reaction.

"Look, I'll just bug you both until you tell me anyway."

They both continued to stare at me.

One beat, then two.

Ten seconds ticked by, then Ransom turned to Harry. "You were saying, time of death?"

"Best right now, say between ten last night and four this morning. I will know more after I open her up. Looks like she fought back, some skin under her nails. Scratches."

"Cause of death?"

"Bullet to the head most likely. She has a contusion on the

back of her skull, not sure which came first. Like I said, know more later."

Ransom jotted down notes. Looked like he had an entire page full from before I walked in. At least from what I could tell from where I stood. I stepped closer and leaned in. It didn't help. Neither did him snapping the book shut.

"Thank you, Dr. Fleet," he said. "I look forward to reading the full report."

I nodded sagely, in agreement.

"Not you, Lisbon," they said in tangent.

"Fine. Not like I want to read an autopsy report."

I followed Ransom into the anteroom.

He stopped me before I could stop him. "What else do you know?"

"I was going to ask you the same thing. You were with Harry much longer than me. Certainly you know more."

"Of course I know more. I am the lieutenant, you are the witness. Only the witness. Do you hear me?"

"Don't get all bossy, Ransom. I'm just asking a question or two. You know I'm already involved."

"In an egg hunt, Lisbon. Not this." He stepped closer. His jaw set so tight, I thought his teeth might crack.

"It could be connected," I said.

"Out."

"Fine. I have to tell Gilbert about Jaime anyway." I casually waltzed toward the door to the visitation room.

He grabbed my sleeve and yanked me back and I nearly fell on my ass. "Wait. Goodsen's here and you didn't tell me?"

"Why would I tell you? You think because you're the lieutenant, I have to tell you every little thing. It doesn't work that way." I struggled out of his grasp. "Besides you told me you were starting without me. How am I supposed to know what you know when you won't tell me what you know?"

"I will deal with you later," Ransom said and swung open the door.

"You should be ashamed, you bastard! You cheated my father!" The Whitaker daughter screamed at Gilbert Goodsen in the middle of the room. She pushed Gilbert, hard, into a row of chairs.

The other Whitaker tried to pull her away, but she moved out of his reach and bumped into the nurse.

"Kat, Alex, really," Gilbert said.

Ransom stepped in front of Kat as a shield between her and Gilbert.

"You killed my father," she sobbed. "You will rot in hell for this."

"Stop, Kat," Alex said softly. "Stop it. Dad wouldn't want this."

The nurse put her arm around Kat, while Alex took his place on the other side.

"I'm sorry about your dad, truly," Gilbert said. He looked shaken and jittery. His feet tapping against the side of the coffee table. He ran a hand through his hair. "I should go."

I glanced at Ransom. One of us needed to tell him and I didn't think it would be me.

"Mr. Goodsen, could I see you for a moment?" Ransom asked.

Gilbert was so relieved to get out of that room, he didn't even wonder why a police lieutenant wanted to talk to him, or why he chose the interior morgue room to do it in.

I followed them, the door softly swinging shut behind me.

Gilbert Goodsen slid to the floor when Ransom told him Jaime was dead. Killed on his boat.

"The *Tiger Shark*?" he choked out. He scrambled to his feet and grabbed both my shoulders. "When? Were you there? The egg?"

Ransom pulled Gilbert's hands from my shoulders. "I have a few questions." He turned to me and said, "Without you."

"And I have questions for you, too, Gilbert."

Ransom pushed me toward the door.

"Meet me at my office in, about, in..." Gilbert said.

"Thirty minutes, tops," Ransom said.

I nodded and left. Gilbert was falling apart and not just from Jaime's death. There was more to this egg and he was going to tell me one way or another.

THIRTEEN

(Day #3: Sunday Late Afternoon)

I zipped across the island with a quick stop at Taco Bell for lunch (two bean burritos, extra sauce, extra cheese, plus a large Pepsi) and use of the facilities, and I still arrived at Gilbert's office before he did. The front door was locked; Mary-Louise must have been enjoying a Labor Day without any labor.

I sat in the parking lot and pondered the case while I waited. Jaime's death added a new dimension. A horrible and tragic one. Somebody clearly wasn't happy with her. Or with Gilbert. Did they intend to kill Gilbert, but killed Jaime by mistake? Middle of the night, black as pitch in that cabin, Gilbert is the one who was supposed to be on the *Tiger Shark*, not Jaime.

So why *was* Jaime there? Reconciliation seemed unlikely as Gilbert was out of town. Unless she wanted to surprise him. Though after dumping his burned clothes all over town, I couldn't imagine Jaime planned a pleasant surprise. Was she in the middle of vandalizing when the killer stopped her? Was the killer the same person who shot Gilbert?

And yet, Gilbert still asked about the egg before asking what happened to Jaime. Screwy priorities, or did he already know the answer? Did I dare ask him?

Time to find out. Gilbert pulled into the lot driving a car smaller than the Mini. I stared, slackjawed. I'd never seen any motor vehicle smaller than mine. A Smart Car. Lime green with tiny wheels and no rear end, as if someone whacked off the back half of the car. He parked next to the Mini (which now looked like a limousine), but as soon as I got out, he backed out. He waved at the front door to the office and putt-putted around the building and out of sight.

Five minutes later, he unlocked the door and yanked me inside. He locked the door behind me. "Someone's following me. I needed to change cars, something inconspicuous."

"You're driving a pedal car, Gilbert. It's pretty conspicuous."

"Please tell me you found the egg. *Please*," he pleaded.

I followed him into his office, then sat in a chair facing his desk. He picked up a letter opener, mindlessly tapping it against a round crystal paperweight.

"I have not found the egg. But there's more to this story and you need to tell me. The whole thing, if I'm going to help you."

He tucked the letter opener behind his right ear and gripped the paperweight. "It's a rotten egg. Been stinking up my whole life since I got it."

"So not a family heirloom?"

"I'm sure it's someone's family heirloom, just not mine." He tossed the small crystal ball into the air, then caught it with both hands. "The insurance business isn't what it used to be. Regulations, competition, online cut-rate internet knockoffs. To really succeed, to really make a name, you need to be creative."

"How creative?"

He tossed the weight into the air, then caught it again. "Some clients would rather sell their valuables than insure them. You know, they call me up to drop it off their policy, see how much they save. I ask them if they have a buyer. If not, sometimes I pitch in. It's nothing illegal, no insurance fraud or anything."

"So you bought the egg from a client?"

"Yes. He needed money right away, no time to wait for an auction—"

"Why the rush?" I interrupted.

"I don't know. Everyone has problems, right? I'm a problem-solver." He studied the crystal ball as if looking for answers, then threw it into the air. "One day, a client brings me an appraisal from a local pawn broker who wanted to buy his Fabergé egg, but the pawn guy backed out of the deal at the last minute. I matched the pawn price, bought it right then, here in the office. The egg and this tray of trinkets. Like a grab bag." He pointed vaguely at the cabinet door where he kept them. The *unlocked* door.

"You matched the price? Didn't you want to get your own appraisal first?"

"Nah, I know the broker. He always cheats by half, a little extra padding. I knew I could flip it quick for a small profit. My way of being creative, keep me and Jaime afloat."

"How much in dollars are we talking?" I remembered the figure scribbled on the pawn slip, $60,000, but I wanted to see if Gilbert would be honest with me.

"I'm not comfortable talking all of my finances with you. But let's say mid five figures."

I took out my notebook and skimmed my notes. "We have to talk some finances, Gilbert, you've got me chasing down an egg for no conceivably good reason. At this point, you have dozens of items much more valuable in your possession. Was it stolen? Someone needs to sell a pricey bauble with an 'appraisal' from a pawn shop? That means stolen."

"No, not stolen. At least I don't think so. It's from a reputable elderly client, one I've bought things from before."

"Then why didn't you report it stolen when it went missing?"

He sighed. Heavily. And tossed up the paperweight. "I didn't get a chance to insure it. Besides, I know Jaime has it, and I'll get it back, then insure it." He missed the heavy ball and it clunked onto the desktop. "Had it," he said softly. "Jaime had it."

I waited a moment until he picked up the crystal paperweight, studying it in his hands. "Gilbert, you're an insurance agent. How did you not insure it? And not to be one who promotes fraud, but why not back date a claim or something? I thought for insurance agents, the line between legal and illegal was drawn in pencil."

"Are you crazy! I can't do that, I'd lose my license. And my reputation. Of all the offensive accusations. Elliott, I'm a decent human being." He leaned back and began tossing the ball again. "Besides, I only had the egg for two days. Who knew? I hadn't taken a photo, and you can't get it insured without it."

Ah, a decent human being without a sense of urgency. At least until it was stolen.

"Why so desperate now?" I asked. "Why is this the most important thing to you?"

"I already flipped it."

"Flipped it?"

"To a buyer. A collector. And he thinks I lied. But I didn't lie. I had it and I need it back." He gripped the paperweight and I could practically see his thoughts whirling behind his eyes. "Elliott, I need that egg."

"Who is the client, the one you bought it from?"

"I can't tell you. I'd love to, El, really. But it's confidential. I can't blab all over town. Gilbert Goodsen's lips do not sink ships." His face deflated, almost caving in on itself. "Oh, Jaime. No more ships."

I, too, remembered her on the boat as he said it, and immediately felt a twinge of sadness, with a hint of guilt. I'd been so convinced she was to blame for everything, I ignored how much danger she had been in. My throat still hurt from her madman boyfriend choking me. I coughed and sat up straighter, to break the spell we'd wandered into.

"I understand discretion better than anyone on this island, Gilbert. I need you to trust me. If you want me to find the egg, which could've been taken by literally anybody who's ever been in this office, you need to tell me."

"It doesn't matter who! The client in no way, form or shape wants their egg back. Ever. They were happy to unload it and they do not care about it. Elliott, the client absolutely has nothing to do with it. Please stop focusing on all the wrong things and find my egg!"

"It's only been like two days," I said. "Why so urgent? Why is this taking over everything? Spit it out already and let me help you."

He studied the paperweight as if it were a crystal ball. The magic kind, not the hold-down-papers-in-case-a-strong-breeze-blew-through-the-windowless-room kind. "It's for a patent on Gil-animals. The final amendment to the app is due in three days. I didn't have the cash to pay, these things are expensive, and I've been waiting nearly four years for it to come through. I owe the government filing fees and my back attorney fees. Unless I pay him everything I owe, he won't file. But I knew he collected these things. Has two eggs already. So I offered an exchange. He gets the fire opal egg, marks me paid in full and files the app."

"But it was stolen before you could get it to him."

"Yepper. Now he thinks I'm stalling, so he's refusing to pay the fees. The patent application will lapse and I lose the whole thing. My legacy. The big one. I even got a line on a New York department store that wants to license."

"And what exactly is Gil-animals?"

He leaned forward. "Only the coolest fashion system ever created for a man's wardrobe. He picks a color for the day, say it's the red sticker. He picks any tie with a red sticker on the box, then any shirt with a red sticker, same with the pants. He can't go wrong! Men be stylin' with their stickers."

"You mean like Garanimals? Where kids match the tags to dress themselves?"

"Yep. Men don't always know what's in style. Gil-animals makes them snazzy dressers no matter who they are. Put the system in place last year, but couldn't get any investors. I use it myself, tell everyone about it when I can. This patent will change everything. Like I said, New York. Filled with folks needing to look spiffy in a jiffy. Dazzle without the hazzle."

"Sure, sure. Who wants hazzle?" I said, nodding at his jazzy catchphrases. I thought about the high-end shops in Manhattan, filled with expensive suits and chic ties and plenty of salesmen to dress a man up. Why would they need a color-coded system? But what did I know about fashion? I still wore leggings as pants in emergency situations. Like no clean pants.

"I'm scraping the bottom of my piggy bank. If I don't get that egg, I'm busted with nothing for the future."

"What happened to your viatical monopoly? Shouldn't that have kept you flush? Or at least enough to pay the bills?"

He leaned back with a sigh. "The bad economy hurts even the dying. You'd think business would be booming."

"You'd think."

"And with Jaime gone, it will all have been for nothing." He stared at a dent in the wood where the weight hit earlier. He ran his finger over the depression. He had a trace of anguish in his eyes when he looked up at me. "She really hated me, didn't she?"

I didn't know how to answer that, and nothing good could come of that conversation now. "I think she seemed angry at you, maybe not hated you. She definitely took issues with Gil-animals. I noticed color-coded boxes in the master closet and they weren't exactly sorted properly."

The phone rang and Gilbert jumped. The crystal weight bounced off the table, then rolled onto the floor. He gripped his hair with both hands like a maniac.

"What's wrong?" I asked and the phone rang again.

He looked at me with wide eyes, but made no move to answer it. "I'm being harassed. Chased, followed, phone calls. I was shot!"

The phone rang again, the shrill old-fashioned bell echoed in the quiet room.

I reached across the desk and picked it up. "Goodsen Insurance."

"Yes, hello," an elderly lady said. "My name is Willa Farnesworth. Is Mr. Goodsen in today? I know it's a holiday weekend, but he gives me such good advice. I've got two more items I know he'd like." The woman had a sweet voice and sounded no more than one hundred and ten years old.

I handed the phone to Gilbert. "Willa Farnesworth."

I watched him while he spoke, the tension slightly easing

from his face. Was he really being harassed or was he just nuts? I studied his mismatched clothes. His Smart Car keys dangled from the top pocket. Was he paranoid? Didn't Mary-Louise mention something about Gilbert being crazy some other time? Could he be Jaime's killer? But then who shot him?

Gilbert hung up the phone and turned to me. "Just a client. This time."

"Who is harassing you? And why?"

"I don't know. I don't know," he said. "I know you've got a dozen wild theories in your head. About me and my egg and my clients and my staff and my Gil-animals. I know what people think about me, but I know what I know, and I'm telling you Jaime stole the egg. No one else knew about it. If my attorney stole it, there'd be no reason to be on my case every minute to turn it over. If my client stole it back, well, no need." He gestured to the phone. "Plenty more things to sell. That only leaves Jaime. She's the only one who could've stolen the egg."

Or the antiques appraiser or Mary-Louise. Or anyone else Mary-Louise told. "Well, then, if that's the case, it's easy. You were still married and you'll inherit all of the property. You can search everything now."

"I have! I've looked everywhere and it isn't anywhere and what am I supposed to do? I'm losing my mind and Jaime's dead!" He leaned across the desk, nearly crawling over to grab my hands. "Help me. Please. You have to help me."

I squeezed his hands and helped him stand. I patted him on the arm. "We have plenty of options, we'll find it. It's just an egg, it won't be that hard. Call the local banks. All of them, from here to Charleston. Ask if Jaime had an account there. Or call your attorney. Family attorney, not patent. See if Jaime had a safe deposit box. You're entitled to the contents, assuming she didn't have a will that says otherwise."

He hugged me so tight, I got a Charlie horse in my neck. "I'm on it, I'm on it. Good idea, El. Good idea. They're closed today and tomorrow's Labor Day, but I can call Tuesday."

"Perfect. Did Jaime have any family? What about close friends?"

"Her sister in Charleston, Judith Durant. Owns a shop on King. Durant's Antiques, I think. But they haven't talked in years. I guess someone should call her and tell her." He paused. For a long time.

"Gilbert, *you* need to call her. It will be so much easier for her if she hears the news from family. What about Jaime's friends?"

He nodded slowly, then leaned on the desk. "I'll call her after you leave. And Jaime's pretty close to Alicia Birnbaum. Her doubles partner and the one who really pushed Jaime to divorce."

I groaned on the inside. I'd forgotten about Alicia Birnbaum and her pushiness. "I'll talk to her. Anyone else?"

He went from nodding to shaking his head, then smacked his forehead with his palm. "Miranda Gaines. How could I forget? They were good friends, not like Alicia. Miranda never said a cross word. Crossword! I don't know where my mind is. Jaime and Miranda played cards or ping pong or something. Maybe bridge? I don't even know. No wonder Jaime hated me."

"This must be very hard on you," I said. "Let me talk to her sister and her friends, see what else I can find."

He plucked his Smart Car keys out of his pocket and tossed them on the desk, then dug around for a pen. "Maybe I am being paranoid. This will work out, right?"

"I'm not giving up, but not everything can be done in a day. Be patient."

"It's really important, you know." He rummaged through his desk, wrote on the back of a business card, and then handed it to me. "Their numbers. Judith, Miranda, Alicia. So you can call."

He walked me through the offices to the front door. "Thanks for not asking if I killed Jaime."

"No one thinks you killed her, Gilbert. It's simple logic. Why kill her on your boat, leave her on the boat, then put it back in the slip?"

"Yeah, I guess."

"One last quick question," I asked. "What were you and the doctor arguing about at the hospital earli—?"

A knock on the door interrupted me and Gilbert's face lost all color. Either from the knock or my question.

I opened the door to Nick Ransom, Corporal Parker, and two uniforms standing on the sidewalk.

"Are you following me all over town?" I asked. "I told you we should team up. Maybe we could carpool."

"Mr. Goodsen, I need you to come with me. I have some questions, down at the station."

"You already questioned him at the mor—, hospital."

Ransom leaned in and whispered in my ear. "By the way, Mimi might be able to help you."

"Really!" I nearly squealed.

"What? What's happening?" Gilbert asked. "Is that bad or good?"

"Sorry, Gilbert, different matter," I said.

"Maybe. Call her, she wants to do lunch."

"Lunch? With your mother?"

Ransom stepped away from the front door and Parker took his place near Gilbert.

"And Lisbon, don't bother coming to the station. You won't be able to talk to him until Tuesday."

"I thought you said no one thinks I killed her," Gilbert said as he locked the door behind him.

Corporal Parker took his arm and walked him to the back of a cruiser.

"Gilbert, call your attorney," I hollered before the door shut.

Ransom turned to me. "So you think he's guilty. Interesting."

"He's at the police station, he needs an attorney."

"Stay out of this, Lisbon."

Stepping closer, I whispered in his ear. "See you at the station." Then I spun around and climbed into my Mini.

I hoped Gilbert heard me before the door slammed. And I hoped he took my advice. In his crazed state, who knew what he'd say to Ransom. I felt terribly guilty. This man's life was literally falling apart and Mr. Ballantyne personally dispatched me to help him.

And I was going to. Ransom or no, I was going all in.

I studied forensics in college. I wanted to be an investigator (before I realized the extent one must encounter germy surfaces and gory situations, and apparently I faint at the latter and freak out at the former). I'm happy performing minor inquiries for Ballantyne supporters and leaving major investigations to the Sea Pine police. But my client, my one and only client, got shot and now arrested. Actually, got his egg stolen, then shot, his wife murdered, now arrested. How could I ignore everything? Certainly it wasn't a stretch to expand the scope of my investigation. It was practically my duty.

FOURTEEN

(Day #3 & 4: Sunday Afternoon/Monday Morning)

I rushed down Cabana Boulevard, hoping if I stayed close to Ransom's racer and the patrol car parade, then I wouldn't get pulled over for speeding. The department only had about sixteen cars out on patrol at any given time, so odds were in my favor.

The City of Sea Pine gave the department a shiny new station about ten years back as part of the Island Civic Complex, on the north side of the island near Oyster Cove Plantation. The library took up the west end of the complex, while the police station occupied the east.

We all arrived at the station in less than fifteen minutes. They went in the back while I went in the front. I slid the lanyard with my temporary PI credentials over my neck and entered the small lobby. Even though all the volunteers in reception knew me, I thought it played better to look professional.

One of the senior volunteers greeted me, a man about ninety who once served his country in the Second World War.

"Hey there, Elliott Lisbon, what brings you 'round these parts?"

"Looking for Parker. I followed her into the station."

He reached for the phone with a mildly shaky hand and punched in an extension. After a brief exchange, he turned back to me. "Go on back, then. I'll buzz you in, you know where to find her."

"Thank you," I said and opened the door to the main station room. I walked down a narrow hallway, the walls lined with bulletin boards, most covered with flyers. Bikes for sale, both of the beach cruiser and motorized racer variety, random furnishings for sale, even a motor home.

Once past the enormous shredder and around the corner, it opened up into a large square room divided into ten cubicles. Parker's was the largest cube, near the back, centered between the doors to the Lieutenant's office and the Captain's. Both their doors were open, but the offices were empty.

I plopped into the chair next to Parker's desk and she looked up from her keyboard where her fingers had been rapidly typing.

"I can't tell you anything," she said. "And you know the Lieutenant won't let you see him."

"What kinds of questions is he asking? You don't have to tell me specifics, just the topic. The shooting? Jaime's death? The egg?"

Parker sat straight as a pin with her hair pulled into a long blonde pony. She turned back to her typing. "Can't tell you, Elli. You might as well go home. We'll be here a while."

I leaned forward. "Tell me this, did Gilbert at least ask for an attorney?"

She glanced at me and shook her head once.

I sighed and thanked her. I pointed to an empty conference room up the hall. "I'm going to make a quick call, be right back."

Gilbert needed an attorney. Not because he was guilty of anything. At least I hoped not. But because he needed guidance. And someone to keep him from blurting out all his crazy.

Believe it or not, the police didn't actually throw tantrums about people asking for attorneys, at least not like on tv and not on Sea Pine Island. They didn't necessarily talk suspects into calling one, but they also understood the benefit of having an attorney present. Especially when things advanced to a trial and the jury saw the client wasn't coerced or threatened or abused or whatever. Win, win.

I sat in the metal chair and debated who to call. Gregory Meade was a big shot criminal attorney out of Savannah who helped me out on my last big Ballantyne murder investigation, but I knew he was wrapped up in a major murder trial involving grave robbing, voodoo, and a ring of senior citizen museum volunteers. Probably wouldn't be able to spare time on a holiday weekend to help me out. The only other criminal attorney I knew, and was comfortable calling in a favor from, was Busy Hinds. She of the swirly cape and mistaken table confirmations. I hoped she'd answer.

"Hello, hello, Elliott. I was just talking about you," she said, with a trio of high-pitched dog yips in the background. "Now, Sugar Pie, you'll get yours in a minute."

"Oh? Good things, I hope," I said. "But listen—"

"I know I goofed up those darn chairs, but I don't want you to worry one bit. I've got a surprise!"

"Tables! You found tables! How, when, where? Wait, I don't care, thank you, thank you," I said, Gilbert completely forgotten.

"Even better, come by the kitchen first thing and you'll see what we're doing for the tea. It's berserk, and gorgeous. No one will even notice the missing chairs when they see what Carla and I came up with. I told her straight out, you'll love it. And so will Janie."

I sighed even deeper than before. No chairs or tables. But Mimi Ransom might come through. Ransom! Get in the game, woman. One crisis at a time.

"Sounds fantastic, Busy. But that's not why I'm calling. Are you free this evening?"

"Sure, sure. You want to meet for drinks, talk Wonderland? I know a darling new spot in South Pebble Beach, makes a killer pomerita."

"I need an attorney, criminal case, and I need you tonight. Right now, actually."

"Good Lord, Elli, don't bury the lead. Is this your one call? Which station you at?"

"Not for me, for Gilbert Goodsen. He's in for questioning right now on the island and I need—"

"I'm on my way. You tell whoever is handling that I'll be there in two shakes and to stop the questioning. They'll wait until I get there. Now hurry, hurry...you, too, Sugar Pie. Mommy has to go to work," she said and hung up.

Parker wasn't at her desk, but I found her in front of the main interview room talking to Officer Prickle. They stopped as soon as I approached.

"Busy Hinds, Gilbert's attorney, is on her way," I said. "Can you let the Lieutenant know?"

Parker nodded and slipped into the interview room.

Prickle put his hands on his utility belt. "Who are you to call his attorney? Seems like you should be arrested for interfering in a police investigation. Or pulled into your own interview room." He moved one of his hands very close to the handcuffs.

"You know, I've been around this police station for more than a decade, and I've never seen you before the other day. Are you fresh out of the academy?"

He raised his finger about an inch and a half from my face. "I'm none of your business, but I'll make it my business," he said. He spun a full one-eighty and marched into the main station room.

I decided I'd better wait in the lobby for Busy. I had no idea what this cracker was talking about, and I didn't want to find out.

Busy arrived in less than twenty minutes, flying past me in a whirl of carry-alls: handbag, briefcase, laptop satchel, and some sort of box case that looked as if it might hold a projector. She tossed me an air kiss and went straight to the interrogation room.

After hanging around the station another thirty minutes, but getting no more information, I drove home. And then, after still no word after another six hours, I finally went to bed.

I woke to a text sent at 7:27 a.m.: *He'll be out on Tuesday, let's talk later this morn. Tate Keating says hello.*

A. I did not want to be up at 7:27 a.m.

B. Especially if Tate Keating's name was invoked.

C. Tuesday!

I quickly texted back. And by quickly, I mean it took me four minutes to get my message typed out. Auto-correct kept fixing things incorrectly, and I hated abbreviations. I hit send, then called her.

"Good morning, Elli, was just texting you back," she said, all chipper and cheery. "Want to meet for breakfast? I can be at Sunny Side Up in ten minutes."

I glanced down at my jammies. "I'm in another meeting right now, but can you give me the quick scoop on Gilbert and Tate Keating?"

"Yeah, yeah, of course. It's nothing terrible, but the holiday is working against us. Court's closed until tomorrow morning. Gilbert's resting in holding, but the Lieutenant got a call about another suspect, he's checking it out now. So there's a wee chance they'll release Gil early, without an official arrest and arraignment. I have to run take care of Sugar Pie, but I'll be back in a flash. And Tate Keating arrived about a half hour ago, talking about deadlines. I gave him nothing, but you know Tate. Nothing means something."

"I'll head to the station," I said and hopped out of bed. I balanced the phone against my shoulder and grabbed a clean tee and shorty pants from the closet. "They tell you anything on this other suspect?"

"Not much, but I'm sure they'll dish by the time you get here."

I thanked her and jumped into an ice cold shower. No time to let the water warm, not with Tate Keating chatting up the volunteers at the front desk.

And no time for Cheerios, either, I thought as I drove to the station. This early on a Monday, the break room should be stocked with plenty of pastries. The frosted kind with a hole in the middle and sprinkles on top.

Tate's yellow MG roadster sat right up front near the station door. Must be something tantalizing to get him here this early on a holiday.

He nearly knocked me flat on his way out the door while I went in. "'Killer Board Strikes Again.' Sounds like a grabber, right?"

"Jaime Goodsen wasn't on the board," I said to his fleeting back. "And we've never had a killer at the Ballantyne!"

He either didn't hear me or he ignored me, but without a wave, he zipped out of the lot and down the road.

I considered chasing him down, but just then Parker came into the lobby from behind the station door.

"I can give you five minutes with Gilbert if you want."

"I want," I said and followed her through the lobby, the main station, to the very back where they kept a small cluster of cells.

"*Elliott!* You're here," Gilbert said. Both sleeves on his bowling shirt were ripped and his orange swim trunks were on backward. And he wore no shoes.

He hugged me tight through the bars, and it took every ounce of humanity to hug him back. He smelled like urine, mildew, and day-old barf.

I looked at Parker over his shoulder and raised an eyebrow in question. "What the?" I mouthed.

"Quiet night, except for crazy pants, here. We had old man Kipper sleeping off a bender," she said. "He hadn't been home in a week. But seems Gilbert needed someone to talk to, so they huddled together most of the night."

"Gil, it'll be okay," I said. "Busy's on the case, and I'll do whatever it takes to get you out." And I would, too. Gilbert got shot, his wife murdered, and landed in the pokey in a span of three days, and I couldn't even pick up a clue on my egg hunt. I definitely needed to get it together, because arraignment and prison loomed in this man's future.

"It's not too bad in here, Elli," Gilbert said. He gripped the bars and squeezed his face through the gap. The thought of the germy metal pressed into skin made my palms twitch.

"You go rest, okay? I'm going to talk to Corporal Parker, amp up my investigation."

He nodded, squishing his cheeks with each movement, then crept over to a cot bolted to the wall.

Parker led me out to the lobby and handed me off to Ransom.

He stood at the desk, tapping his hands on the countertop, talking with the day's senior volunteer. "Well, Elliott Lisbon, you're up awfully early."

"It's like eight thirty. I've been up for hours. Maybe three at least." I discreetly glanced down at my shoes, made sure they matched.

His smile lifted in a half-smirk as if he knew I was full of shit, then gestured to a waiting area in the corner of the lobby.

He rested on the arm of a sofa, casually crossing one ankle over the other. He smelled like morning: a zesty fresh shower, a Downy-crisp shirt, and a hint of dark roasted coffee.

I smelled like someone who just hugged Gilbert the jailbird.

"So what's going on?" I asked. "Busy said you had a suspect. Other than Gilbert Goodsen, who we both know did not do this. He's not capable."

"Good morning to you, too. I do not know that Gilbert didn't do this. He's the beneficiary on a million-dollar life insurance policy for his wife."

"He's an insurance salesman. For an insurance guy, a million bucks is practically chintzy. And he probably has policies on every item he owns." Except the extremely valuable Fabergé egg, I thought. I kept that morsel to myself.

"Uh-huh," Ransom said. "He doesn't exactly present a picture of innocence."

"His picture isn't one of guilt. He's stressed. It's been a rough couple of days."

"I'm aware. A robbery, a shooting, and a murder. With one Gilbert Goodsen dead center."

"A robbery?"

"The egg hunt. Any luck on that front?"

"I'm actually making quite a bit of progress. But I'd really like to know about this other suspect Busy Hinds mentioned. It must be good or she wouldn't know about it."

He stayed silent, watching me, and I resisted the urge to shift from foot to foot. "Come on, Ransom. I'm asking nicely. Give me *something*."

The look in his eyes shifted slightly and I felt a flush rush up my neck. Before he left for the state training facility three months ago, he would've offered up a snappy suggestion on what he'd like to give me, but he just nodded slightly instead. "I suppose I could share some things, as a courtesy."

"Because I'm an investigator in training?"

"Because Busy will tell you anyway."

"Good enough for me."

"Gilbert's secretary, Mary-Louise Springer, called into the station late last night in a panic. She had told her boyfriend Bobby Falco about the Fabergé egg—"

"The egg? I knew it was connected. Wait, Bobby? From the pink trailer over at Fisher's Landing, the one Parker wouldn't tell me about? I'm running an investigation, too, Ransom."

He ignored me.

"So Bobby stole the egg?"

"Not exactly. Or at least Mary-Louise isn't admitting that right now. She said she told Bobby that Jaime Goodsen stole Gilbert's expensive Fabergé egg. Bobby hatched the brilliant plan to call Gilbert, say Jaime gave *him* the egg, and he'd sell it back to Gilbert for fifty thousand dollars."

"Jaime just gave Bobby the egg? And Gilbert believed it?"

"Didn't even question it."

"So when they met at Tug's on Friday, Gilbert thought he was buying back his egg. He told me the money was down payment on a new boat."

"Nope, he was buying back the stolen egg. But there was no egg. Bobby probably panicked when he saw the bag of money and shot Gilbert right there. He took off and hasn't been seen since."

"But Mary-Louise has seen him, right?" I asked.

"Neither seen nor heard from him. Guess Bobby didn't want to share the cash from the bag."

"Interesting. So why did Mary-Louise call last night?"

"She heard we brought Gilbert to the station and quickly panicked, thinking she'd be an accessory when this whole Bobby scheme came to light. Wanted to get out in front."

"Okay. But if she said Bobby killed Jaime, then why is Gilbert still locked up?"

"She didn't say that, rather she was worried she'd get swept into the mess. She talked so fast, I barely kept up. Who knows what crimes those two are capable of, including murder."

"Exactly. Gilbert is not in their league. Did you bring her in for questioning?"

"We searched her house this morning," he said.

"But she's not here. That's what you're not saying."

He conceded with a nod. "Mary-Louise is gone. Cleared out after her call last night is my guess. No sign of her or Bobby or the egg. But we were able to find a photo of Bobby, who matches the shooter's description from Tug Boat's."

"Can I see? I'll follow you back, grab a donut." Or three. "I'm starving," I said.

"Sorry, Elliott. We ran out of donuts an hour ago." At my sad and shocked face, he added, "they always go fast on a holiday. And give us a day or so on the photo. We just got it ourselves."

I didn't want to push it, since he was offering to share it with me. Just not as soon I wanted. But I was a beggar, not a chooser. "I guess I should find someone to cover Goodsen Insurance. Even if we get him out tomorrow, he'll need a few days to get back on his feet."

"Going to be a while before he's on his feet."

"He may be under some stress—"

"That man is one mismatched sock away from the Cuckoo's Nest," Ransom said.

"—but that doesn't mean he killed his wife."

"What's this 'we' get him out? Before you start thinking about gathering evidence on your own, don't."

"I won't step on your toes, but I'm an investigator—"

"In training."

"All the same."

"Yours is the case of the missing egg."

"I'm beginning to think it's all about this egg. Can you at least share your working theory?"

"I've shared quite a bit already. I think it's your turn to give me something, Red," he said and stood.

The flush returned and I felt like I was in the middle of a hot flash.

He stepped closer. "Don't you want to know what I want?"

I nodded.

"Your promise to stay out of this. Continued promise, to continue staying out of this."

"Ransom, I can't promise that. My client is in your jail. What kind of investigator stays out of it?"

"One in training." He chucked my chin lightly. Like one would do to a child. In a fifties movie involving a good sport. He started to walk away.

"Don't underestimate me. I'm quite resourceful."

"Indeed you are," he said and waved at the volunteer to buzz him through the door.

"Wait! One last question," I said. "At least tell me your theory on how Jaime was killed."

"You're resourceful, you'll figure it out." And with that, he was gone.

I hurried to the counter. "Can you buzz me in real quick?"

"Well, now, I'm not one to eavesdrop, but I don't think the Lieutenant would appreciate that," the elderly volunteer said. "I like my job here."

"How about Corporal Parker? Will you see if she'll give me like two seconds?"

That he was willing to do, and Parker came out a minute later.

"The Lieutenant mentioned you weren't going to step on our toes."

"No stepping, only asking. And I made no promises," I said. "One quick question and then I'll skedaddle. What's your theory on Jaime Goodsen's murder?"

She pulled me to the side and lowered her voice one octave. "Someone, likely Gilbert, caught Jaime vandalizing his boat. They struggled and Jaime ended up dead."

"Or Bobby went to the boat to look for more money. Or the egg. And thought Jaime was Gilbert, or Jaime saw him and he panicked again. Bobby doesn't hold up under pressure. Remember? He shot Gilbert."

"I remember, Elliott. We're working on it. Watch the toes, okay?"

"Sure, sure. No worries," I said.

I walked out of the lobby just as Busy parked her red hot Alfa Romero next to the Coop.

"Hello, hello! I'm back. How's our Gil?" she asked

"Not terrible, but in trouble, that's for sure."

"So Lillie filled you in?"

Lillie? "Oh, Parker, yeah. She and Ransom. I'm caught up. The insurance policy doesn't look good. But I'm pretty sure the Lieutenant thinks Gilbert's too crazy to be involved. I need to see what I can find to convince him absolutely Gilbert's not involved."

She gathered up her entourage of belongings and whisked into the station.

I called Tate Keating at the *Islander Post*, but it went straight to voicemail. I left a message, plus asked the receptionist to leave a written note on his desk about Gilbert not being involved in the shooting or his wife's murder, but I had a feeling it wouldn't matter much at this point.

I sat in my car with the top down, still trying to rationalize getting involved in Gilbert's shooting and his wife's murder. I actually do believe in coincidences. Case in point, Carla once commented that my new sunglasses reminded her of the Blues

Brothers. Later that same day, Sid called to say she was renting the movie Blues Brothers and did I want to watch with her? When was the last time you even thought of the Blues Brothers, much less discussed them twice in one day? Total coincidence.

But larger events tended against happenstance. I thought it earlier, Ransom said it earlier, and now I couldn't let it go. A priceless bauble stolen, a man shot, his wife killed. All within two days. Three terrible traumas, not three random anomalies. And might as well toss in Gilbert's claims of harassment as a fourth. It's all connected. It had to be. I wasn't saying Bobby stole the egg, shot Gilbert, killed Jaime, and was now harassing him. Though, maybe why not Bobby? Where was he anyway?

And Mary-Louise Springer. I didn't like that this Bonnie and Clyde duo were on the loose, but perhaps they were in Rio by now. While reassuring, it didn't get Gilbert out of jail or solve my egg case.

Unless they lied and really did steal the egg. Just because Ransom didn't find it, doesn't mean I couldn't. Now that's motivation.

FIFTEEN

(Day #4: Monday Morning)

Since I missed out on the morning donuts, I swung through the Donut Hut myself. Right outside the gates to Oyster Cove Plantation, they made their dough fresh every day, and I swear the frosting on each donut contained half a stick of real butter. I ate in the parking lot while I figured out how to locate Mary-Louise. She was now my number one candidate for egg thief, even if she didn't confess it to the police. Easier to snitch on your runaway boyfriend and blame him for everything.

The best place to start was Mary-Louise's house. I didn't know where she lived, but the island was small and without conspiracy theorists who were afraid to make their info public. I started with the obvious: the Google machine. Her address came up in less than ten seconds. I may not always use/enjoy/appreciate technology, but it was kind of like magic.

After a glimpse at the Sea Pine island map in my glove box, which was faster than GPS since I knew nearly every neighborhood on the island, I found her address on Bent Tree Road, off plantation, in a more rural part of the inland island. Marsh Grass Road split the island nearly in two, starting at Cabana Boulevard just north of Palmetto Plaza.

I took Marsh Grass about two miles, then went left on Bent Tree Road. It started as a lone drive, with overgrown oaks lined up in front of miles of marshland, tall thick grass forming a dark green prairie, before I entered a loose subdivision of tiny houses lined up on compact streets.

Mary-Louise's was about four blocks in, a weathered white bungalow wedged between identical homes on each side. The yards were mostly overgrown, and I doubted a weed whacker had ever been wielded in this neighborhood.

I parked on the quiet street, a good block down from her house. Seemed as if most folks already went to work, as it was closing in on ten a.m. The air was thicker with humidity and higher heat so far from the ocean, and I could smell the briny scents coming off the salt marsh.

After a quick tuck of my phone and a pair of gloves into both pockets, I locked my car and moseyed on up the road over to the narrow drive. It was empty. No car or bicycle or other mode of transportation. The concrete on the walk up the porch was cracked, as was the porch itself. I pushed the round plastic doorbell and waited.

No answer.

The rusted screen door squeaked in protest when I opened it to knock on the front door, but again, no answer. And it was locked. I casually leaned to the left to glance inside the front window, but heavy sheers made it impossible to make out anything.

I surveyed the neighborhood from atop the porch. Still quiet, no sounds or traffic. Just an old white van parked at the curb three houses down and a lone dog barking, maybe from the block behind, but certainly not from Mary-Louise's backyard.

There wasn't an attached garage, but a wide wood fence wound around the side of the house, all the way to the back. I clunked through the gate, a splintered wreck barely hanging on to its metal latches, and shoved it shut behind me.

The dog kept barking, but now I could see the top of its red Irish Setter head as it tried to jump the fence directly behind Mary-Louise's house. Boy, that guy could jump. The fence was about six feet high.

The rear area was squat. A patchy square of yellowing grass, a narrow slab of raised concrete. And by raised, I mean like five inches from the soil. Two white plastic Adirondack chairs were arbitrarily placed near the center and four terra cotta planter pots decorated the four corners, each with a wilted geranium inside.

The back door was locked, but the handle was cheap and rattley and was probably once a shiny gold. It looked like the push button kind. Not very secure. I rattled it and shook it, but it stayed locked. Curtains hung over the windows, pulled tight on the inside, so no peeking.

The sun was full up, and so was the heat index. Without a tree or a breeze or a patio umbrella in the backyard, I might as well have been standing on the surface of the sun. I wiped my forehead with a glove from my pocket. She had to have hidden a key back here. Everyone does. And lest the world think me an opportunistic burglar or crime scene wrecker, I was neither. With Mary-Louise on the lam, and the police already through the house, I was simply taking a quick looksee to see if I could find a clue for my own investigation.

I checked each of the geranium pots, scoring a brass key beneath the one closest to the door. In one quick twist, I was in. I placed it back under the pot so I wouldn't forget and take it with me.

Wearing my gloves, I eased the door shut. It was dark and cool and smelled like old house: a mix of mold, heating oil, and aged paper. And the place was a mess. Clearly, Mary-Louise left in a hurry.

I could also see the results of the warrant-driven search. Drawers and cabinet doors not quite shut all the way, and everything looked slightly shifted, as if moved from its original spot. I looked inside each kitchen cabinet and the trash can and the refrigerator. No egg. She probably wouldn't have tucked it inside the bologna drawer, but couldn't hurt to look.

The back door opened into a galley kitchen with a two-seater vinyl dinette pushed into the right side wall. Three steps later and I was smack in the middle of the living room. Two doors opened from the left wall. A bedroom and a compact half bath.

I scoped the bath first. Just a sink and a toilet. No medicine cabinet or shelving, only a simple round red rug on the floor and a matching towel set on a bar behind the door. I checked my watch: been inside five minutes. I gave myself another ten, then I needed to get out of there.

The master, and only, bedroom was larger than I expected. The bed was made, a pretty pink and blue quilt set on top. A barely used recumbent bike sat in the far corner, dusty and neglected. I peered inside the closet. Only about a third full, all women's clothes, mostly shoved in the back. The front part held about thirty empty wire hangers.

I took one minute to spy the master bath, but nothing much left behind. And what was left, was all female-oriented. No stray razor, cologne, after shave, sport deodorant, nose hair trimmer. No egg, either.

With only a handful of minutes left, I checked the living room. The cushions were already upset, so I figured the police probably found what was to be found, but I checked anyway. Lots of crumbs, but nothing else.

I tugged on all the carpets, nothing loose, and lightly pounded on the walls, nothing loose there, either. No hidden compartments or floor boards or mysterious staircases leading to secret rooms.

I saved the best for last. Her desk. A slim writing-type desk, pushed against the front window, between a curio cabinet and towering light fixture with ten lamp arms twisted in ten different directions.

The desk held a messy mix of miscellaneous papers (receipts, coupons, flyers, postie notes) and unopened bills. Guess she wasn't worried about her credit score, since she rushed out without snatching up her mail.

And since the envelopes were all addressed to the house I was standing in, no need to jot anything down. No drawers to look inside either.

A glance to my watch told me I had about a minute left, and really, no other place to look. The curio held an interesting array of ceramic collectibles, mostly cats. Also a shiny pair of gnomes, a sparkly ballet dancer, a woven basket, a porcelain chicken, and at least a dozen other farm animals. An odd assortment that agitated my inner compulsive self. There was no symmetry. Two gnomes, a dancer and a chicken? How can she live in such disorder?

As I reached for the curio cabinet door, I heard a car pull into the driveway. I glanced through the dark sheers. A police cruiser. Oh shit.

I whirled around to run and slammed right into the sofa, going face first over the top. I rolled onto the floor, cracked my head on the coffee table, and scampered on all fours so fast, I'm not sure my knees ever touched the ground. In less than five seconds, I was outside, from curio to back door.

I quickly dusted off my pants, which were coated with about three years' worth of dust bunnies, and shoved my gloves down the front of my pants. Didn't want them in my pockets, in case they searched me. Not sure who would search me, but when you're panicking, you're panicking.

I started talking into my phone as I walked through the gate. "I'll just leave a note on the front door," I said as I hip-checked the gate back into place. And noticed my phone was upside down.

I righted it, then turned to see Deputy Prickle blocking my way down the drive. He pointed his finger at my face. "What are you doing on this property?"

"Oh, me? Looking for Mary-Louise. I thought maybe she was out gardening when she didn't answer the front door," I said and squirmed past him.

"You think we'd miss her coming back? Or maybe we searched the place all morning, but didn't notice her gardening in the backyard?" He made an unmanly swervy move when he said "gardening." "I know Lieutenant Ransom told you all about the search this morning. Including the part where Mary-Louise was not home."

I spied the white van across the street. I thought I knew all their surveillance vehicles. The police must be watching the house, then called Prickle in when I didn't come back up the drive.

"She might have been at the grocery or something," I said. "No harm in me coming by to check."

"You listen here. I won't have you obstructing my case."

"Your case? I thought this was Lieutenant Ransom's case."

"Police business is not your business."

Uh-oh, back to the whole not-my-business routine. Time for me to leave.

I nodded and scurried down the drive. I put one step into the street when an old green Plymouth sped by, and I fell back on my butt.

"*Hey!*" I yelled, scrambling up and wiping gravel from my pants. I turned to Prickle. "Why not make *that* your business?"

He ignored me.

I stomped back to my car, waving to the white van as I passed. Tattletales.

I started up my Mini and zoomed away, following the same path the speeding old Plymouth took. The car looked familiar. I was sure I'd seen it recently, but I didn't get a look at the driver. Though on an island, you ended up seeing every car at least once.

It hadn't taken much time, but I still felt like I'd wasted the morning. I didn't want to admit it, but I kind of expected to find the egg at Mary-Louise's. Maybe hidden in plain sight. But unless it was disguised as a ceramic cat, it wasn't there. So either she hid it better than I anticipated, or she didn't steal it.

Who did that leave? Who else even knew Gilbert bought the egg? Jaime obviously knew, and Gilbert still considered her the only culprit. And she could've blabbed to her friends or her sister. Either they took it or knew where she put it.

I debated whom to call: Jaime's sister or her friends? Did these people even know about Jaime's death yet? It'd only been twenty-four hours. Though knowing the island gossip network, everyone probably knew. I bet even the third grade class at Sea

Pine Elementary already heard the news and school hadn't even started yet.

I pulled out the card Gilbert gave me with contact numbers and made a quick call to Miranda, Jaime's best friend on the island, but she didn't answer. I left her a short message, asking to call me as soon as she could.

Then I called Jaime's sister, Judith Durant, the antique shop owner in Charleston. Also left a message, but made a mental note to drive out and see her. I was tired of leaving messages all over town and not getting any return calls.

I circled out of Mary-Louise's neighborhood and back onto Marsh Grass Road. Might be able to find the egg faster than I thought. An antiques shop was an even better spot to hide a Fabergé egg in plain sight, especially one owned by her sister. And it wasn't my only lead. Two other people definitely knew about the egg: the pawn broker and the antiques appraiser. They both saw it, held it, appraised it. And wanted it.

But maybe they didn't want to pay for it.

Sounded like motive to me. I needed to stop in at the Big House for a quick check, then I could be back on the trail by mid-afternoon. For the first time all day, all weekend really, I was feeling pretty good. Gilbert may be in jail, but I had two solid leads. Things might actually start to come together.

SIXTEEN

(Day #4: Monday Afternoon)

I walked into the Big House and straight into a fight in the foyer.

Carla stood to the right of the staircase, brandishing a supersized whisk, waving it willy-nilly at Jane, who did not seem the least bit intimidated.

"I demand to know what the hell you're doing with all that frosting," Jane said and pointed at five buckets of colorful frothy confection, in colors Willy Wonka himself would appreciate. Strips of masking tape adorned the side of each, marked with names like flamingo pink, buttercup yellow, and leprechaun lime.

"You don't demand anything of me," Carla replied, pointing her whisk back at Jane. "You need to stop disrupting my kitchen."

"I'm the chair of the board, I don't disrupt, I lead."

"You'll lead yourself right out of my kitchen," Carla said.

"Jane, can't you trust Carla on this one?" I said and stepped between them, though slightly closer to Carla. "You know she'll do right by the Tea."

"Trust? This isn't a party for Sandra Dee, Elliott, where we pinky swear, then braid our hair," Jane said. "It's a business. Start treating it like one. I expect a full menu on my desk by this afternoon." She glanced down at Carla's whisk, then walked away. She may have muttered "amateurs" on her way across the foyer.

"That girl is wound so tight, her head's going to spin off," Carla said.

"Don't I know it," I said. "How's things?"

"Fine. Jane-zilla just wasted half my morning, we still have no furniture for the Tea, and Edward left you a message. Tate Keating tracked him down for a comment on tomorrow's headline."

I didn't know which was worse: the lack of tables or the headline.

"And Zibby came by to check on her tea set."

I grabbed Carla's arm. "Oh shit, the broken teapot. I completely forgot."

"I told Zibby it was already in pre-set up holding and she'd have to wait to see it on Wednesday, along with everyone else."

"You're my hero," I said.

"I'm aware, chicken. Now let me get back to the kitchen before Jane climbs through a window. You better solve some of these problems. I've got enough of my own."

She tucked her whisk under her arm and picked up two buckets, then walked toward the kitchen.

Carla was right, I needed to start solving problems. That was my job, and usually, I was quite good at it. Which is why the Sea Pine Police agreed to be advisors to my PI license. As long as I produced results and kept local squabbles off their desks, they signed my PI paperwork.

Until Lieutenant Nick Ransom came back to town.

I wondered if he was the reason I'd been so distracted lately. It was as if I couldn't focus on the task before me. Any of the tasks before me. I once thought maybe he was the love of my life, but a twenty-year hiatus without communication tends to change relationships. And ours was more complicated than ever. Considering the last time I talked to him, he arrested my client.

Oh! The last time we talked, he mentioned his mother had tables. I wanted to slap myself. What was happening? I used to be able to juggle six wet cats while balancing a bowl of Jell-O on my head. Now I couldn't locate a cat if I stood in a barn with a can of tuna in one hand and a mouse in the other.

I plopped into my chair and dialed Mr. Ballantyne. While the line rang, I looked up Mimi Ransom's number in my rolodex.

Proving to myself I could still multi-task. If two tasks constituted a multi.

"Elliott? Are you there?" Mr. Ballantyne yelled into the phone.

"Mr. Ballantyne! How are you, sir?"

"Doing dandy, my dear," he shouted, his voice booming as if phoning from the space station. "We're just leaving the most amazing bale of turtles. A dozen hatchlings!"

"That sounds wonderful, sir," I shouted back, even though I heard him just fine.

"Carla mentioned the Tea was progressing splendidly, said she has a big surprise for the children."

"Indeed, going to be a stunner," I said, as if I knew exactly what the surprise was. Which I didn't. But unlike Jane, I trusted Carla and her culinary vision.

"I don't have a lot of time, my dear, but I'm worried about our Gilbert Goodsen. Been told he's in jail. Arrested for murder? Does that sound right?"

How does word travel so freakin' fast? The man's in Alaska for shit's sake. "Not arrested, sir, he's a cooperating witness," I said. "Doing everything he can to help the police with his wife's death. He's a trooper, our Gilbert." A bit of a fib, but Mr. Ballantyne wouldn't be home for a week, and it would all be over by then. I'm nothing if not optimistic.

"Bravo, then," he shouted. "And his missing egg? Unless you've found it? Can't be too difficult, right, my dear? Nothing like a rousing egg hunt," he said with a chuckle.

"Agreed, sir. I haven't tracked it down yet, but I'm getting close. Actually have quite a few solid leads I'm working on today."

"Good to hear! We don't want donors to think we don't care. He's part of the family! And how's that short list for the board coming? I hear there's a new name."

I thought of Gilbert in his torn clothes and broken demeanor. Probably not a viable (or stable) candidate anymore. But perhaps Busy made progress getting her name penciled in after all. "Busy's been a big help, for Gilbert and for the Tea, sir."

"She's a charmer, that one. Vivi adores her. Be good to see her, and you, my dear. We'll fly home tomorrow for the Tea. Going to arrive late, but Zibby convinced Vivi she's winning the Particularly Peculiar for her tea set. The top prize! We wouldn't miss it!"

And with that, he was gone.

I was so relieved he didn't mention Tate and whatever outrageous headline he was planning, it took a full minute before I realized what Mr. Ballantyne said.

They were flying home tomorrow. For the Tea. For which we had no tables. Or a winning teapot for Zibby, Vivi Ballantyne's cousin.

I quickly dialed Mimi's number.

"Mrs. Ransom," I said when she answered. "It's Elliott Lisbon, from the Ballantyne Foundation."

"Elli, dear, how are you?"

"I'm well. But in a pinch."

"Yes, I heard. I might be able to pull a string or two. Are you available for lunch tomorrow? Say twelve-thirty at the Palmetto Café, inside the Charleston Place hotel?"

I made a sound, a cross between a choke and a gag. She really wanted us to lunch? Seriously? Me and my ex-boyfriend's mother? Our paths had crossed maybe once or twice over the last twenty years on the South Carolina fundraising circuit, but we hadn't actually shared a meal since the Thanksgiving before Ransom abandoned me and our relationship a week before Christmas. I recalled a minor mishap with a pan of brown sugar carrots and Mimi's silk dining chairs.

"I would love to," I replied. I was a professional and I did what needed to get done.

"Lovely. See you tomorrow," she said.

She hung up before I could ask more about the tables. It was cutting it close, but close didn't mean it wouldn't get done.

Not one to put all the eggs (I knew the location of) into that particular basket, I made four more calls to party rental places.

Three still closed for the holiday, and one answered, but nary a table to rent or a chair to spare. Charleston for lunch was my top option.

I opened my lower desk drawer to find my folder of Charleston maps, and saw Zibby's broken teapot, now slipped into my desk. Carla always had my back. I jotted down a description of the pot including the maker's mark stamped on the bottom.

I had just tucked it away when Jane passed my open office door.

"Jane, wait," I hollered.

I scrambled up to catch her before she disappeared down the hall, but she had actually stopped when I hollered, and I nearly chest bumped her in my doorway.

"What is it now?" she said, standing a mere six inches from me.

"It's about the Fabergé egg, the one I mentioned yesterday."

She turned and started walking away, and I quickly followed.

"Unless you're about to tell me exactly what Carla's concocting in the kitchen, I'm busy," she said over her shoulder.

"I don't know what she's doing in the kitchen, but I need—"

She whirled so fast we actually did chest bump that time.

"What do you mean you don't know what's going on in the kitchen? What kind of rumpus house are we running?"

"I mean, Carla has a plan, and I have complete faith—"

"Your faith fails to impress me." She blinked slowly, waiting for me to continue. Clearly unimpressed by any of me.

"Back to the egg," I said. "I know I saw one in your shop, or at least something like it. It was ruby red?"

"Yes, I'm aware of the Fabergé egg in my own shop."

"What's the value?"

"Worth more than your faith."

"I'm serious, Jane, what value did you assign to that egg?"

"That particular egg was worth close to four million dollars."

I choked. "Four *million*?"

"Yes, it was an Imperial egg." At my blank stare, she

continued. "Carl Fabergé created eggs for the Romanov family, given as gifts to their wives at Easter. Forty-two survived the Revolution."

"What about all the other eggs?"

"Other eggs?"

"Aren't there other Fabergé eggs? I'm thinking in the fifty-thousand dollar range."

I thought she'd laugh at me, but she didn't. "Carl's grandson made limited edition eggs, many years after the fall of the House of Fabergé. While not one-of-a kind Imperial eggs, they still hold value. Also, some elaborately adorned Fabergé 'style' eggs range from fifty thousand up to the millions."

"My investigation centers around a missing egg, this is helpful. Thank you."

"Any other antiquities I can help you with? Perhaps you discovered the lost Ark of the Covenant at a yard sale?"

"One last question. How would you sell another egg, if you got it?"

"After verifying provenance, auction, of course. Unless I contacted a private seller."

"So not a pawn shop?"

"Only if you are an idiot." With a slight emphasis on "you," she walked back down the hall.

Regardless of the opinion of one Jane Walcott Hatting, I was not an idiot. However, I wasn't the one trying to sell a Fabergé egg, Gilbert Goodsen was. Or at least his client was.

I went back to my desk and dialed Sid. Like most professional PI's, every now and then I needed backup.

"It's all over the senior's phone tree," Sid said. "You wrecked Gilbert's boat, found Jaime Goodsen drowned in the harbor, got stuck in a bucket of chum and Detective Handsome arrested your client. Good Lord, woman, tell me all about it."

I rolled my eyes. "How you believe any of that nonsense is beyond me."

"Uh-huh, sugar. How much is incorrect?"

"Jaime's body was on the boat, which was not wrecked by me, I'm guessing by Jaime, and I may have accidentally gently kicked a tiny pail of fish. Barely made a splatter." I shivered as I remembered the fish juice splashing from my shoes to my face. "Besides, that was yesterday. I've got new problems. I know it's Labor Day, and you're probably celebrating on Milo's yacht, but I need a quick favor."

She sighed. "Not today, though I wish I were. Stuck working at the hospital again. What's up?"

"How about a day in Charleston tomorrow? We can do some shopping, have a little lunch…"

I opened the folder of Charleston maps and started rifling through the stack.

"You? Shopping?" Sid said. "What's the catch?"

"I need to track down Judith Durant, Jaime's sister. She owns an antique shop in Charleston, but she might know something about this egg I'm trying so unsuccessfully to find. While we're there, we need to find an identical teapot to match the one I broke of Zibby's at some kind of pawn parlor, and then also have lunch with Mimi Ransom, who may or may not pull a string to get me tables for the Wonderland Tea on Wednesday."

"Oh, is that all?"

"For now, but I'm off to a different pawn shop, so who knows what else will come up?"

"A pawn shop? If money's tight, sweetie, you know I'm here for you."

I found a thin pamphlet naming all the local antique shops in downtown Charleston. "Bingo!" I said, and circled Durant's Antiques, then focused back on Sid. "Not me. Not yet anyway. The Fabergé egg. Gilbert had an appraisal from a local pawn shop. Seems too lowbrow for such a valuable heirloom and I want to check the place out, see if maybe Jaime went there, too."

"Jaime? Why would she go there? Aren't you supposed to be finding Gilbert's egg, not investigating his wife's murder? Won't Lieutenant Handsome be unhappy about this?"

"I'm not fully investigating her murder, just her possible involvement in the case of the missing egg. Plus, Gilbert's in jail and I can't let him sit there. Something's not right with this egg, Sid. After my last fiasco investigation, I'm not ignoring anything. Or skipping any steps."

"Yes, Elli, please remember the last fiasco. You can skip a step if it means staying safe from the crazies."

"I've yet to encounter a single crazy," I said, then thought about Ransom wanting to stick Gilbert in the looney house. "Mr. Ballantyne expected me to fix the Goodsens. Now one spouse is dead and the other's in jail. That's not mending the fence. I have to find this egg. Period. If Ransom doesn't like it, he can suck it."

"Uh-huh. Do you have to be so competitive?"

"Ransom called it an egg hunt, for shit's sake. And the worst part is, I haven't even found it yet."

I sailed over the bridge and into Summerton before lunch. With the top down, but the windows up, the air conditioning kept the interior cool while the warm air swirled my hair into a wild wig of wonder. I carefully reached around to the compartment net behind my seat and plucked out a fisherman's hat to stick on my head.

I turned off Cabana Boulevard near the downtown traffic circle in Summerton and into a commercial part of town. Strips of industrial warehouses and machine shops fronted a half-dozen seedy streets. Rusted dumpsters sat on weeded patches of broken asphalt near the curb. Two dogs roamed around an old Winnebago, the once orange W now faded to a weathered gray.

According to the pawn slip tucked into the folder on Mary-Louise's desk, Bucky's Pawn and Cash Exchange appraised the Fabergé egg nearly three months earlier. For whom, I didn't know. And how it figured into someone stealing the egg, I didn't know. Gather information first, answer questions later. Not every tidbit mattered, but I wouldn't know which ones did until it was over.

I located Bucky's at the end of E Street between a tattoo

parlor and an old-fashioned barber shop with a chipped red striped pole in front. Bucky's was closed, but the cardboard clock sign on the door indicated he'd be back at eleven twenty-five. A fifteen minute wait. Which gave me plenty of time to huddle in the Mini and strategize.

How in the world was I going to get Bucky the pawn broker to tell me about a Fabergé egg he appraised three months ago? Maybe as an interested buyer? I could pretend to be a wealthy collector who heard a rumor he'd nearly acquired the rare egg. I glanced down at my cargo capris and faded tennies. Throw in the tiny Mini Coop and the fact I hadn't even worn makeup, a wealthy collector might be a stretch. A scout for a collector, like a shill? More like a lackey. That might work.

I still had ten minutes to wait, so I cleaned out my hipster, dumping two empty Tic Tac cans into my Mini litter bag. Organized my CDs. Both of them. Checked my voicemail. One message from Judith Durant saying she'd be in the shop all day tomorrow, I was free to call anytime. Perfect, though I'd planned to pop over, not ring back. I might actually find the egg before Mr. Ballantyne returned to the Big House.

A shiny black Cadillac SUV pulled into the lot, backing into the space directly behind mine. Now there's a wealthy collector. If he headed into the barber shop, the owner might assume the Caddy was mine. I quickly hopped out of my convertible, eager to disassociate myself with the go-cart I drove up in.

The driver door opened and a husky man with a long white beard slid out. He looked like a cross between a guitarist from ZZ Top and Santa Claus. He crossed the lot, straight to the pawn shop door, with a ring of keys large enough to open every lock in a tri-county radius.

"Morning, ma'am. Come on in," he said and held the door for me. "Help you with something today?"

He ambled over to the other side of a long glass counter case and flicked a row of switches on the wall, then punched a series of numbers into a blocked code box.

"Good morning. I'm here about a Fabergé egg."

"You wanna sell it or pawn it?" He took a handgun from a drawer and stuck it in the back of his waistband.

I cleared my throat. "Neither. I'd like to buy it. Buy one. If you have one, of course."

He slowly looked around the shop with a skeptically raised bushy brow.

There were guns everywhere. So so many guns. On the walls. In the cases. On the shelves. Shotguns, rifles, handguns. Probably BB guns, nerf guns, glue guns, and squirt guns. If it could shoot something out the front and had a trigger down below, I bet this guy had one.

And guitars. Rows of guitars. And guitar-like equipment. Amps, speakers, tuners. Old wagons, vintage tools, and more electronics than Best Buy. It was all so manly. Even the jewelry. Very clean, but all chunky gold and thick watches. Not exactly Fabergé egg compatible.

"I see your point," I said. "But I heard you recently had one here in the shop. Blue enamel with an orange fire opal?"

"Don't believe I ever acquired one for the shop." He sat on the short stool behind the counter, hands folded across his round middle, patiently waiting for me to spit it out.

I was sure the ticket I glanced at for all of one second in Mary-Louise's file said Bucky's Pawn on the top. "Maybe you didn't acquire it, but perhaps you appraised it? Possibly?"

"Well, now. I do lots of private consultations for folks. But, like I said, those'd be private." He glanced down at my handbag, then back to my face. "Confidential like."

Now I'm getting somewhere. I quickly brought out my wallet, the old-fashioned method of obtaining information. One didn't need a ruse, one needed cash.

Unfortunately, my bright orange floral pouch held seven dollars in paper money and approximately nineteen cents in change. I smiled up at him. "Do you take Visa?"

"Yep. Take a look around. I've got something for everybody."

"And if I find something I'd like to purchase, you think you'll remember the egg?"

"Quite possible."

Well, I certainly wasn't about to buy a gun. Or a guitar. Even though I detest shopping of any kind, I do have a weakness for vintage games. My collection includes a Batman radio and a 1940s Parcheesi board. But nothing of the sort in this shop. Though he did have a shelf of books.

I moseyed over to the bookcase in the far corner. "I like to read, I guess."

"There's a first edition Stephen King right there."

I pulled out a hardcover edition of *Pet Sematary*. "I don't really read him." Except I totally did. *Pet Sematary* was the very first King book I ever read. And the number one reason I'll never own a cat.

"It's a collector. Rare, and signed."

I shrugged as if rare and signed meant nothing to me. "How much?"

"I could let it go for around six and a half."

Holy shit. I started to put it back on the shelf.

"I think I remember the egg you're talking about. Full size, turquoise blue, right? With gold trim?"

I tapped the book in my palm and wondered how I could possibly charge this back to the Ballantyne as an expense. "I'll give you three-fifty."

"Five-fifty."

"Four and a quarter."

"Five, and that's the best I can do."

"Tell me about the Fabergé egg. Who brought it in?"

"Fella brought it in, oh, I guess goin' on about three months. Right around Father's Day I s'pose. Real nice looking egg. Good condition. He had a few other Russian trinkets to go along with it." He held out his hand for my credit card and I handed it over.

"Can you describe this fella?"

"Don't believe I remember that much. Besides, I run a

confidential shop. Folks prefer discretion when selling their belongings for cash."

"I understand," I said. Gilbert referred to the client as "he," so no big loss of information. "Did this fella want to pawn it?"

"Sell it. Worth about sixty tops, something like that. Gave him a written appraisal and offered him full price. I know a collector in Charleston. Almost had a deal, but my guy backed out, so I did, too. Never saw it again."

After I signed the slim two-part receipt, I tucked my money pouch back into my hipster. "Anyone else come in asking about the egg?"

"Don't remember."

"A woman, perhaps? Thin, small, short hair?"

He simply shrugged.

"Uh-huh," I said, and looked around his shop. "No offense, but why bring such a beautiful piece here? Unless it was a fake?"

He sat back on his stool, his hands once again clasped across his middle. "Definitely not a Carl Fabergé, though I'm not an expert in Russian antiques. Lots of repros out there. I know it was real gold and a real stone. So a guy wants fast cash, and we're always open. In this economy, everything's for sale and we're always buying."

I thanked him for his time and the Stephen King and walked out to the lot. An interesting establishment. But it lined up with Gilbert's story. Mostly, anyway. I'm sure a fancy New York auction house would be a better bet to sell a treasure, but a slower payout. If you take a jewel-encrusted egg—even one valued at a paltry sixty-thou—to a pawn broker, then you needed cash fast.

Unless you needed to keep the sale off the grid.

Back to my Gilbert-bought-a-stolen-egg theory, I started to call Corporal Parker for an update on her nationwide search for stolen Fabergé eggs, but clicked off before she answered. Probably not smart to remind her of my theory: Gilbert bought (fenced?) stolen property. At least not while he sat in jail. Better to follow my own advice and keep gathering information.

SEVENTEEN

(Day #4: Monday Afternoon)

After a swing through the McDonald's drive-thru (cheeseburger, ketchup only, fries and a small Coke), I crossed back over the bridge at half-past noon, eating while I drove, headed to the south side of the island. The other appraisal in Mary-Louise's folder was from Bygone Wishes, an antiquities shop. I'd never heard of it, and after twenty minutes of brake-slamming and u-turns, I thought I'd never find it. But I finally did.

An ornate Victorian house, tucked behind the post office off Ocean Boulevard and way down a skinny gravel drive, bore a lovely large green canopy over the front door, "Bygone Wishes" printed along the front. A tiny bell jingled when I opened the door, and I walked into a dusky room.

Parlor chairs from an erstwhile era flanked the entry way, sitting on the edge of a threadbare rug. Worn nearly through in some spots, though probably quite expensive back in its day. Sometime when Aladdin flew the skies.

I approached a wide glass case. It nearly stretched the width of the room, but only held a smattering of select items. An interesting set up. Carefully arranged items, very few actually out for me to see, the low lighting, the dark carpet. Bygone Wishes? I'd walked into Stephen King's *Needful Things*.

I peered over the top of the case just as a tall, older man appeared from behind a heavy curtain. Charming, friendly, familiar.

Oh my God, I thought when I saw him. It's the evil Leland Gaunt, straight from Stephen King's pages.

He smiled warmly and approached the case. "Good afternoon," he said. "And welcome."

"Good afternoon," I replied and dialed back my imagination. "What an interesting shop you have here."

"Undeniably. A little bit of everything." He folded his hands on top of the slim counter.

Three things were spotlighted in the center: A 1930s Russian Pelikan fountain pen, a vintage Mickey Mouse watch and The Elvis Presley Game, new in the box circa 1957. Three things I'd love to own, that fit perfectly into my collections.

My nerves started to hum. If he tried to hand me something, I wasn't just leaving, I was moving off the island.

I gripped my hipster with both hands, casually, I hoped, and told myself to get it together. "I'm interested in a Fabergé egg," I said. "An acquaintance of mine brought it in for an appraisal awhile back. He suggested I contact you."

I had considered using some kind of ruse for information, but I couldn't think of anything and I was pretty sure my credit card couldn't handle another purchase.

"Ah. The turquoise egg with the fire opal clasp," he replied. "I remember it well. I believe I provided the gentleman in question with a written appraisal report."

"Yes, of course. I read it, but I'm afraid I don't trust printed reports. Anyone can type one up and slap on a fake logo. I was hoping you could walk me through it, before I bought it."

His hands clenched together. "You are purchasing the egg? I didn't realize Mr. Goodsen was seeking another buyer."

Another buyer? Interesting. "Possibly, depending on the appraisal. Were you also interested in purchasing it?"

"Perhaps, but I only saw it briefly. It looked to be a genuine Fabergé. Theo, not Carl. The gemstone was of the right quality. The clasp worked beautifully. Reminiscent of the House of Fabergé. Mr. Goodsen was supposed to leave it for a more formal appraisal, but he never did."

"Could you place a value on it?"

"Not without closer inspection. I held it only briefly."

"But if it were authentic? What value would you assign?"

"As I wrote in my report, I estimate somewhere in the one hundred-fifty range. A truly pristine specimen, I'd love to see it again if you find it."

One hundred-fifty was nearly triple the pawn shop price, and I wondered why Gilbert didn't sell it to this guy on the spot. What was Gilbert hiding?

"One last question, did a woman come in about the egg?"

"Other than you, no. You're the only one."

"Thank you for the information," I said. "For verifying the appraisal report."

He nodded once and leaned across the case. "Here, I have something for you."

I knew it! He would hand me something and it would ruin my life.

I reached into my hipster and dug around for my keys as I started walking backward. "I'm good, not really a collector of anything. Tight budget..."

He held out his card. "Horace Lovecraft. In case you wish to contact me."

I stumbled forward and snatched it out of his hand. I mumbled thanks and flew out of there as if chased by children playing in a field of corn.

As soon as I slammed the door on the Mini Coop, I locked it. Of course the top was still down, but I felt safer. And he didn't come out after me. The parking lot sat empty, other than my own car, so I took out my notebook to jot down what I could remember. The one-fifty price tag certainly stuck in my mind. Why such a discrepancy? Because of the type of establishment? He certainly sounded like he knew what he was talking about. Close to what Jane said. Also, did he say if you *find* it? I never said it was missing.

I went to tuck his card in a back slot of my bag when I noticed a logo on the other side. Seabrook Preparatory. Now what did that mean?

Seabrook Prep is a private school located in Harborside Plantation, close to the island's landmark lighthouse. It looked fresh from a Roaring Twenties picture postcard with its red and white striped base and round lantern room perched on top. Wouldn't take but five minutes for me to stop over to the campus and ask about Mr. Horace Lovecraft. However, as it was both Labor Day and still technically summer, I doubted anyone would be around to answer my questions.

Which also gave me a fabulous excuse to talk to Matty Gannon, my best friend slash the hunk from the Regatta who also happened to be the Seabrook Prep Headmaster. And I had an idea of just where he might be: Bay Harbor Yacht Club.

Matty looked handsome, rugged, tanned from days spent on the ocean waters. He wore torn cargo shorts and his Oakleys on his head and he knelt against the side rail of the *Fire Escape*, his brother's sailboat.

"Hey, sailor!"

He looked up and smiled, low and easy. "Elli Lisbon."

I walked along the short pier until I stood across from him. Me on the dock, him on the boat. He had a box of supplies behind him. Towels, a large cooler, sunscreen. "Heading out or coming in?"

"Out. Beautiful afternoon for it. High sun, calm seas. Been craving the she-crab chowder over at The Cotton Exchange in Savannah. But hey, never seen you two days at the docks in one weekend. Must be something special to bring you down here."

He was right, even though we lived on an island, I rarely visited the docks or sailed the open seas. I'd been afflicted with motion sickness since my first stroller ride, and even thinking of a rocking boat made my head light and my knees heavy.

"I just met someone I thought you might know," I said. "I couldn't resist the opportunity to come by. Horace Lovecraft, proprietor of Bygone Wishes Antiquities."

"Sure. He's a guest lecturer at Seabrook. Teaches a course for the art department."

"So he's reputable, you'd say?"

"Highly. Eccentric, but knowledgeable. His class fills up fast. You thinking of him for the vacant Ballantyne board seat?"

"Not exactly. I came across Mr. Lovecraft while researching an heirloom quality valuable bauble for a donor who needs my assistance."

The explanation sounded lame to my own ears. Me trying to delicately avoid stating the obvious, that I'm involving Matty, and his school, in one of my investigations. I questioned him about a student in the Hirschorn murder investigation and it didn't go so well. I offended him, alienated him, and I'm pretty sure I insulted him, too.

He glanced at the dock behind me, then down at the long rope he was winding. "Well, then. Sure good to see you. I should finish up if I'm going to push off soon."

I noticed he hadn't asked me to join him. While he may be very aware of how seasick I get on boats, rafts, canoes, docks, pool floaties or anything touching the water, I had a feeling he already had a sailing companion. A twinge of jealousy stirred in my stomach and I feared he was already over me.

"Matty? I'm so sorry I blew our lunch date yesterday. It's this case, well, not really a case, an inquiry. It's more complicated than I thought. I'm not making excuses, really. But I miss you. Can we try again?" At his raised brow, I added, "Lunch. Can we try lunch again?"

He finished coiling the rope, then stood, leaning against the railing. "Sure, Elli. I miss you, too. How about tomorrow?"

"Yes! Wait, no. I'm having lunch with Mimi Ran—with, well, a lady trying to get me tables," I inexpertly finished. Ransom might still be a sensitive subject, and I didn't want to complicate it further by mentioning lunch with his mother.

"No problem, Elli. You have the Tea on Wednesday and school starts Thursday. We'll just do it another time."

"Okay, Matty. I'm going to hold you to me. I mean, *it*. Hold you to *it*."

He smiled and hopped onto the *Fire Escape*, then walked along the side of the sailboat.

I sighed as he left, wondering how to fix our friendship, or if I ever could. And if it was friendship I wanted, or something more. Especially since seeing him with Nurse "call me El" Elaine. He disappeared from view, so I turned and crossed the dock, walking across the patio to the clubhouse.

I was so distracted, I nearly plowed into the perky nurse in question. She didn't see me, thank God, and I jumped behind a potted palm. I wasn't sure if it was because I didn't want her to know I just saw Matty or if she might grill me about Gilbert Goodsen. Either way, I stayed hidden until she was out the back door. Not the most mature moment I'd had this week, but probably wouldn't be my least.

EIGHTEEN

(Day #4: Monday Night)

The day had stretched on longer than I intended and I'd done absolutely nothing for the Wonderland Tea, and Labor Day weekend was now nearly over. I'd left everything in the hands of Carla, Jane, and Busy, a woman who couldn't tell a Tuesday from a Sunday. Yes, this is the same woman I put in charge of Gilbert Goodsen's defense.

I called for pizza delivery on my way home, and it arrived in my driveway when I did. Lest you raise your eyebrows at my back-to-back junk food meals, I did vow to ride my bike to the Big House for the next month. Well, at least for the next few days. Some exercise is better than none, right?

I ate over the sink and had just finished the last slice of BBQ chicken with extra cheese when the phone rang. Miranda Gaines, Jaime's friend, returning my call.

"Oh Elliott, what awful news," Miranda said in her soft drawl. "Of all the terrible things, you discovering Jaime on that boat is just the worst." She said it, wurrrrrst.

"I know. Everyone at the Ballantyne is in shock. A complete surprise." I waited a beat, then continued. "Do you have a minute to talk with me? A little background for the piece the Ballantyne would like to put out for Jaime."

"Of course, Elliott. Maybe before the Tea on Wednesday. Though it won't be the same without Jaime there. She had the most adorable pinstriped teapot she was bringing."

"Actually, we wanted to say a few words about her at the Tea, so I was kind of hoping we could get together sooner. Like maybe tonight?" I made a quick note in my notebook to remind myself that I needed to say a few words about Jaime at the Tea.

"Well, I've got the girls coming over for mahj in a minute. I suppose you could stop by."

"Mahj?"

"The Haverhill Ladies Mah Jongg League. I'm hosting tonight. It'll probably be the perfect time for y'all to stop by. We're putting together an impromptu potluck in Jaime's honor. I'm sure the girls wouldn't mind, especially for the Ballantyne."

"I really appreciate this, Miranda. I'll be over in a bit."

I'd barely clicked off when the phone rang in my hand.

"Hey, El. What time we going to Charleston tomorrow?" Sid asked. "You picking me up or want to swing by?"

"Swing by the Big House and we'll take the Mini."

"For a two hour drive? I barely fit, even with the seat all the way back. Let's take my X6. It's roomier, plus plenty of space for all our shopping bags."

I groaned out loud. I'm not a happy shopper. "Roomier, yes, but my top comes off and yours doesn't. But listen, I can't chat now. I'm off to a mah jongg game in Haverhill. Can we decide—"

"I'm on my way."

The phone went dead in my hand. I dialed Sid back.

"Two seconds, I'll be at your house. Seriously, do you know how hard it is to find an open game? They're down a seat now."

"Ouch."

"Sorry, sweetie. But it's like New York real estate, you gotta move or someone else will get there first. See you in ten."

It actually took Sid fifteen minutes to arrive, then another fifteen for us to zip over to Haverhill Plantation. We picked up our pass from the gate guard, the same well-armed soldier from Friday when I slid through with Ransom.

I drove around to Magnolia Drive, but turned right instead of left, away from the yacht club, then another right onto Cypress

Court. Several houses lined the short block, each designed in a different architectural style. We passed a Colonial and Tudor before pulling into a white Georgian with four tall columns across the wide front porch.

"This looks familiar," I said and nodded to the French country estate next door. Sid and I once scaled the estate's courtyard wall in the middle of the night and nearly got shot trying to charm the bodyguard in the driveway.

"Milo wants you to know you're welcome to join us for poker anytime. Though he'd rather you use the front door."

"Hey, you were with me, sister."

Sid straightened her pale pink sweater set and pulled out a string of pearls. "Too much? Or not enough? I also have a cameo brooch."

I shoved my keys into my hipster and swung open the door. "It's a card game, Sid, not tea with the queen."

She mumbled something that sounded suspiciously like naïve and adorable, then followed me up the brick drive.

Miranda opened the door before the bell chimes stopped ringing. And damned if she wasn't wearing pearls. And a little black dress that would've made Coco Chanel herself stop and stare. I tried not to feel uncomfortable in my cargo capris and pink tee, or the fact that my sneakers squeaked on the shiny marble floor while her kitten heels delicately clicked.

She showed us into an enormous formal living room with a two-story wall of windows overlooking a spectacularly green rolling golf course. Three leather card tables with silk high-back chairs were set up amidst oversized floral sofas.

"Ladies," Miranda hollered into the other room. "We have a special guest with us."

Several women poured into the living room, each carrying a glass of wine and a small plate of appetizers and petit fours. Not your typical potluck. And yes, all dressed as if visiting the queen.

"Elliott, I didn't know you were joining us," Deidre Burch said.

I was happy to see a familiar face, and one not adorned with pearls. She wore her reading glasses around her neck on an orange and yellow decorative chain.

"You must be here about Jaime," Deidre said.

"Lord Almighty, poor dear Jaime," another woman said. She clicked over to me and balanced her wine and china plate in one hand and shook my hand with the other. "Caroline Walsh."

"Nice to meet you," I said in return. "Were you close with Jaime?"

She took a seat at the leather card table closest to the window. "Oh, I'm not sure any of us were close to her. More like committee friends than close friends."

The other ladies made quick introductions, then took seats at the tables. Sid and I grabbed a glass of wine each, then sat down with Deidre and Miranda, behind Caroline and the others.

"The last group is running behind," Miranda said when she noticed me glancing at the vacant third table. "We'll start without them. It's actually good you're here, so much more fun to play with a four than three."

"Have you ever played mahj?" Miranda asked. She dumped a hundred small tiles onto the table and started mixing them up, face down like dominoes. The other ladies quickly started arranging them in rows near their trays.

"Never. I actually thought it involved cards, like gin rummy."

Sid kicked me under the table. "You've sat with me before, Elli. I used to be in mahj league with the hospital. It'll come back to you."

"Sure, sure. Looks easy enough."

Deidre raised her brow and handed me a paper card folded into three parts. Dozens of crazy sequences ran in lines across the three sections, down in columns, all in different colors. Deidre started explaining about Bams, Craks, Pungs, Kongs, Dragons, and Dots. I thought my brain might explode.

She patted my hand. "Just follow us, sweetie. You'll be fine."

I played along with the tiles dealt to me, but let's face it, no way I knew what I was doing. I arranged them by matching colors and numbers and tried to bury my intense competitive nature. Even though I was there for information, I really wanted to win. No matter that I had no idea what I was doing.

A lady at the next table began to sing the first line of an old tune from the forties, something about a young life lost too young. She hummed the rest.

"Dear Jaime," she sang.

I leaned back to see her. She wore a quilted cardigan with a beaded necklace and her gray hair coiffed to perfection.

"Isn't it just a shame? Should've been that goof Gilbert to go down," another player at her table said. "Five dot." She clacked down a tile so fast I almost didn't see it. Then I realized I wasn't supposed to be watching their game, I was supposed to be playing my own.

"Probably killed her himself. You know he lost his marbles some years ago."

"That's right! A three-day hold at Island Memorial, if I recall."

Miranda shook her head and slapped down a tile. "Three crak. Picked up wandering the golf course in his boxers and missing a shoe. Odd duck that one."

I picked up a tile and studied it like I knew what I was doing, then selected a random tile from my tray to discard. I could do this all night. Pick up one, discard another. "Odd duck?"

"Jaime didn't say much to us over the years," Miranda replied.

The singing grandma chimed in. "Four bam. Yes, but remember the cooking conversation." She continued humming.

Another lady at her table picked up the thread. "She alphabetized everything in the refrigerator! Not just every cupboard in the kitchen, but also the produce drawers."

Deidre looked at me over her orange polka dot readers. "Embarrassed the poor girl. Didn't realize no one else organized their kitchen that way. Gilbert had a revolutionary idea for grocery shopping."

I looked down and it was already my turn again. Jesus, these gals moved fast. The game would be over before I even asked my second question.

"Boy, she was hot over that," a lady at the other table said.

"First she got mad," the singing grandma said. "Then she got revenge."

"Revenge?" I asked, trying to squeeze in a word. The conversation was flying faster than the damn tiles.

"Took his favorite driver and melted it into a knot."

"Threw him out like a fox in a hen house. Then started on his clothes."

"And kept on going," Miranda finished. "Red dragon."

My ears perked up. "Oh?" I asked casually and slung out another tile.

The grandma sang another tune about boots and walking. "Sold his baseball card collection on eBay, too, I think."

I made a mental note to check eBay out later. "I heard she took his Fabergé egg," I said. I threw out two tiles just to catch up.

Sid kicked me again and I yelped. She gave me back the tiles. "Not your turn, sweetie."

I glanced down and realized I had only half the tiles the other ladies did. Maybe I should sneak a few from the pile to even it back up.

"Fabergé egg? Jaime never mentioned that," Miranda said as the doorbell rang and the door swung open behind me. The other contingency of Mahj players.

"Hi girls, sorry we're late!"

"What the hell is she doing here?"

I glanced at Sid. From the look on her face, I gathered I was the "she" in question.

I slowly turned and faced Alicia Birnbaum, Jaime's tennis bff. I smiled and wiggled my fingers in a friendly wave. "Hi, Alicia. Good to see you, too."

"This is a regulation Haverhill Women's Club League game and you are absolutely not sanctioned to be here." She turned to

Miranda with an ice cold smile. "Miranda, darling, you know we could lose our position if she's here."

Alicia stepped forward and gripped my chair. "I do believe that's your signal to leave."

Sid firmly studied her mahj card, but every other woman firmly studied me.

"Thank you, Miranda," I said. "You are a gracious host."

I pushed my chair back so I could stand and accidentally rammed it into Alicia. I may have scooted with everything I had.

Alicia wobbled into the singing grandma behind us. She grabbed the table to steady herself and flung tiles across the room.

"How dare you!" Alicia shouted, her face so red with anger I could feel the heat from two feet away. But she closed the distance fast and shoved me back with her right hand.

I stumbled back and knocked into my own tray of tiles. I recovered in two seconds and shoved her right back. Both hands right in the middle of her chest. She flew over the empty silk high back and straight onto the sofa. One of her shoes fell off and I swear I saw her entire head of hair move, like a wig about to be displaced. She struggled to her feet and lunged.

"Watch it, bitch," I said and threw up my hands. "I know kung fu."

"That's assault!" she screamed. "Miranda, call the police. I want her arrested."

"Hey, you started it," I shot back. "You can yell at me all you want, but don't touch me."

"Oh, I'll yell! You're a wretch, coming here when Gilbert murdered Jaime."

"He didn't kill Jaime!"

"Yes, he did!" Alicia yelled. "She was kindly returning his boat so he'd have a place to sleep and he killed her."

"She stole his boat and nothing kind about it," I said. "She was destroying it in the slip."

"So now you're saying she deserved to die?"

"Of course not, but I'm not letting an innocent man get

accused of killing her."

"Let me guess, you're 'helping' him." She said "helping" with an unattractive sneer. She picked up her shoe and pointed it at my face. "You're the worst PI in the South. All your clients land in jail."

Sid pulled me back before I could knock the shoe right out of Alicia's hand.

"And since Gilbert's already there, nothing more to argue about," Sid said. She quickly handed me my handbag and pushed me toward the front door. She whispered, "Did you say kung fu?"

"I meant to say tae bo."

"Since when do you know tae bo?"

"I don't. But I think it's more believable than kung fu. Though I'm pretty sure I have a yoga mat someplace."

She gave my arm a squeeze, then raised her voice when we neared the foyer. Every lady in the room stood behind her. "You should feel lucky that Alicia Birnbaum is kind enough to let this slide. She has such class." She winked at me.

I sighed.

Fine. Better to let Sid stay and get what info she could. I raised my chin in the air and put my hands on my hips. "You're choosing Alicia over me?"

Alicia stood smug behind Sid.

I whirled on my sneaker and walked out the beautiful front door. Sid better get the good stuff, I thought, as the door shut firmly behind me.

After two wrong turns, I sped out of the Haverhill Plantation gate and onto Cabana Boulevard. It was after eight, but the air was still warm from the sun which already disappeared into the horizon.

It sounded as if Jaime had been extremely private, at least with this crowd. And this crowd seemed to be her closest circle of friends. Didn't Miranda call Gilbert an odd duck? Someone sure did. I'm not sure I'd argue. But odd isn't necessarily a bad thing. Unless you're trying to impress the tea-with-the-queen set.

Alicia said Jaime was returning Gilbert's boat the night she died. Those two were as thick as thieves. Literally. Alicia probably helped Jaime steal the boat.

I also wondered about the two appraisers I met with and the fight Gilbert had with the Whitakers, the ones who were unhappy about their viatical payout. They seemed awfully angry, especially the daughter, Kat. I thought Gilbert originally said she was quiet. Was she the type to harass, then murder? Steal the egg? Probably not steal the egg, then harass him about it. If she thought it would save her father's life, it would be long gone now. Sold for money to pay for treatment. No need to harass Gilbert or kill his wife.

It didn't take long to drive to my cottage and get tucked inside for the night. I had another big day tomorrow: the Ballantynes were coming home. But late, probably well after dark, so I had all day to make progress in Charleston. No need to update Mr. Ballantyne with every twist and turn. Better to wait until after the Tea, and after I'd found the egg. And if I couldn't find the egg by then, I'd burn my bunny slippers.

NINETEEN

(Day #5: Tuesday Morning)

I woke Tuesday to a crisp Carolina blue sky sparkling through the skylight above my bed. The sounds of seagulls flying low along the surf drifted through the open window. I loved the end of summer. The days became cooler and the island visitors headed home. Part of me wanted to throw on my sweats and tennies and hop on my oversized three-wheeler, riding my bike along the hard-packed sand. I could get in three or four miles before I needed to be at the Big House.

But that was the procrastinator in me. I didn't have that kind of time. If I hurried, I could make one quick stop before I hit the Big House. I needed to get up, get out, and get it together.

Since my culinary palate resembles that of a third grader, my first stop was the Sonic drive-thru for French toast sticks with extra syrup and a large Coke. It was barely half-past eight, but a serious sugar kicker was my reward for getting on the road so early.

After a short drive down Cabana, where I spotted two suits and a pair of boxer shorts in an azalea bush (clearly Gilbert hadn't retrieved his entire wardrobe), I pulled into the Sea Pine Civic Complex. I turned to the west and parked in an empty spot near the library entrance, opposite the police station. I left the top down in the shady lot and hoped I wouldn't return to find a family of squirrels nut-hunting in my back seat.

The library is considered the largest in the county. Though

"largest" only applies if comparing it to a library you'd find in a one-room schoolhouse. The Library Guild manned the inner lobby, selling used books on racks and tables. I waved as I passed, then entered the main (and only) room. It was packed.

Not sure what I expected to see first thing on a Tuesday morning thirty minutes after opening, but certainly not so many people. The sun was shining and the beach was only a mile away. I stood in line behind a woman and two children, all gripping more books than they could carry. The two ladies behind the counter didn't seem overly friendly to the customers, more like harried grocery store clerks than librarians, and not likely to waste time answering my random questions. I stepped out of line.

I slipped into a low chair in the magazine section. What was I even doing there? How could I figure out why Gilbert was sneaking over here conducting secret research? And what did it matter? This was nuts. I had to go to the Big House, get to Charleston, find a teapot, question Jaime's sister, have lunch to secure tables for the Wonderland Tea, which was in less than twenty-four hours, and greet the Ballantynes at the Big House.

I was about to leave when I spotted Deidre Burch at the information desk at the far end near the back wall. Her bright glasses perched on her nose, her gray bob tucked behind her ears.

"Deidre, I need a little help," I said. I am nothing if not persistent.

"Why, Elli, what a surprise. Two days in a row. Sorry about the mahj, sugar." She patted my hand. "But it didn't look like it was your type of thing. Though Sid's a natural. She won two of the five games."

"She must've been thrilled," I said, then remembered I was fake mad at her, and waved my hand all willy-nilly. "Whatever. What's with the crowd here, you guys giving these books away?"

She smiled. "You should come by more often. We're always this busy in the morning. Especially the week before school starts. Why do you think I'm here and not at the Big House? Which reminds me. You hear about the dustup over at the Big House this morning? A real showstopper, I heard. I'll head over in an hour. You, too?"

I walked behind the long desk and slumped into the worn visitor's chair. "My next stop. What happened?"

"Busy Hinds wants on the board. Tod wants to nominate her and Jane's pitching a fit like a pageant mother back stage."

"To her face?"

"Oh no, honey. Behind her back. Jane's a true Southerner."

The Ballantyne board short list was turning into a neglected plant, only the more I neglected it, the more it grew. "I'm actually here about a different candidate. Suspected murderer slash candidate, Gilbert Goodsen. I hear he was frequenting the library over the last two weeks and I'm wondering why."

She looked over the top of her glasses at me. "And you find this suspicious?"

"I do. Can you help?"

"Absolutely," she said. She wiggled her fingers and started typing on the keyboard below the counter, surreptitiously glancing around at the other library volunteers. She perched her tangerine readers upon her nose. "Let's see. Gilbert Goodsen registered for a card in August, but no books on record. Checked out or otherwise."

I stood and glanced over her shoulder at the screen. "I guess it affirms my anonymity theory. He didn't want anyone to know what he was up to."

"You know, I did see him in here a few times, using the desktops."

I studied the long bank of computers down the central aisle. At least a dozen, all occupied.

"He favored the one in the back, near the Large Print." She clicked off the screen and pointed to a section tucked in the corner. A kid sat at the desk near the window, tapping on the keyboard.

"Thanks, Deidre. See you tomorrow."

"We going to have tables at the Tea? Not sure Edward will enjoy eating on the grass. Though Vivi will."

"I'm working on it," I said and left her at the desk.

With a tiny library comes a tiny catalog resulting in half-empty bookshelves. I tiptoed over to the Large Print section, then moved two books to the shelf below, ignoring the sign requesting I not re-shelve the books because I'll put them out of order. I peeked at the kid. A boy, maybe twelve. Backpack, notebook, iPod. Doing homework a week before school starts? Goes to the library instead of the beach? What world am I living in? And how do I get him to move?

I scooched to my left, two wide steps, then a third. Grabbed three books, and peeked again. This time I saw the monitor. Some sort of video game. Ha! All was right with the world.

Except he'd never get up, not the way he was battering the keys with one hand and clicking the mouse with the other.

A woman cleared her throat from six inches behind me, and I jumped. I dropped the books on my foot and screeched. Damn hardback smashed my baby toe. The woman shushed me (quite loudly, I might add) as she selected a book from the shelf above me, then walked away.

I sat on the floor holding my throbbing foot, then leaned over and checked on the kid. Still battering and clicking.

I wasn't leaving without getting on that stupid computer. I did not sustain a painful book injury for nothing. His finger tapping taunted me from behind the bookcase and I was still sitting on the carpet. The dusty dirty public carpet that probably hadn't been shampooed since the grand opening some thirty-five years earlier. I scrambled to my knees.

One's perspective changes when one is squatting on the floor. For instance, there were no books on the bottom shelves. I had a clear view of the kid's feet and his backpack. And the computer's power cord.

It ran from beneath the desk, along the back wall and over to a square outlet box at the edge of the Romance section.

I stood and walked over to the tall cases opposite Large Print. Chose a particularly thick book. An antique brass clock with cracked glass and Scotsman kilt on the cover. *Outlander.* I casually leaned against the wall and pretended to read the opening page. No one noticed me; only one man could see me. He sat in a low chair two rows down reading a paperback.

I slowly slid down the wall, pulled the computer's power plug out of the socket, then strolled down the aisle toward the kid.

He jabbed the on/off button, then smacked the side of the monitor, all the while mumbling words his mother would object to.

"Network went down," I said with a knowing nod. "This computer only. Lady at the info desk said it won't be back up until tonight, maybe Wednesday. First day after Labor Day, the guy's backed up with tons of work orders." I shrugged vaguely and went back to the case, slowly re-shelving *Outlander* in its proper place.

The kid shoved his notebook into his backpack with his iPod and shuffled over to the entry hall. After hovering around the other busy computers, he walked out the front.

I quickly plugged in the power cord and snagged the seat in front of the computer. When the screen came to life, I clicked on the web icon. I started with something easy. Party rental companies, searching large and small from Alabama to Tennessee. Not as many as I'd hoped. I printed the short list, then moved on to Gilbert and his clandestine searches.

It only took me thirteen minutes to find the history option from the browser menu.

Lots of gaming sites, medical diagnostic pages, travel sites, Wikipedia entries, Google searches, and the *Islander Post* website. Funny, since the actual newspaper was less than twenty feet away.

I started with the *Post*, paging through dozens of links to the classifieds. Next I checked the Wikipedia entries. Nothing interesting or helpful, but I got lucky with the web searches.

A series of articles on Fabergé eggs. I skimmed through them, ending up with basically a longer version of Jane's history lesson. Tsar Alexander III commissioned Carl Fabergé to craft an Easter egg for his wife in 1885. She adored it so much, Alexander continued the tradition, as did his son, Nicholas II, after his father's death, until the Revolution in 1918 (when his entire family was viciously murdered). Known as Imperial eggs, Fabergé made about fifty, though most agree only forty-two survived. Each was currently accounted for, and each was worth in the several millions. Fabergé also designed eggs for his private clients, though it's unknown exactly how many. Or where they were.

Plus there was a surprise. Literally. As in each egg contained a surprise inside. Hence the clasp, because every egg opened. The very first Imperial egg was the Hen egg. Crafted of gold and covered in white enamel, it opened to reveal a gold yolk, which opened to reveal a colorful hen, which opened to reveal a teeny tiny replica of the Imperial Crown, complete with diamonds and a ruby pendant. Both the hen and the crown surprises were lost, only the golden yolk remained.

Gilbert's egg did not include a surprise, diamond or otherwise. Did this mean his egg was a fake? Or simply a lost surprise?

After the Revolution, things got hazy—and pilfery. The Fabergé business was seized and nationalized. The family fled Russia, and Carl Fabergé never designed again, so the story goes. Many years later, his grandson, Theo, designed his own elaborate works of art, first for pleasure, then by commission. He fashioned original eggs for the White House, Royal Air Force, and many a Duke of wherever.

Then there were the eggs under the Fabergé brand, acquired in the eighties. Crafted by a contemporary of Carl Fabergé, these eggs were sold to a "members only" type crowd. No names and not many descriptions or pictures.

I searched Google images, Pinterest pages, and eBay for an egg. Over three thousand results! I was hoping to find one like Gilbert's with gold trim and a fire opal clasp. I scrolled through pages, but I got bupkis.

Except to surmise that Gilbert's egg was not a long-lost true Carl Fabergé heirloom smuggled out of Russia. Likely it was a one-of-a-kind by either Theo, a modern Fabergé, or one of a dozen other designers creating "Fabergé style" eggs.

Probably exactly what Gilbert figured out when he sat at this same computer and read these same articles. The values lined up, ish, with the appraisals. Somewhere between fifty and one hundred fifty thousand, depending on who was buying.

But why a secret search at the library? Seemed like extraordinary measures for an egg he bought on a whim with a plan to sell immediately.

I put my head in my hands and took a deep breath. Again I asked myself, what bothered me about Gilbert going to the library in secret? People do odd things all the time for innocent reasons. And Gilbert researching the value seemed right in line with trying to sell it, no harm done.

Except somebody ended up dead.

That's what bothered me. Was he hiding his behavior from Jaime or from the police or from Mary-Louise? Was Gilbert being paranoid, even before the egg was stolen? So what did that mean?

It meant he knew that egg was trouble *before* he bought it.

I checked my watch. The internet is the most helpful researching tool on earth, and yet sucked up time faster than a black hole sucks air. I needed to get on with my day. I considered heading back to eBay to search for a tea set like Zibby's, but I didn't have the time to search or to buy and receive.

I clicked my way out of the Google machine and ended up at the *Post*'s home page.

HUSBAND KILLS WIFE FOR BALLANTYNE SEAT? by Tate Keating.

Son of a bitch, I thought. Two full pages about Gilbert Goodsen, his divorce, Jaime's death, and Gilbert's vocal campaigning for the open seat vacated due to the murder of Leo Hirschorn last May. The splashy article spelled out more details than I cared to read.

Impatient bugger didn't even wait for my quote.

I waved to Deidre on my way out and stalked to my car. No squirrel family in the back seat, but plenty of fallen leaves and a handful of Spanish moss.

I climbed in the Mini, mumbling to myself how Tate Keating skewed everything to put the Ballantyne in a disparaging light. Gilbert didn't have a shot at the Ballantyne board any more than Jaime did, not once they filed for divorce. We'd never put ourselves in the middle of that mess. I knew that, Tod knew that, the entire Ballantyne board knew that—and I bet even Tate Keating knew that.

I stopped just before I hit the start button. But did Gilbert know that? Would he have killed his wife to get the seat? I tried to shake it off as ridiculous, but wondered if the supposedly missing egg was just a way to get closer to me. Gilbert set up our initial meeting on Friday, the day he got shot, to talk about him taking the empty board seat. Maybe I got it all wrong and it's been about the Ballantyne this entire time.

TWENTY

(Day #5: Tuesday Morning)

I stopped at the Big House shortly before nine a.m. Sid was due in thirty minutes, so I had to cram two hours' worth of work into a short window. I was fairly optimistic until I entered the foyer.

Tea sets sat on tabletops, bookshelves, chairs, settees, and gasp, the steps of the staircase. I peeked into the library and the parlor, both stacked high with teapots and teacups and matching saucers. Those four foot tables I drudged out of the attic barely held a third of the china.

"You absolutely are not leaving today," Tod said as I walked into my office. He stood in the doorway, hands on hips.

"What makes you think I'm leaving?"

He gestured drolly to my outfit. "Set up does not require silk shantung."

I smoothed my gorgeous floral print tunic. "I'm having lunch in Charleston, but I'll be quick. You won't even miss me." I moved two teapots off my chair and sat.

"I don't miss you now," he said and walked away.

"Don't be so melodramatic, Tod," I hollered toward the doorway. "You've got Jane and Busy and Carla to help."

"Jane left for the day, sugar," Carla said from the hall.

I reached for the hand-sani. "Is she sick?"

"She's protesting," she said, her voice fading as she continued by. "But I know she'll circle back, trying to sneak into my kitchen."

With both Jane and myself out for the day, there'd be no one to boss everyone around. Not good. I was counting on Jane to cover for me, even though I hadn't asked her. She would've said no.

The only way to cancel lunch with Mimi and stay at the Big House was to secure tables. I pulled the list of party rental companies from my handbag and started dialing. By the seventh "sorry, ma'am," I gave up. On the calls, not my hope. I was sure Mimi Ransom would come through.

Tod was not.

"Should I start arranging for plastic tablecloths to be spread across the grass?" Tod asked. "Doesn't sound like you made progress." He strode into my office and set another tea set on the desk.

"Those calls were just insurance. I've got a contact in Charleston, and I'm positive we'll have tables."

"Uh-huh. The Ballantynes arrive at four thirty this afternoon. In case you'd like to be here."

"I'll be here," I said, opening my desk drawer. I found the pamphlet of Charleston antique shops in my desk and tucked it in my bag. "Do you happen to know which shop Zibby bought her teapot?"

"Nope."

I stood and threw my hipster handbag over my shoulder. The edge caught a teacup and started a chain reaction of rattling, fine porcelain jostling against even finer porcelain. "It'll work out. I'll get the tables," I said. "And Tod, you're in charge this afternoon."

"I'm always in charge," he said.

I left Tod and the teacups behind and found Sid talking to Carla in the foyer.

"Carla, do you know where Zibby bought her teapot? The shop name or street or anything?"

"She called it a pawn parlor, someplace in Charleston," Carla said. "But she did say she had a meeting at the grocery, that's where she found it. I'm sure that helps."

"Maybe I should call her," I said. "I just don't want her to know it's broken. But I can't find a replacement without knowing which shop. Which only she knows. Ideas?"

"Can't reach her anyway, sugar," Carla said. "She's off hunting bobcats."

"Hunting bobcats?" Sid said.

"Not with a gun," I said. "With her conservation group. They search the forest preserves on the island. Like a safari, making sure there are no game hunters or traps, that they stay protected."

"Sure, sure," Sid said.

"No worries. In fifteen safari hunts, they have yet to spot a single bobcat."

We said our goodbyes and climbed into Sid's BMW X6. Half SUV, half coupe. And all white. Shiny white paint on the outside, soft white leather on the inside. So white, it made me nervous to sit on the seats, convinced the blue pen placed securely in my bag would somehow end up marking them. "Are you sure we shouldn't take the convertible?"

"I'm not driving two hours in the soup can." She powered open the sunroof and cracked the windows. "See? Just as airy as a convertible. But with twenty-four-way seats."

"Yes, well, perhaps. Your electric seats may be snazzy, but my seats have hand pumps. Way more fun."

She gunned her V8 and zoomed us out of Oyster Cove Plantation and onto Cabana Boulevard. Before long, we sailed over the Palmetto Bridge connecting us to mainland South Carolina. The tide was in. The water was so high and lively, sailboats from the marina visibly rocked in their docks. Sid was right, with the sunroof open, the briny sea salt scented air drifted in the same as in the Mini with the top down.

We hit I-95 a smidge after nine thirty and sped north. Sid kept the radio turned low and the speedometer on high.

"How was the mahj game?" I asked.

"I won two out of five. Deidre says I'm a natural."

"A natural competitor."

"You know it, sister. And those gals know what they're doing."

I remembered the women slapping tiles on the table with vigor. "Seriously. Any bits come up on Jaime?"

"Not much." She hit the gas and passed a semi rumbling in the slow lane. "Alicia seemed hit the hardest, but didn't want to talk about Jaime or Gilbert. Or anything really. She didn't say much all night."

"Even about me? After our skirmish?"

"Skirmish? You threatened kung fu fighting."

"Accidentally."

"Yes, well, she may have said something about you and what you could do with your kung fu. Miranda was a delightful host, though."

"Which gets me no closer to the egg." I stared out the window, the tall pines whizzing past. It was peaceful and calm and I hated driving in the car for two hours. I sighed. Loudly. And started to fidget with the air vents, then my seat extender.

"Tell me what you've got so far," Sid said, clearly trying to keep me busy. "On your egg hunt."

"Gilbert says he promised the egg to his patent attorney and will lose everything if he doesn't get it by tomorrow. Or maybe Thursday, with the holiday. I'm not sure."

"Lose everything? A murdered wife, a vandalized boat, a stolen heirloom, a destroyed wardrobe, a new residence in the clink..."

"Yeah, he's pretty much lost everything. But he created a clothing thing and patented it. The filing fees have now come due. Pay up or the filing expires."

"A patented clothing thing? Odd. But I guess it sounds like something Gilbert Goodsen would do."

"Indeed. He thought he'd win back Jaime, but with her gone..." I said and shrugged. "Maybe he's fixated on proving it to himself. Jaime thought he was a failure. Even with her gone, maybe because she's gone, he really needs this to work out in his favor."

"So who took his egg? You got a suspect list?"

"Firstly, I've got two appraisers: a pawn shop owner and a creepy antiques dealer. I'm guessing the pawn shop guy thought the egg was stolen or fake and wanted nothing to do with it. But the creepy guy really wanted the egg."

"Creepy doesn't mean guilty."

"It means something. Like maybe he knew it was genuine," I said. "Apparently fake Fabergés are more prolific than knockoff handbags. Secondly, we also have Jaime's friends, Miranda and Alicia, and her sister, Judith, whom I've never met."

"Miranda seemed oblivious at mahj. Not even a casual lean in when Gilbert's name came up. I vote she's too much of a longshot to be a suspect."

"Maybe, but Alicia Birnbaum is no longshot. She has the most motive so far. She would've done anything to help Jaime, and she really, really despises Gilbert."

"Agreed," Sid said.

"On the list of folks closer to Gilbert, we have his assistant Mary-Louise and her boyfriend Bobby, the guy who tricked Gilbert out of fifty thousand dollars, then shot him and ran."

"Wait," Sid said and sped around a minivan going the exact posted limit on the sign. "You know who shot Gilbert? Seems like he'd be the number one egg suspect."

"Yeah, but Mary-Louise ratted him out. She says it was only a scam. Bobby didn't really take the egg."

"Scam or no, his saying it's a scam could be a scam. He's definitely still on the list," Sid said. "And you haven't listed the obvious suspect: Jaime. The vindictive spouse who threw Gilbert out on his ass?"

"Yeah, I hear you. It's totally in line with the rest of her nasty attack on all things Gilbert. The torn clothes, the vandalized boat. So yeah, why not prevent his life's work? Steal the egg and ruin everything."

"And it's working. Gilbert's meltdown centers around this egg. Jaime certainly knows Gilbert. Well, knew him."

"Right. Knew him. She didn't attack herself. Someone killed

her and someone is harassing Gil. Someone has that egg. And you don't kill someone over a fake Fabergé."

I sat up straighter and adjusted the headrest. "Okay, here are my top three suspected egg robbers: Jaime, Jaime's boyfriend, and Alicia."

"Jaime had a boyfriend?"

"Yep. And it's possibly Bobby, Mary-Louise's boyfriend. The guy gets around. And if it's Bobby, he not only shot Gilbert, he also strangled me in the Goodsen's closet."

"What?!" Sid hit the brakes, then punched the gas pedal to make up for the lapse. "Who strangled who where?"

"Didn't I mention that? Saturday night—"

"Saturday night, after the regatta? When I asked how your night went, I recall you said something like 'oh, I'm good, getting nowhere fast.'"

"I may have glossed over a bit or two. I went to calm down Jaime, found the Goodsen house in serious disarray, and the remainder of Gilbert's wardrobe shredded in the closet. Then someone clobbered me from behind and started strangling me. He yelled that he wanted to get Jaime back. I think he thought she and Gilbert were reconciling on his boat, when actually she was vandalizing said boat."

"Next time, you don't gloss. What did your sexy lieutenant say? Did he investigate? Come to your rescue?"

"Sort of," I said. "He told me to butt out."

"How's that working?"

"Calm down."

"Well, not a whisper about Jaime's boyfriend at mahj. And actually, not much gossip at all for a ladies league on Sea Pine Island. I expected better. They could've been reserved with me there, a new recruit. They gossiped freely when you were there. Though Alicia glared at anyone who mentioned Jaime's name. Might take me a week or two to get in tight."

"I have one day," I said and watched more pines whiz by.

Sid took the Highway 17 exit east. We were halfway to

Charleston and making seriously good time. The road was beginning to fill up, but nothing Sid couldn't weave her way around.

"Where did Gilbert get the money to buy the egg in the first place, if he's so strapped for cash that he can't pay his patent attorney?"

I thought about Gil and his lifestyle. Ordinary. Not extravagant, not moneyed. I've seen moneyed. I've been to houses where the sofa cost more than my car. Actually, any one object cost more than my car. And it's a nice car. Turbo. But the Goodsen house was very middle. A middle plantation with a middle hotel, the kind with some sort of kids eat free package. A middle-sized house in the middle of the subdivision, not near the beach or on an extra-wide corner lot. So where *did* he get the money? And was it my business?

You know it. You hire me, it's my business.

"He makes money on insurance payouts, buying and selling expensive heirlooms," I said. "He's running a dozen whacky schemes."

"How does that fit with the missing egg?"

"Lots of unhappy clients, that's how."

"Lots, huh? Your list is kind of long."

"I'm aware."

We crossed the Ashley River and rolled onto Cannon Street. Charleston is the most Southern of Southern cities. Streets lined with charming manors and towering palms. A culture rich in exquisite cuisine, fabled architecture, and mannerly residents. It's nestled square between Sea Pine Island (two hours to the south) and Myrtle Beach (two hours to the north). And like another Southern charmer, Savannah, Charleston offered a glimpse into its distinctive history with tours of cemeteries, gardens, and ghosts.

It was nearly half-past eleven. Only one hour until my lunch date with Mimi Ransom. Plenty of time to meet Judith and find Zibby's teapot.

Sid squeezed into a spot on Market, a lovely street lined with charm and hospitality. We walked a block to Durant Antiques and a tiny bell tinkled when we walked through the door. The shop consisted of one narrow room, crammed with kitschy finds from the forties through the seventies. Books, dolls, gadgets, linens, canisters, jars, and jewelry decorated every surface and wall space.

A woman with the tightest curls since Barbra Streisand rocked her *A Star is Born* perm emerged from the back. She wore cat-eye glasses and her bright pink lipstick feathered around her lips. She maneuvered a set of wide hips through the tight space and never once bumped a table edge.

"Help you ladies?" Her eyes were rimmed red behind her glasses.

"Judith? I'm Elliott Lisbon, from the Ballantyne. I know it's a bad time, but I was in Charleston and was hoping we could talk about Jaime. If you've got a minute?"

"Sure, I guess." She looked from me to Sid, who didn't introduce herself. "As long as it's not too personal."

"You two go ahead," Sid said. "I'll be over here out of your way." She walked over to a display of vintage cookbooks and started browsing the faded cloth spines.

"I appreciate this," I said. "I'm so sorry about Jaime. Were you and your sister close?"

"Not so much anymore. You know, time passes. You grow apart." Judith paused, then sighed. She picked up a chipped coffee cup with lipstick decorating the rim. Took a long sip. "Who am I kidding? We weren't ever really close. Not like I thought we should be," she said with a wistful tone. "I watched every episode of *Little House on the Prairie*. Mary and Laura shared everything. I wanted that."

"But Jaime didn't?" I asked softly.

"We were so...different. We were raised in a little town out near Greenville. I loved it, never wanted to leave it. But Jaime, she was itchin' to get out. Loved to go to the big city."

"New York?"

"No, Charleston. This big city. She'd beg our mama to drive us here, practically every Sunday after church. Something about the bustle of the port and the pretty window displays, even walking down the streets drew her in. Even way back when."

"But now you live here and she doesn't," I said.

"Life's funny like that." She gazed out the picture window into the street. "After mama sold the house, which was to pay for the home we put her in, which didn't matter none since mama died later that summer..." She looked back at me. "Jaime convinced me to move to Charleston. She had such a slick way with words. She could twist them 'til you didn't know what you were agreeing to. But then she met Gilbert at a fancy golf tournament down in Sea Pine. All very cosmopolitan. She never came back."

I kept my expression neutral at calling Sea Pine Island "cosmopolitan." But perhaps it was when compared to a small town in rural South Carolina. "Jaime loved Sea Pine," I said. "We weren't very close. I'm closer to her husband, Gilbert. I'm helping him...get through this."

"Gilbert's a fine man. Makes a good living selling insurance, but Jaime always wanted more. Not to speak ill of my sister, but her sights were always set higher. She liked the finer things."

"Do you know if she had a Fabergé egg?"

Judith laughed, spontaneous and short. "Hardly. She doesn't have the Hope Diamond either. Her sights were high, Miz Lisbon, but not that high. She wasn't aimin' to be the Queen of England."

I nodded and casually glanced around her shop. A fancy blue egg would stand out like a rose bush in a junk yard. "Gilbert claims Jaime took it from him. Blackmail in the divorce, knew it meant a lot to him. Maybe she gave it to you to hide? No disrespect," I added.

"None taken. Sounds like my sister. She didn't always play nice as a child. Though if she took it, she wouldn't give it to anyone, not even to hide it."

Judith probably wouldn't have told me if she did have it, but I believed her. She stood wilted, holding her cracked coffee cup, with her Streisand curls and outdated glasses, missing her sister and the relationship that never was.

"You ever heard of a pawn parlor?" I asked.

"You mean like a pawn shop? Not on this side of town."

I tried to picture Zibby with her orange hair and her enormous Cadillac trolling the streets in the wrong part of town. It scared me how much trouble that woman could get into.

"But there's dozens of antique shops up and down Market. I wish you could stay, I've got a lovely selection myself, but I need to close up. Jaime's visitation's tonight on the island. Will I see you at the viewing tomorrow or the funeral Thursday? It's at Bennett's on Sea Pine. You know, Jaime so wanted to be on your Ballantyne board."

"She would've been a wonderful addition. I'm sure I'll see you, Judith. Thank you."

Judith took her coffee and zigzagged through the hutches and cabinets toward the back.

I found Sid outside and checked the time. "We've got forty-five minutes before we meet Mimi at Charleston Place. Where should we start?"

"Judith mentioned a bunch of shops out here on Market," Sid said.

I raised a brow.

"You know I listen."

We stood on the sidewalk in front of the shop, looking up and down the narrow street. Market Street. "Carla said Zibby talked about a meeting at a grocery store," I said. "Grocery, Market, pretty close, right?"

"And Meeting Street is only a few blocks from here. A Meeting at the Market."

"It's got to be one of these shops. Let's split up, we'll make better time."

"I have no idea what this teapot looks like."

"Orange poppies in a kind of chintz pattern."

"That doesn't help."

"Right. Stick together."

We found six potential shops on the opposite side of the street, but none had a teapot even close to Zibby's. On our way back toward Judith's, three other shops didn't sell fine china, and another two only sold artwork.

I called Zibby.

She must have still been out hunting the bobcats, because it went straight to voicemail. I left a vague message, implying both urgency to return the call immediately and irrelevancy that nothing major was at stake. Like her injured teapot.

We were almost at the last shop when we came across a tiny storefront with fancy script on the window. The Boardroom: Consignment & Collectibles. Every Deal is Negotiable.

"Hey! I bet this is it," I said. "We call the Ballantyne Boardroom the parlor. This must be what Zibby was talking about. Consignment is like pawn, right? Luck is turning our way! Finally."

"Not really, sweetie," Sid said and pointed at a sign taped to the door.

Closed for Holiday.

"Like Labor Day holiday or like the English call a vacation, like going to university? Labor Day is over." I placed my face near the glass with my hands cupped on both sides of my face, peering in to see what I could see.

Not the exact teapot, but several tea sets through the front part of the store. Something to hope for.

I dialed the number etched into the glass. No answer. No surprise, since they were probably across the pond enjoying tea and crumpets.

"Sid, this is it. I know it," I said. "We have to get this teapot. I have to get inside this store right now."

"We have to be at lunch in like five minutes."

"I know, but this is more important. And it's right there."

"You don't know that. What about the tables?"

"That'll be more important after we get the teapot. My boss, my mentor, the closest person I have to any family, is flying home from Alaska, today, specifically because his dear favorite cousin

Zibby thinks she's winning the Wonderland Tea's Peculiar Prize for this teapot. The one I broke and then hid like Peter Brady who broke mom's favorite vase after she said don't play ball in the house."

"Uh-huh. I believe they all confessed. They were good like that. They didn't hide it and buy a new one."

"Well, they should have. I have to get that teapot. I have no tables for the event and my one client is sitting in jail. The only sure thing is that teapot is most likely right inside this door."

"Most likely isn't a sure thing, sweetie."

I dialed the store number again, alternately pacing in front of the window and peeking through the glass.

"Check this out," Sid said and waved from a spot ten feet away.

I walked over to a slim alley between the two buildings with The Boardroom on the right. And an open window on the second story.

Sid pushed back the rickety rusted iron accordion gate blocking the entrance. I barely fit frontways, and Sid, who's built like a professional athlete, six feet of tone and tension, scooched behind me.

A soft concerto floated down from the window. Its sophistication no match for the stench emanating from the alley. Sour vegetables, urine, rank body odor, misery. While no reason for this alley's existence came to mind, a trash truck or delivery van couldn't service the shops from it, I'm pretty sure Charleston's less fortunate sought shelter, and solace, in the tight space.

"Hey!" I yelled. "Helloooooo!"

Sid and I stared at the open window, our necks tipped back in unison, but no one appeared. We shouted louder and louder until nearly hoarse.

I stretched my arms, trying to reach the cement sill, but no go. Not even Sid's ridiculously long arms came close. I put my hand on her shoulder.

"Don't even think it, sister. We're having lunch at the

Palmetto Café. You're not putting those grimey shoes on my person."

"I'm not going to stand on your shoulders, for shit's sake. I'm not aiming for the roof. I only need an extra couple feet. I'll sit."

"Try shouting again. Or throw a rock."

We scoured the ground, neither of us wanting to actually touch anything. Sid didn't. Since it was my desperation, it was my mucky rock. I found a lump and palmed it. "Not enough room to really wind up," I said.

"It's not a baseball. You'll break the window."

I aimed and flung. My elbow slammed into the brick behind us. The rock missed the target, but cracked the edge of the sill, raining dust down on me.

"I'm climbing, Sid. The clock is ticking and we have to do something."

She stared at me a beat. "Fine, but take off your shoes."

I left my ballet flats on the ground and hoisted onto Sid's shoulders in the most unladylike way possible. I pulled her hair and smacked her cheek.

We tottered forward, then backward. "Don't slam into the wall, Sid, I'm wearing silk." My pants were wrinkled, and I knew I had alley wall particles in my hair, but my outfit remained lunch-worthy.

I gripped the gritty sill, stuck my face in the open window, and hollered.

Judith Durant popped up from behind a cabinet and scared the crap out of me. I screamed, Judith screamed, Sid screamed. Then Sid ran, leaving me hanging from the sill. Judith rushed over and opened the window all the way. "Good Lord in Heaven, what are you doing out there, Miz Lisbon?"

She grabbed both my arms and yanked. My bare feet scarcely gained traction as I scaled the wall. As soon as I was halfway through, Judith tugged me like a sumo wrestler going for the gold and I flew ass over teakettle into her lunch. Tuna fish salad and cold coffee. I was so grossed out by the combination of smells, I barely heard Sid pounding on the door downstairs.

Judith ran out and I plucked a dozen thin sheets from a tissue box on the desk, mopping up coffee splashes from my arms to my face. When neither Sid nor Judith appeared in the upstairs office, I went down to the shop.

They were chatting near the front between a painted china hutch and stack of colorful Moroccan silk pillows.

"I told y'all I was closing. Then I walked over here to close this shop up. I own a third, in case you need to break into another one later today."

"No, we're good," I said.

Sid handed me my shoes. "Looks like we found the pawn parlor," she said, pointing at a row of teapots.

Adrenaline perked me right up. "That's it!" I walked over to delicate tea set adorned in hand-painted poppies with green leaves. It truly resembled silk chintz fabric. A whimsical orange poppy sat atop the lid and the handle was covered in porcelain leaves. "I've been searching for this exact pot. It's to replace an identical one purchased here a while back."

"Why didn't you just tell me you needed a teapot like Zibby's? I sold it to her myself."

"I didn't realize you knew Zibby Archibald. She called this shop a pawn parlor," I said, then added before I offended her, "we call our board room the parlor. Zibby mingled the names. But a pawn shop is pretty close to a consignment shop." Mentally adding, you could've mentioned it when I asked because they're nearly the same.

"Not close in the least. Different clientele," she said, as if an expert in all things pawn related. "Jaime sent Zibby my way, told her about my collection. I think Jaime was trying to make friends on the board."

"Well, I'd love to buy it. How much?" I flipped over the paper tag hanging by a string from the handle. It said $250 written in red pen, then SOLD AB.

"It's already sold. Twice already. Once to a buyer in London, then to Alicia Birnbaum who said she had to have it. She thought it would be fun for her and Zibby to have matching pots at the Tea."

Alicia Birnbaum wasn't invited to the Tea. And she knew full well the Tea was about originality. So why sabotage Zibby? Or was she really trying to sabotage me?

"I'll double what she paid if you let me take it right now," I said.

"Oh, I don't know. I'm giving it to Alicia today..." her voice trailed, her face in full negotiation mode now. "You know, Alicia and Jaime were like sisters. Alicia wanted to be just like her. Probably thought she'd help her out with the board. I'd hate to interfere."

"There must be a dozen other things that will bring Alicia Birnbaum closer to Jaime than a teapot she recommended to Zibby Archibald."

Judith stood silent, slowly shaking her head.

"I'll triple it," I said.

"Done." She pointed to a pretty turquoise peacock pot. "Alicia had her eye on this one, too."

I whipped out my credit card before she could change her mind. This egg case had cost me more than a thousand bucks in a single week. The teapot counted as part of the case because Jane exasperated me whilst discussing the egg when I dropped Zibby's original set.

Judith wrapped it carefully in bubble wrap. I thanked her again and we left. Standing on the sidewalk, I checked my watch.

"Oh crap, we're forty-five minutes late!"

I stashed the teapot in Sid's car and ran the three blocks to the Charleston Place Hotel. I hurried around the stone fountain in the drive and burst into the lobby, Sid three steps behind me. I slowed, so as to not draw attention.

The elegant marble floors shone with a generation's worth of polish. An enormous crystal chandelier hung between two sides of a grand double staircase covered in heavy rugs, held in place on each stately step with a heavy brass bar. A floral arrangement sat center, understated and delicate, and yet somehow still dominated the space.

I asked the bellman for directions to the closest powder room. He visibly stepped back at my appearance. And smell. I was filthy, disheveled, tattered, and reeked like a dock worker who slept in an alley.

He pointed across the lobby, and as I followed the direction of his gloved hand, Mimi Ransom stepped into view. With Alicia Birnbaum by her side.

TWENTY-ONE

(Day #5: Tuesday Afternoon)

"I'm out," Sid whispered and fled.

"You just want your mah jongg seat!"

Before I could also flee, Alicia spotted me. She wore a tailored shift straight from the fifties. All that was missing were a pair of gloves and pillbox hat. She turned to Mimi, who if possible, was her fashion superior in a tea-length suit and draped silk scarf, and helpfully pointed me out in the lobby.

Embarrassment burned from my insides out. A flash that simmered in my gut and crept up my neck. I started to sweat, which made everything worse.

I didn't dare look down at my sullied outfit. If it were as clean as a just-cleaned whistle, I couldn't compete. As is, security was certainly on their way to escort me from the lobby.

"Look what the cat finally dragged in," Alicia said in a low voice as they approached.

Mimi Ransom leaned in and kissed my cheek. I'm positive it tasted like coffee and tuna. "How delightful to see you again, dear."

She was as kind and gracious as I was awkward and inappropriate—in my appearance, in my timeliness, and in my smelliness.

"My apologies, sincerely," I said. "Take me two shakes to get cleaned up. I had a bit of a scrum behind an antiques store."

They raised brows. "Oh?"

"Helping a Ballantyne board member," I said.

"Helping them hide the body?" Alicia asked.

I thought about mentioning the teapot I just bought out from under her, but didn't want to ruin the surprise.

"I'm sorry, Elli, but I'm on the run. Something came up at the stables," Mimi said. "And I wish I had better news about your tables. I thought the staff here at the hotel might help. They had a cancellation, but booked a replacement event last minute."

I fought back panic, swallowing and blinking. No lunch, no tables, no time.

"It was lovely to meet you, Alicia," Mimi said. "And Elli, we simply must get together soon." And with that, Mimi Ransom walked out the glass doors, taking my hope with her.

Alicia smirked. "Guess you should've looked for tables at that antique shop." Then she strode off in the other direction, heels clicking, attitude clacking.

I literally snapped my fingers in an Ah-Ha! moment. Who knew Alicia Birnbaum's snark would save my day?

With a quick spin toward the lobby doors, I dashed outside and chased after Mimi in the drive near the fountain. "Mimi, wait," I said, waving her down. "Do you have any restaurant connections? Maybe Moroccan or Indian, who have a spare fifty squat tables?"

She smiled. "I like your style. Now that I can do."

"You're a saint. And I promise to be on time in the future." I looked down at my outfit. "Well, and cleaner."

"You're lovely, Elli. Say hello to my Nick for me."

I agreed and went back inside the hotel to the powder room. I needed to scrub off some of the stench and muck before Sid made me sit in the way back for the ride home.

What I really needed was a tall glass of something ice cold and boozy to wash away my mortification. My life with the Ransoms was one long line of humiliations and indignities. From spending the majority of our forensics class with my head between my knees to backing into the family mailbox on Thanksgiving Day. But hey, even twenty years later, I still got it.

My makeup took the brunt of the coffee splatter. Mascara ran down my left eye, the eyelashes themselves a droopy mushy mess. The blush I'd carefully applied now had random blank circles where the liquid washed it away.

Lord help me, this is what I looked like? My hair mussed and dusty, my tunic stained and mottled. And the horrendous smell. How could she kiss me? And not gag or wince or flinch? What would she say to Ransom?

I had just turned on the hot water when Alicia came out of one of the stalls. She stopped, stared, then went to another sink.

"I do not for the life of me understand why so many people think you're so damn amazing," Alicia said, swirling her hands in soap. "Show up late. Looking like...like...like I don't even know what. What the hell were you doing?"

"My job."

"You deserved to lose those tables."

"I didn't lose anything. I actually got an even better idea out of this mishap."

"Mishap? You're a dump. An embarrassment. A menace. You think you can do whatever you want. All in the name of the Ballantyne—a bunch of—"

"Watch it, Alicia." I pointed a soggy towel right at her face. "Don't mess with me or the Ballantyne."

"Or what? You going to slug me? Oh wait, you don't have your best friend here to protect you." Her voice shook when she said "best friend." She threw her towel in the bin. It missed. She grabbed it with a trembling hand and slammed it down the chute.

I had my best friend and she didn't. "I'm sorry Jaime's gone," I said. "I know it's a terrible loss."

"How dare you try your Ballantyne act on me," she said. "You know nothing about my loss."

I finished with my towel and tossed it into the bin. "Both my parents died when I was twenty. One right after the other," I said. I looked at her full on. "You feel empty and lost. As if some unseen anchor, one you never even realized was attached, has disappeared, leaving you alone and adrift."

Alicia let go. Her posture folded in on itself and she leaned on the sink counter. Tears streamed down her cheeks. "She was my family. I don't know what to do. We're supposed to play in a tournament this weekend. How can I ever go to our club again? It won't be the same." Anger rose to the surface and she pointed her finger at me. "She loved our club, the one place Gilbert could never go. And now I can't go either."

She snatched another towel and covered her face as she cried.

"I'm sorry," I said and slipped out the door.

Words couldn't help her. I didn't reassure her things would be okay. Because they wouldn't. Not for a very long time.

I walked back down Market Street and found Sid waiting for me in her car. She'd moved the tea set to the rear, put a garbage bag over the entire front seat, headrest to bottom, and another down in the foot well. "It's that or you sit in back."

Using her fancy electric buttons, she rolled down all the windows and the sunroof and we hit the highway at full speed. Without a hat, my sometimes curly auburn hair would be blown snarly when we returned to Sea Pine, but at least we didn't have to smell me.

"I'm starving," I said.

"Yeah, I skipped breakfast. More room for the Palmetto's she-crab soup and lobster mac and cheese."

"There's a Zaxby's just off the highway," I said, fiddling with her GPS screen.

"So not the same," she said.

The GPS lady directed us, and with only a twenty minute delay to scarf down two orders of Chicken Fingerz, we were back on the road.

Ransom called before we even hit I-95. "Mimi says you were quite impressive."

"Don't make fun of me," I said.

"Seriously. She said you had a genius idea for tables." He paused. "Why? What did you do this time?"

"No 'this time.' I'm a genius remember?" I said and quickly changed the subject. "When are you releasing Gilbert?"

"He's already out," he said. "Released this morning."

"Really? You caught Jaime's real killer?"

"No, we just don't have the evidence to arrest Goodsen for it. Yet. But I'll tell you what I told him and Busy Hines: he should not leave town."

"He's not leaving town."

"Yeah, I doubt he's capable of leaving town. But with your help, on the other hand..."

I hung up.

"Great news," I said to Sid. "No evidence to arrest Gilbert, so he's out of jail. Just in time for the Ballantynes to arrive tonight and the Wonderland Tea tomorrow!"

"He could still get arrested, sweetie."

"Well, not tonight he can't. Wait, forget I said that." I started looking around the car. The dash, the doors, the center console.

"Whatcha doing?"

"I'm looking for wood to knock on."

Tod phoned as we passed the gated entry to Oyster Cove Plantation back on Sea Pine Island. He was tied up with a topiary emergency and couldn't meet the Ballantynes at the Big House, who were due to land any minute.

Sid dropped me at my cottage door and I ran inside. Not to pat my own back, but I was killing it lately in the abbreviated shower get-ready-fast department. I was dressed in linen pants and an eskandar button down shortly before four thirty. I popped into my garage and remembered, once I saw it empty, that my Mini was back up at the Big House.

I climbed onto my three-wheeler, tossing my hipster handbag into the basket, and pedaled as fast as I could without breaking into a literal sweat. I parked my bike near the front steps two seconds before a float of a car rambled up the drive. The

Ballantyne's Rolls Corniche. Vivi waved with both hands from the front seat and Mr. Ballantyne honked the horn.

Vivi Ballantyne was a petite seventy-two year old dynamo, not a frail bone in her delicate body. She wore a pretty pink pantsuit with Chanel flats and tucked her arm in mine once she hit the pavement. "My lovely Elli, oh we missed you so!"

I kissed her soft cheek. "And I, you."

Mr. Ballantyne lifted the massive trunk lid and removed their luggage, five leather bags ranging in size from shoe case to steamer trunk.

"What's the twist, Elliott?" Mr. Ballantyne shouted. He was six feet of stage presence, robust and commanding and captivating. Think Jimmy Stewart on Broadway.

I wasn't sure which twist he was referring to, since we had so very many for the Wonderland, but a bright red and orange truck backed up the driveway, an Indian restaurant supply company name painted in fancy script along the side.

I wanted to jump and shout! The tables arrived! Hallelujah PTL. "You'll love it, sir. Something fanciful to take advantage of our perfect weather."

"I bet you ordered it up special," Vivi said.

"Indeed I did," I replied. I made a mental note to send Mimi a gift and an invite to the Palm & Fig Ball this Christmas. And a second mental note to look my very best.

We walked through the Big House. Where once there was chaos, now complete order. The tea sets were gone. All of them. I did not know where, but I did not care.

Mr. Ballantyne opened the patio doors wide and we went outside to see the transformation in progress.

A grungy Tod walked up the path and I quickly held up my arm, palm flat. The international sign for stop, duck, and hide. He jumped into the garden hedge just as the Ballantynes surveyed the scene.

Beyond the lap pool and patio, dozens of crape myrtles, massive oaks and towering magnolias spread out among the greens of the back lawn. Heavy strands of Spanish moss dangled from the oaks' branches, along with twelve-arm crystal chandeliers and oversized brass keys on long ribbons.

We watched as the crew unloaded squat tables and stacks of square poufs, ornately decorated with intricate embroidery and rolled edges.

"I love your imagination! Such a twist, indeed," Vivi said. "The children will adore sitting on pillows for tea."

"Wholeheartedly agree, my dear," Mr. Ballantyne said. "Looks as if you've got things under control, as usual." He winked at me and I felt my cheeks burn. Did he know how out of control things were just an hour ago? Probably.

"I think we'll retire to the residence," he said.

"I'll have Carla send up dinner, then, after you get settled," I said and hugged them both.

They went inside and Tod popped out of the bushes. He had ivy in his hair and dirt on his chin. "A small tussle with the Cheshire Cat," he said as he walked by.

I tracked down Carla outside the kitchen, which was apparently still off limits. A petite sous chef stood guard at the swinging door.

"The Ballantynes are upstairs," I said to Carla. "They'd like dinner when you get a minute."

"Of course. I'm making Vivi's favorite: Seafood tacos with lime cilantro aioli and blue corn chips for snacking."

"Babies, I'm here!" Busy Hinds said and glided into the room. She wore a tall white chef's hat and matching coat. "I'm ready to pipe when you are, Carla."

"I'll leave you two to your piping and tacos," I said.

I started to walk away, then remembered Gilbert and turned back. "How is Gilbert doing? Did you get him tucked in someplace?"

"Like an asylum?" Carla said.

"He's doing fabulous," Busy said. "Full of vim and vigor and can't wait to hit the street. Says he has his own plan and might not need you at all."

"His own plan?" I asked, but they'd left for the kitchen and left me standing in the hall.

Nothing good could come of this.

With the Ballantynes tucked in for the night, everyone in place, crews handling the tea set up, and me freshly showered, I had time to visit Gilbert and see exactly what this "plan" was.

I popped into Tod's dark office beneath the stairs. It had a tall ceiling, but not much square footage. A rickety chandelier hung over his desk and archaic door knockers hung on the wall. Very Addams Family meets the Haunted Mansion. He liked the imagery.

"I'm heading out, won't be gone but an hour. Two tops," I said.

He waved me off. "Take the night. You saved me an embarrassing moment."

I stood shocked, my eyes duly wide, my hand on my chest. "Are you saying *you* owe *me*?"

"I'm saying leave before I change my mind."

I left.

With the top down, I zipped out of the gate and onto Cabana Boulevard, heading south to Sugar Hill plantation to visit Gilbert. But as I waited my turn with the gate guard, I saw Gilbert's squished white and green Smart Car zoom past me.

The Mini was the perfect vehicle for stakeouts and car chases. I only needed half the room of a normal car to make a u-turn, whilst still in line. I whipped around and followed.

I stayed three cars back, which was difficult. I overestimated his speed when I used the term zoom. More like a smooth putter. I almost accidentally passed him twice.

He drove north on Cabana to Old Pickett Road, then turned right, following it around the creek. He pulled into the parking lot of the Wharf, a swank restaurant on the Intercoastal Waterway with a spectacular view of the Palmetto Bridge.

I parked in the far corner, far enough from the entrance it had to be staff parking. I tucked the Mini between two mid-sized SUVs. I could've parked next to Gilbert and asked him about his plan, but I wanted to see what he was up to. It's what investigators did.

Gilbert certainly looked more put together than he had of late as he walked across the lot and into the restaurant. Only one mismatched shoe, and though his shirt was inside out, he wore normal pants.

I noticed Ransom's slick silver racer parked by the door. Maybe he had the same idea I had. But before Gilbert even arrived?

A young hostess in ridiculously high heels greeted me at the door. I told her I was meeting someone and casually checked the dining room. Square tables set at angles faced a wall of windows, each table covered in a white cloth. Nearly every table was taken, fine diners preparing to enjoy their five-star meal while watching the sun set over the bridge.

Gilbert wasn't in the main dining room. I casually walked toward the bar and spotted Ransom on a high-backed stool. He lifted his drink in greeting. I slid into the seat next to his.

"Riesling, please," I said to the bartender.

She uncapped a bottle of Loosen Bros, poured, and set the glass in front of me on top of the requisite white napkin square. Then topped off Ransom's drink from a bottle of Pellegrino.

"Water?" I asked.

"I don't drink when I'm on the job."

"PI's don't necessarily follow those rules."

"I find you don't necessarily follow any rules."

"You're hilarious."

"And you're watching Goodsen," Ransom said. He tilted his head toward the patio.

I leaned forward and looked at Gilbert on the deck. He sat alone, half facing the railing, half facing the glass door entrance to the restaurant.

"Be careful," Ransom said. "You'll get us made."

"Not if we're on a date."

"So now you're ready to date me?"

"All in the name of the hunt."

"Uh-huh. How's that coming along?"

"We've been here before, Ransom. You tell me, I tell you."

"I think it was you show me yours, I show you mine."

"That sounds like an evasive answer."

"The only kind you give me," he said.

I sipped my wine, slowly. It was sweet and crisp and delicious. I leaned forward again for a better view of Gilbert. A man joined him at his table. Dr. Locke, the one who I'd seen arguing with Gilbert at the morgue. I took another sip of wine to hide my reaction.

"You know him?" Ransom asked.

I set my wine on the napkin square. "He looks familiar."

"You're a terrible liar."

Gilbert and Dr. Locke sat close together, huddled almost, at their four-top. They looked like two people plotting something nefarious.

I shrugged at Ransom. "You know him?"

"Looks familiar," he said.

"Good evening, Nick," a woman said in a sultry voice. "Been waiting long?"

I looked over his shoulder at Alicia Birnbaum. She wore a black dress with black heels. All sleek and sexy, and, if I'm being honest, slutty.

He pulled a pen from his sport jacket and signed his tab. "Nice consulting with you, Red. You take care."

With gritted teeth, I tipped my glass at them both. Those were the last words he said to me twenty years earlier. He left them on my answering machine a week before Christmas. That and some nonsense about not being our time.

I took a gulp of wine, trying to look like I could give a shit, and went back to watching Gilbert, my client. He looked stressed and unhappy and in the middle of an argument. Seemed as if Dr. Locke was giving him the business.

Did the doctor steal Gilbert's egg? And what, now he's harassing him about it? Someone's harassing him. Though probably not to his face over short rib empanadas and a butter bibb salad. Besides, if he was telling Gilbert he had the egg, Gil would've leapt over the tabletop and searched him.

But something wasn't right. This was the third time I'd seen them like this. First the emergency room, then the hallway outside the morgue waiting room.

I glanced over to the dining room, involuntarily, and saw a smirky Alicia enjoying a bottle of wine with Ransom.

So I guess the on-the-job part of the evening was over.

I handed over my credit card to the bartender. Time to get out of there.

The sun colored the sky in a mélange of warm hues from burnt orange to velvet red. The sharp salty air blended with crisp pine as the temperatures slowly fell. It was another beautiful evening in paradise.

I hiked across the lot and passed an old Plymouth Fury one row from the Mini. I stopped. I know that car, I thought. It nearly ran me down at Mary-Louise's house. Seeing it parked so close to the line jogged another memory. The emergency room on day one.

Walking backward, I checked out the license plate. South Carolina plates, not personalized, registration current. I'd write it down when I got back to my car. I walked around the driver's side and peeked in the window.

Horace Lovecraft popped out of nowhere, his face an inch from the glass.

Oh my God! I freaked out, clamped a hand over my own mouth to keep my screams inside and flung myself backward into the car in the next spot.

Horace slowly opened the driver's door and slid out. "You startled me. My keys slid down beneath the floor mat." He stared down at me, calm expression, hands clasped in front of him. "May I assist you, Miss Lisbon?

My own hands shook as I waved him off. "Nope, I'm good," I

said and again walked in reverse, not wanting to turn my back on him. When I hit the last row, I found the Mini and jumped in.

"I'm out. Forget it. It's just an egg and no doubt Jaime hid it and it'll turn up," I said out loud. I jammed the key fob into the slot and jabbed at the start button. "That dude is way too scary. Probably keeps the bodies in his basement."

I knew I should feel bad about leaving Gilbert alone to face Horace in the lot, but he had Dr. Locke to help him and I had the Ballantynes and the Tea. I checked my rearview and saw Horace get back into his car, just as I zipped onto Old Pickett Road.

Strange. Unless Horace was leaving the restaurant. Except I sat at the bar with a view of the nearly the entire restaurant and never saw him inside.

Never mind, I thought. I'm not going back.

I flipped the car around before I'd traveled a quarter mile.

What kind of investigator gives up because of a creepy Leland Gaunt-like man? He's probably the stalker freaking out Gilbert and I practically caught him doing it.

I didn't want to pull back into the same lot where Horace might see me, but I could get close. Luckily the Wharf is basically on the same property as the Crab Hut with only a thick row of bushes and crape myrtles dividing the two parking lots. I found a spot about halfway down the row and gently clicked my door shut after I got out.

Pushing branches aside, I snuck through the hedge. One whipped back and slapped me in the face, another scraped my forearm. But the soft ground muffled my steps as I crept from one lot to the other.

Horace's Fury sat right where I left it. And like before, it looked empty.

Fallen keys under the floor mat, my ass.

I crouched down and scurried to a staff car. I peeked over the row and saw Gilbert crossing the pavement. He walked straight to the Fury. The door opened, and this time Mary-Louise popped out. She looked around, quickly, as if making sure they were alone.

I dropped to the gravel and hoped the cars really were staff cars. I didn't need diners finding me flat out face down by their tires as they exited the grounds. Or one Lieutenant Nick Ransom.

Carefully, quietly, I sat up and knelt on my knees. I had a decent view, even though a thousand shards of gravel stabbed through my thin pants. Mary-Louise and Gilbert stood about two feet apart. Before they could say word one, Dr. Locke appeared.

Interesting. But Mary-Louise didn't even acknowledge him; he simply pulled Gilbert to the side, and closer to me.

I heard snippets.

Dr. Locke: "...tomorrow...in my office already."

Gilbert: "...fix it.."

Dr. Locke: "...hospital...pulled files."

Gilbert: "...got a plan."

Dr. Locke nodded once and left, ignoring Mary-Louise. A case of see no evil if ever there was one.

As he walked away, the Fury pulled forward out of its space and slowly drove across the pavement. That must have been the cue for Gilbert and Mary-Louise, because they started shouting at one another. Even though I couldn't hear exactly what they were saying, their body language said they were pissed.

I scrambled up and ran over to them.

"How many people you meeting in this parking lot?" Mary-Louise said, checking the area again. "I thought you were alone."

"What are you doing here?" Gilbert asked me. "Are you spying on me?"

"Of course not. I just had a lovely dinner at the Crab Hut." I figured neither knew I would rather eat Play-Doh for dinner than seafood. "I heard you yelling. Keep it down, the whole island can hear you."

"He thinks I killed Jaime," Mary-Louise said. She looked exhausted. Hair limp and unwashed, clothes wrinkled and unkempt. "I swear on my grandma's grave, I did not kill her."

"Well, I think you did," Gilbert said. "I think that's why you ran and left me to take the heat."

"No, Gil, honest," Mary-Louise said. "I wouldn't kill anyone."

"But Bobby would?" I interjected.

"Never. I don't think so. I don't know," Mary-Louise said and started crying. "He can't be a murderer. I love him."

"He shot Gilbert and stole his egg, probably killed his wife," I said.

"Bobby didn't take the egg," she said and dug a tissue out of her sweat pants. "But yeah, he shot Gilbert. That doesn't mean he hurt Jaime."

"Then you obviously took my egg," Gilbert said. "And tricked me into thinking Jaime took it."

"I swear I didn't steal it. Maybe a trinket, but not the egg," Mary-Louise said. "I wouldn't jeopardize your Gil-animals. I know you need the money for the patent."

"Then why run, Mary-Louise?" I asked. "You called the police, then ran. That makes you look guilty."

"I know, I know. I don't know what I was thinking. I panicked. Bobby didn't show up and didn't call. I thought he was talking to the cops, so I called them to give my side of things. But then, they didn't have Bobby, they had Gilbert—"

"So you were just going to leave me there?" Gilbert said.

"No! I was heading to the station when Bobby showed up. He came back for me, Gilbert. What could I do?"

I nodded sagely. "Leave with him."

We stood in a tight triangle alone in the lot, except for Horace driving slowly between the rows. "Where is Bobby now? And why are you here?" I asked.

"I had to tell Gilbert I didn't hurt Jaime," Mary-Louise said, pleading at Gilbert.

"And..." I said.

"And I forgot my passport when I left, so I couldn't go to Canada. Bobby went without me and I came back."

"I don't buy it," Gilbert said. "You can go to Canada without a passport. You only need a driver's license. You need the passport to come back, not leave. It's the law."

"I'm not lying, Gilbert," Mary-Louise said. "And that's not true. Bobby said."

"You can travel to Canada and then back to the U.S. without a passport. It makes it easier," I said. "Wait, what am I saying! You can't go to Canada!"

"I'm not," Mary-Louise said. "I'm going to Mexico. I want to be as far away from Bobby as possible. He might be a murderer." She put her face in her hands. "I can't handle this."

"Mary-Louise, listen to me," I said. "You have to get in front of this. Or at least as much as you can now. Talk to Lieutenant Ransom or it will be so much worse. You'll be a fugitive instead of a witness." I gently put my arm around her. "He's right inside."

She jumped back and flung off my arm while Gilbert spun around in a full circle and grabbed at his hair.

"He's here?" They said in unison.

"Yes, he's here. See the half-million dollar Mercedes with the personalized license plate that says RANSOM parked in the very first spot?"

"He'll arrest me!" They again said in unison.

"He won't arrest either of you," I said.

"He thinks I killed Jaime," Gilbert said.

"No, he thinks I killed Jaime," Mary-Louise said.

"He doesn't think either of you killed Jaime," I said. Before the words left my lips, Mary-Louise took off running. The Fury picked her up halfway down the entrance drive and they drove away.

Gilbert ran in the other direction, straight for his car.

"Gil, wait," I shouted, sprinting toward him. "Why are you running? If Ransom wanted to arrest you, he wouldn't have let you go."

"He's hung up on Jaime's insurance policy. He doesn't believe me. I didn't know. I thought she changed it, made her sister the beneficiary."

"Didn't you manage it for her?"

"Originally. But she took it over years ago, wouldn't let me have anything to do with any of it."

We stood in awkward silence. Their relationship fell apart years ago if she wouldn't let her insurance salesman husband administer her own insurance.

"I've got to go," he said. "I've got a plan."

"What's this plan? Gilbert, I'm the investigator. Let me handle this."

"Just find my egg. Handle that. I've got more than just eggs in the frying pan." He whipped open his door and climbed inside.

I slowly walked back to the dividing hedge. I wasn't about to walk up to Alicia Birnbaum in the restaurant sporting two tears in my top and gravel stains on my pants. Not twice in one lifetime. Or at least the same day.

I called Parker instead.

"Let it be known that I'm sharing information as soon as I received it," I said when Parker answered. "I'm a cooperating investigator."

"Whatcha got?"

"Mary-Louise Springer is on the island. I just saw her with Horace Lovecraft in his Plymouth Fury. I didn't get the plate."

"Got it," she said. I heard her fingers furiously tapping a keyboard in the background. "When did this happen?"

"Minutes ago," I said.

"How many minutes?"

"Five. Ish. Nearly almost immediately. I'm cooperating."

"I'll tell the Lieutenant. You coming by for a statement?"

"I can tomorrow if you need me. Right now I'm heading to the hospital. Not injury related," I added before she imagined me beaten on the side of the road. "But I'll be home after that if you have questions."

"Got it," she said again and hung up.

With my civic duty done, I crawled through the stickery bushes. I brushed off the leaves and dirt before getting in my car. It was time to see what Dr. Locke was up to. Him and his "pulled files" and Gilbert's big plan.

TWENTY-TWO

(Day #5: Tuesday Evening)

Before I hit the road, I searched all things Google on my phone for a listing for Dr. Locke. Nothing, not even with alternate spellings. It occurred to me I never saw him actually treating patients, just saw him in a white coat with a name badge. As someone who has perhaps done an impersonation before, I know better than to trust the validity of every badge pinned to a person.

When he and Gilbert were in the lot, Dr. Locke had said the word hospital, so I drove to Sea Pine Memorial, about a mile down Cabana. The annual board meeting was tonight and Sid would definitely be there.

I texted her from the lobby and met her by the welcome desk. She stuck a visitor sticker on my blouse and we walked toward the elevators.

"You know a Dr. Carl Locke? Gray on top, a little doughy around the middle?"

"Sure, he's in oncology."

"So he's a real doctor? I didn't find him listed on Google."

"Yes, a real doctor," Sid said. "His office is here at the hospital. He doesn't have a private practice. He doesn't see a ton of patients, but he's always around somewhere."

"He around tonight?"

"You need to talk to him?"

We stood in front of the elevator bank. The halls were quiet, especially on the first floor. The emergency room took up a good chunk of space, along with a bright waiting room, plus offices, labs, a gift shop, cafeteria, and miles of hallways.

"Not exactly." I stepped closer and lowered my voice. "I'm thinking I need to visit his office."

"Without him in it."

"Yep."

She thought about it for two seconds, then punched the up arrow for the elevator. "He's on three. I'll walk you through the maze."

"You have a key?"

"It's probably not locked," Sid said. "Patient records are computerized. These offices generally hold knick knacks and photos. What do you think you'll find?"

"I'm not sure, but a guess? Something to do with viaticals." At Sid's questioning look, I explained. "It's where one buys the life insurance policy of a dying person, at a discount. Say he's got a two hundred thousand dollar policy, so a guy buys it for one fifty. Win-win. The dying guy gets to spend his own money while he's still alive, the buying guy makes a very nice return when the policy pays out."

"I know what viaticals are, I am technically in the medical field. I didn't know you knew. But they aren't all win-win. Some kids get pissed their dad sold out their inheritance."

"Yeah, but maybe dear old dad spends it all on them. Could do a lot of good, spending time with the family."

"A trip to Paris for everyone. First Class."

The doors to the elevator opened on the third floor and I followed Sid through a series of turns and stretches of hallway.

"But wait, there's more," I said. "A life insurance buyout can pay for experimental treatment not covered by regular medical."

"Drug trials do cost a fortune, and hospitals don't generally offer payment plans."

"Plus, they can use the cash to pay off his debts early, rather than his family having to wait until after probate."

"Save your wife's credit score and your kid's college

education. I can see that," Sid said. "And you figure Dr. Locke and Gilbert are working on a viatical business?"

"I know Gilbert is, he told me. And who better to supply him with dying clients than an oncologist? The perfect team."

"Yes, sweetie, but for one thing," Sid said. "Who issues a life insurance policy on a dying man?"

We approached a closed door at the end of a hallway, directly across from the nurses' station. A plastic wood-like nameplate was screwed to the door, CARL LOCKE MD etched on the face.

I twisted the handle, but it barely moved. "Locked."

A doctor in gray slacks and a white coat dropped off a chart on the other side of the nurses' desk. He scribbled some notes, checked his watch, scribbled some more, then left.

"Should I just pick it?" I whispered.

"You pick locks now?"

"No, I was hoping you'd say you had a key."

"I can get a key, wait here."

When I remained next to the door, Sid waved me away. "Not so obvious. Act like you're on break from visiting a relative or something."

I paced the hall, trying to blend in. Two doors down was a nondescript visitor's lounge. An old leather sofa, tan chairs, a low table. Coffee supplies on a cart.

Sid waved from the doorway, dangling a key, and disappeared down the hall. Back at the door, she turned a key in the knob and I was in.

"See you tomorrow at the Tea," I said.

"Don't take too long in there," she said.

"I'm a professional."

I clicked the door shut behind me. I'm sure most envision a PI rifling through filing cabinets with a mini flashlight in one hand, while the other tabs through row after row of folders. Not so much here. A windowless office allowed me to flip on the lights, and there was no filing cabinet. It looked pretty much like Sid said. Mostly knick knacks and picture frames.

Dr. Locke's desk took up a third of the room. A reddish maple monster with three drawers, one in the center and two on the side. I started with those.

The top one could kindly be described as a junk drawer. All manners of nonsense were in that drawer. A thousand pens, loose blocks of staples, five kinds of tape (including duct), rubber band balls, Bazooka bubble gum wrappers, dice, what could only be tiddlywinks, golf pencils, and an egg full of Silly Putty. Maybe he treated children?

The bottom drawer held two medical journals. I flipped through the pages and found a folded printout inside. It listed twelve names with a series of columns next to each. Identical diagnoses and blood work. All cancer, all Dr. Locke's patients, and all the phoniest names I'd ever read. Augustus Boxleitner, Carmine Dolittle, Everest Franken, Gladys Holbrook. All adults, no children.

It would take the authorities all of an hour to nail these two yahoos and crack the case wide open. I skimmed the rest of the names and notes.

Who insures a dying man, Sid had asked? You don't. You insure a fake healthy man, then diagnose him and give him six months to live. Now you're in the viatical business. Illegally, of course.

I took two snaps of the patient list with my phone and tucked the info back in the journal, then into the drawer.

Gilbert was having a time of it this week. Now add getting busted for insurance fraud to his list of unfortunate events. Well, possible insurance fraud anyway.

I slipped out the door, making sure it was locked, and turned to face Nick Ransom. He stood statue still five feet away, hands folded in front, no expression.

"What the hell are you doing?"

I looked over the shoulder toward the door, then back to Ransom. "Oh. Just..."

"Just breaking and entering?"

"I had the key, so it's not breaking and entering."

"It is when you steal the key."

I didn't tell him I wasn't the one to steal the key. Best to keep my pie hole shut on the whole where-did-the-key-come-from front.

"Parker called," he said, his voice steely and flat. "You met with Mary-Louise Springer, a fugitive murder suspect, as you well know, and you didn't tell me?"

"You were at dinner."

"Forty feet away."

"No time to tell you. I heard her arguing with Gilbert, so I approached them. We talked for like ten minutes max, then she ran away." My shoulders started to hunch and I didn't like the defensive tone my voice started to take on. I took a breath and spoke more slowly, professionally. "I immediately called Parker and told her every detail."

He stepped closer. "You call the police *before* you engage with fugitives, not after."

"It's not written that way in the handbook."

"This isn't funny."

"I'm not laughing."

"You told her to go to Mexico?" His voice so tight, he mouth barely moved.

"I told her she didn't need her passport to go to Canada. She brought up Mexico, then I told her to talk to you. That's when she ran," I said, looking straight at him, hands on hips. "I assume you found her since you know the details of our conversation, even if they are incorrect."

"Incorrect, my ass. Gilbert Goodsen told me. Personally. When he walked into the Wharf to report seeing Mary-Louise Springer in the parking lot with Elliott Lisbon, rogue investigator."

"I'm not rogue, Ransom. I called Parker." I thought about Gilbert racing to get out of there, mumbling about his plan. I never thought it included the police.

"Why are you here?" I asked.

"To arrest you for obstruction of justice. Now I'm adding breaking and entering. Second time I've caught you on this case alone."

"You can't be serious. You can't arrest me."

"I am and I will. You can't do whatever you want and the law be damned."

"I'm not damning the law."

"That's right, you're not," he said. "Not on my watch."

We stood two feet apart. Him looking down at me, me defiant in his face of barely conceived fury.

"You have no right to threaten me, and you're sure as shit not arresting me." I started to walk away. Ransom grabbed my arm and I yanked it right back.

"You owe me, Nick Ransom."

"That was months ago. I've made up for the danger I put you in. We're square, I don't owe you."

I jabbed my finger into his chest as hard as I could. "You broke my heart on an answering machine. We will never be square. You will owe me forever."

I stalked down the hall, clenching my fists in frustration. I passed Nurse Elaine at the station desk. I looked the other way and hoped she didn't notice me.

"Hey, Elli," she hollered. "See you at the Wonderland Tea tomorrow. It's my first Ballantyne event."

I waved but didn't stop until I stabbed at the down arrow on the elevator.

Matty was bringing a date to my Big House and Ransom was pulling rank right to my face.

Boys suck.

TWENTY-THREE

(Day #6: Wednesday Morning)

Morning makes everything better. As do cupcakes for breakfast. In anticipation, I awoke before the crack of dawn. If half-past seven were the crack of dawn, which it was for a non-morning person like myself. In the spirit of Wonderland, I fancied a dress with dozens of wispy fluffy layers and applique flowers on the bodice. I topped it with pink ballet flats and a hat befitting a royal wedding or a Kentucky Derby.

With the stepladder from my kitchen closet, I climbed up to the ledge in the living room above my sofa, the one where I kept my collection of vintage toys. The left side held old games, from a *That Girl* board game to a pyramid of old lunchboxes. On the right, in the corner, Raggedy Ann and Andy sat at a squat table, enjoying a tea party.

I carefully took down the teapot, then a single cup and saucer. A series of intricate butterflies and dragonflies danced on the surface, painted by hand, by my mother, with a delicate touch and a tiny brush. I remember the day she painted it for me. I'd had the chickenpox and couldn't go to my best friend's birthday party. Real afternoon tea at a fancy hotel. I was devastated, but a teapot painted only for me made it all better. I'd always kept the tea set close. My parents weren't "savers," and I often feared it might get tossed into a donation bag.

I tucked the pretty pot and cup into a padded tote and drove to the Ballantyne.

The weather was script perfect. A bright sun, a Carolina blue sky, and a handful of fluffy white clouds drifting by.

The Big House was in the final flurries of set up. One crew fluffed the Moroccan pillow poufs, while another gently placed tea sets at over two-hundred fifty settings. An army of kitchen helpers in white chef coats put a pink chocolate place card on each plate.

Carla was still piping mini cupcakes as crews set up serving trays in the staging area. I snagged two and popped them in my mouth one after the other. Chocolate with raspberry buttercream frosting swirled high.

"Perfect, Carla, just perfect," I said, my mouth full.

"Don't touch these, they're flawless. I saved you a plate of imperfections over there," she said and nodded toward a silver platter balanced on a chair.

"You're a dream," I said and took another two from the platter, their frosting droopy, but just as tasty.

"Rough night?"

"Aren't they all?"

A line of servers exited the house carrying huge round baskets with vintage medicine bottles stacked inside. Each filled with colorful liquid and marked "drink me" on a tag hanging by a string.

"Babies, I'm here!" Busy said. She wore a dreamy fairy dress with a crown of fresh flowers in her hair. "Are you ready for the surprise?" She clapped her hands like a little girl, so excited to finally share her secret.

Tod and Jane joined me on the patio, both properly hatted and dressed for a tea party. Even Jane was smiling. Sort of.

Busy held out a plate. "First take a petit four."

She didn't have to ask me twice. I selected one with a tiny flower on top. When we all held one in our hands, Busy told us to eat them.

"It tastes like chicken salad," Jane said.

"It *is* chicken salad," Busy said.

Creamy, smooth, with a crunch from the frosting, or really, the crushed cashews dyed and made to look like frosting.

Busy held out a different tray. "Now try a sandwich."

I bit into a bite-sized prosciutto on pumpernickel, but it was really chocolate.

"Surprise! We reversed them! Cakes are sandwiches and sandwiches are cakes!" Busy said. "Isn't it fantastic? Genius, fantastic?"

Jane licked her fingers. First her ring finger, then her index. "It would've been just as fantastic had I known." She plucked another sandwich cake from the tray and walked away.

I hugged Busy, then Carla. "The kids will love them. Alice herself would've been delighted!" I, too, grabbed another sandwich cake and headed down to the lawn.

The gardener had dyed the pool water pink and set to floating dozens of peonies on lily pads. Ribbons adorned a wide topiary arch at the entrance to the party. A seven-piece Dixieland band decked out in red striped vests and straw boaters tuned their instruments and the set up crews started to disappear.

The press arrived first. Tate Keating tipped his newsboy cap and sauntered over to the centerpiece. A nine-foot topsy turvy cake with a tuxedoed white rabbit on top. Tate was quickly joined by the folks from the Savannah and Charleston papers. The Ballantyne's Wonderland Tea would be the talk of all the lowcountry.

A large pocket watch hanging from a pole next to the cake struck eleven and the band started playing. Children, their parents, and their doctors all streamed onto the lawn. The children were shy at first, then started laughing and running, as if walking through the gates of Disneyland.

I made a mental note: next year we need a train!

"A wondrous Wonderland," Zibby Archibald said. She wore two hats, one on top of another, her own nod toward topsy turvy, which matched smashingly with her Nemo-colored hair and gloves. One orange, one pink. And both inside out. If ever an event suited Zibby Archibald, the Wonderland Tea was it.

"You look fanciful, Zibby," I said. "Thank you for being on the committee, it's a perfect party."

"I'm pleased as punch to participate! Oooh, the banjos are playing. I should've brought mine..." she said and hustled toward the crowd.

"You look lovely, Elli," Matty said. He leaned down and kissed my cheek.

"Matty! You made it!" I said, then remembered he was bringing Nurse Elaine. I tried to fight my face from drooping at the thought. "Where's your date? I was looking forward to seeing you both."

He tilted his head toward the photographers at the cake table. Nurse Elaine was posing for Tate, holding the blue peacock pot from Judith's shop, her arm tucked into a young doctor's from Savannah.

"She traded up," he said.

"Ouch," I said. "Better career connections?"

"More money."

"Ah."

Applause went up and we turned to see the Ballantynes arrive on the top step beneath the arch. Mr. Ballantyne dapper in pinstripes and a plum velvet top hat over a foot tall; Mrs. Ballantyne in a lilac wide-brimmed beauty. They welcomed their guests, read a short passage from *Alice in Wonderland*, then strolled through the clusters of visitors, chatting with the children as much as the adults. They never had children of their own, though they treated me like a daughter, but adored kids of any age.

The band played and the children laughed and the sun shone. It was glorious. It was perfect. It was interrupted by crazy pants Gilbert Goodsen. Though pants was clearly used in metaphor.

He wore swim trunks.

And a tie on his head, like a bandana from an eighties aerobicize video.

"Elliott!"

He ran into the middle of the party, hands waving frantically. "*Help me!*"

The topsy turvy cake was directly in front of him. With visions of Gilbert colliding face first into it, I sprinted like an Olympian off a starting block and skidded into him.

The guests around us laughed, thinking it was part of the party, but when Gilbert said "car bomb," smiles faded. I hugged Gilbert, my arms over both of his to hold them down, and said loudly, "Gilbert! You're not due on stage for an hour."

His face went blank.

I turned him around and stuck my arm in his, dragging him toward the pool and patio, away from the party. I spotted Tate out of the corner of my eye. He was running toward us fast, knees high, arms pumping, eyes wide. He looked like a cartoon.

I kept walking, pulling Gilbert with me. "What's going on?" I asked.

"I'm nearly dead, that's what. I need that egg. Today. Now. They bombed my car! They're going to kill me!"

That stopped me. "Who's going to kill you? The attorney?"

Gilbert slapped his palms against his cheeks and left them there. He looked crazed and panicked and desperate.

Tate crossed under the arch, taking the steps up to the pool two at a time.

"Gilbert, honey, give me one minute and I'll help you with everything," I said calmly. "You go inside, okay?"

His eyes focused on me and he blinked.

"You know where my office is?"

He stared at me as Tate approached, then nodded. "The convertible Mini, right?"

"Yep, that's my office. Parked out front. Hurry now and I'll be right there."

Tate snapped a quick picture of Gilbert scurrying away. "What a headline! Ballantyne Board Member Bombs Wonderland Tea."

"What are you talking about, Tate?" I said. "There's no bomb here."

"I heard bomb, Elliott, and that sells papers."

"Good to hear you care about safety first."

I needed a minute to think and I didn't have one. Tate's

headline would undermine the entire event before tea had even been served.

A little girl in a big hat waved to me from the arch. I waved back and brought Tate over to meet her.

"Abby, sweetie, look at how pretty you are."

"I'm Alice at Wonderland," she said. "We're having a tea party. With a rabbit. And a cat. My mama said I could eat dessert first today."

"Well, then so will I!" I said. "Abby, please meet Tate Keating. He's a reporter with the newspaper."

Abby pointed at his camera. "You wanna take my picture? Do you like my hat? I put the ribbons in a bow under my chin. Mama said that's how Alice would do it." Abby twirled around and her hat wobbled and teetered on her head while she giggled.

"But it's too big for you," Tate said.

"Yeah, that's because I don't have hair. See?" She tipped it back to show the top of her head. Only a handful of wispy strands remained. She wiggled her hat again. "The bow keeps it in place."

"It's perfect," I said. "Did you see the band? They have a banjo!"

"A banjo? What's that?"

I pointed to Zibby plucking on the strings of one, wedged between the Dixieland members and the crowd. "Run over there by Dr. Hannah and she'll show you."

"I want a banjo!" Abby said as she ran toward the lively music.

"Tate, that's your story today," I said. "Abby is six years old and she won't live to see Christmas this year."

"But she looks so happy."

"Her parents took her off treatment last month. She was so ill, and it wasn't working. They wanted her to have fun again. Run again, laugh again. If only for a month or two."

He watched Abby a moment, then slowly surveyed the crowd. It looked as if he understood, really understood, who our guests were.

"You have two stories to choose from today: A distressed patron whose grief is causing a minor meltdown, or a child whose last days are spent playing dress up. She deserves the spotlight, Tate. They all do. With the right mix of emotion and exposure, you'll touch the hearts of your readership. They'll donate to the hospital to provide more programs like this one."

Tate nodded, sadness clear on his face. "I get it. I'll delete the photo of Goodsen. But I'll be tracking him down tomorrow."

"His wife's funeral is tomorrow."

"You're all sunshine and rainbows today, Elliott. Lighten up, it's a party," Tate said and walked away.

I spotted Matty talking with Tod near the elephant family topiaries. "I'm sorry, Matty, but I've got to go. Gilbert's yelling about a car bomb. I've got to get him out of here."

"Is that what Tate Keating was racing for?" Matty asked.

"Yep, but that's handled. He's now writing a piece on the children."

"I'll make sure of it," Tod said.

"Maybe I'll see you later?" Matty asked me.

"I'd love to," I said. "Will you find Sid for me, tell her I had to go?"

"Sure," he said.

"Oh, Tod, one last favor. Will you tell Miranda Gaines we'll hold a special luncheon in Jaime's honor next week? I told her mahj group we would say something nice about Jaime here, but I don't think it's the right place."

"Agreed. I saw her arrive a few minutes ago. Be careful getting out of here, the Ballantyne's are back near the front," Tod said.

"Cover me." The last thing I needed was to get delayed. The way Gilbert was spiraling out of control, he might next run through the party naked.

I snuck across the garden, through the Big House, and out to the Mini, which was parked under the porte cochere.

Gilbert sat in the passenger seat, head in his hands, weeping.

"Hey Gil, you okay? Tell me what's going on."

"Visitation is today. The viewing is tonight. The funeral is tomorrow." He lifted his head, tears on his cheeks. "My Smart Car is no more. Neither is Jaime."

"Where's your car?" I asked gently.

"Home. In the driveway."

"It exploded? From a car bomb?"

"It's going to. I heard the clicks and the car wouldn't start."

"And how do you get from that to a bomb?"

He waved me away. "I've seen enough movies to know how this works. I took a chance the seat wasn't a pressure trigger and ran like hell."

I nodded at his quick thinking. "Was it charged?"

"The bomb?"

"The car."

"Charged?"

"It's electric."

"Stop making fun of me!" He shook his fist at me, up near my face. "It's not a golf cart, it's a real car!"

I placed a calming hand on his forearm and lowered it. "I know it's a real car. An electric one. That's what the big plug symbol means, the one on the side."

"Well, I can't go see Jaime alone. I can't. Please. Please go with me. Please go with me. Please. Please go—"

"Of course I'll go. What time tonight?"

"*Tonight?! We can't wait for tonight!*" He grabbed my hand. "Oh Elliott, you have to help me. We have to go now. I was already supposed to be there when I discovered the bomb." He lowered his voice to a near whisper. "No one's there with her."

Sounds of the children laughing and the band playing and the giant clock ticking drifted from the back of the Big House. They didn't need me. But Gilbert did. The best thing would be to help him, not worry he'd distract from the children's merriment.

"Okay, but we need to get you changed. You cannot go to your wife's visitation wearing swim trunks."

"I don't have anything left," he said, still whispering.

"I got this," I said and opened the car door.

Tod's haunted office included a hidden closet behind the hat rack in the corner behind the door. I tapped along the panel until it popped open. Two sets of black pants and crisp white shirts hung inside. No ties, no belts, no shoes. Gilbert's rubber flip-flops would have to do.

He put on the pants and the legs were approximately four feet too long. I rolled them up until they hit the top of his feet.

"That looks ridiculous," Gilbert said, the tie still tied around his head.

"I think it's very chic. Hip, even."

He perked up one notch. "You think I look like a hipster? I knew I could pull it off. Maybe I should add it to Gil-animals."

I agreed and led him back to the Mini and got us out of there before someone caught us. And by someone, I meant Tod. He might literally drop down dead if he saw Gilbert in his Dolce & Gabbana pants with the bottoms rolled up.

Once we hit Cabana Boulevard, Gilbert seemed to have calmed down some. He kept fiddling with the hand pump to make his seat rise higher.

"Tell me about the insurance fraud with Dr. Locke," I asked.

"What?" he asked, all innocent as if he'd never heard such an outrageous claim against his person in all his life. The same reaction he gave when I asked about faking an insurance policy for the egg. I should've known then he was up to something.

"I'm an investigator. I investigate. Sometimes I discover things I wish I hadn't. Can't un-ring the bell, Gil."

"I know not what you speak."

"Here's a hint: You're supposed to meet Dr. Locke today to 'fix it.'"

"Oh shit!" He checked both wrists, presumably for the watch he wasn't wearing.

"Oh shit, indeed. Augustus Boxleitner, Carmine Dolittle, Everest Franken? Those are the most made-up names I've ever heard. Everest?"

"It was supposed to be Everett."

"Uh-huh."

"It's all a misunderstanding."

"I don't think the police will think that."

He grabbed my arm with both hands and squeezed. "You can't rat me out. We have privilege. I'm your client. What we say can't be used against me."

I pried his fingers from my flesh. "There is so much wrong with that and none of it applies. I can't ignore what I found out."

He went to grab me again, then pulled back. He sat defeated, staring out the window.

"Maybe I can help," I said. "Tell me the misunderstanding."

"The viaticals were going strong, real strong. We signed up two, three clients. Made our money back, plus some. But it's hard to find dying people and convince them to sell me their insurance. You'd think everyone would do it."

"You'd think."

"So we thought, why not make up our own clients?"

"Because it's insurance fraud?"

"It didn't seem so at the time. I filed the policies, but immediately regretted it. I'm not a criminal. But the paperwork is in limbo. Mary-Louise was supposed to help me track it down and cancel it, but then this all happened," he said with an arm wave.

"Won't it look suspicious to rescind twelve policies at once?"

"I'm not crazy. I only filed two, Augustus and Carmine. But nothing's going to happen with them, I swear. We aren't filing claims. I'm canceling the policy. I didn't commit fraud."

Except for the initial filing, I thought. Pretty sure that counts.

We rode in silence for the last mile to Bennett's Funeral Home. It was located mid-island, a long winding drive off Cabana Boulevard, wedged between two construction trailers. I turned onto the narrow lane, following it about a quarter-mile to the marsh. A short white building resembling a wide ranch home sat to the side with a black hearse beneath a long black awning. Parking was scarce, nearly every slot taken. So much for Jaime being alone. I found a spot close to the side door, almost on the grass, and we walked inside.

About a dozen people milled in the entry, all speaking in hushed tones. Two sets of double doors were open, each with a spray of flowers at their entries. A small digital sign, as big as an iPad, was placed near each set of flowers. The right said WHITAKER, the left said GOODSEN.

Alicia Birnbaum stood in the middle, shaking hands with a young couple. She saw me. I nodded at her, she nodded at me.

Then she saw Gilbert.

She ripped her hand from the lady shaking it and stormed toward us.

"How dare you show up here," she said to Gilbert.

"She's my wife!" Gilbert said.

"You mur—"

"Alicia, darling," I interrupted and engulfed her in a hug. "I'm so sorry for your loss."

"Oh, I, okay," she said.

I pushed her and Gilbert away from the crowd. I saw a closed door and quickly twisted the handle, herding them both inside.

It was a quiet space adjacent to the other viewing room, filled with dark furniture and formal parlor chairs, and it smelled like lilies and sorrow.

"What the hell is he doing here?" Alicia asked.

"She was my wife," Gilbert said. "I loved her."

"You killed her."

"Whoa," I said and held my hands up to both of them. "Knock it off."

"You don't tell me—" Alicia said.

"I do today," I said. "You two can't act like that out there. I know you want to lash out, assign blame, be the one who hurts the most. But if you do, you take away from Jaime. Everyone will watch and gossip and blab every detail they heard."

They both stood rigid. Sad, but rigid.

I touched Gilbert's arm. "Let the focus be on Jaime." Then I turned to Alicia. "Let people pay their respects to your friend. Let her rest in peace."

Alicia stared me down, processing, eyeballing my overly fanciful dress. She nodded and left.

Gil hugged me tight, then left.

I stayed in the small anteroom.

I hadn't been inside a viewing room since my father's death twenty years earlier. I could handle the lobby and the side rooms, but I wasn't going to enter the funeral room.

Quiet voices carried through the walls, like soft music in the background. I sat in one of the parlor chairs. Even though Gilbert needed to meet Dr. Locke later, I wasn't sure how long he wanted to stay at the funeral home. Or how long his truce with Alicia might hold up.

Something Alicia said the day before rattled around in my head, but I couldn't shake it loose. I felt as if I'd let a clue slink by and it made my brain itch. I replayed what I could remember of our conversation in my head, but the slinky clue eluded me. I sighed in frustration.

A stack of bulletins sat on the side table. I picked one up. It was nicer than the usual two-pager. Several sheets had been inserted, an array of family photos printed on fine paper. They looked professional, but still candids. Must have an amateur photographer in the family because these definitely weren't cellphone shots.

I flipped to the last page. A lovely obituary for Peter Whitaker. Survived by his son, Alexei, and his daughter, Ekaterina. Must be long for Kat. I remembered them both from the hospital morgue viewing lounge. Peter's wife, Galina was a Russian ballerina. As was his mother, who married an American. Russia always made me think of cold. Snowy, blizzardy *Doctor Zhivago* cold. Though Lara was a nurse, not a ballerina.

A ballerina! Something popped into place and I jumped up, a hot flash racing from my knees to my scalp. "Holy shit," I said just as the door opened and Mr. Whitaker's son, Alex, walked in.

He looked at me politely, considering I stood there sweating, cursing, and gripping his late father's obit.

The back of my neck burned hotter in embarrassment. "I'm so sorry for your loss," I said and hurried out.

I rushed to the door, barely noticing the people in the lobby, then sprinted to the Mini. Took two minutes to hit Cabana Boulevard, another five had me racing down Marsh Grass Road. Theories in my head struggled, twisted, and clicked, trying to fit together like colors on a Rubik's Cube.

Peter Whitaker was Gilbert's client. It was his Fabergé egg. Peter's wife and mother were both from Russia. Which was where the original Fabergé eggs hailed from. Was Gilbert's egg a real Russian Fabergé egg?

I shook my head. Figure that out later, I told myself. Keep working the theory.

Peter sold his egg to Gilbert. He was desperate for money. Probably after Gilbert bought his life insurance. That much Gilbert told me. He even said it wasn't enough money for another experimental treatment. So Peter sold his most valuable possession and needed it sold quickly. Hence the pawn parlor, local antique shop, and Gilbert the viatical king.

I turned onto Bent Tree, slowing my speed as I followed the overgrown road.

Peter's wife and mother weren't just Russian, though. They were ballerinas. And I knew where there was a sparkly ballerina figurine: Mary-Louise's curio cabinet. I was betting those sparkles weren't crystals, they were diamonds. Stick that tiny dancer back into the egg and it's worth millions.

But Peter couldn't have known or he wouldn't have sold it for fifty thousand dollars, fast cash or not. The ballerina figurine probably got separated from the egg years ago. A little girl playing with her miniature ballerina, didn't put it back where it belonged. A generation later, no one remembered it was a set.

Peter gets the egg appraised, separate from his tray of trinkets. It's valuable, sure, but not seven-figures-possibly-real-

Fabergé valuable. Not get-as-much-medical-treatment-as-you-need valuable. Not kill-to-own-it valuable.

I arrived in Mary-Louise's neighborhood and parked one street over from her house, about halfway down the block. I casually walked to the corner and peeked down Mary-Louise's street.

The white police surveillance van was still parked at the curb, several houses down from Mary-Louise's.

I walked back to my car and called Mary-Louise. Voicemail. I left a quick message saying I could help her with the police, I just needed five minutes inside her house, did she mind? Next I called Parker, but hung up before she answered. What would I say? I think I found the missing surprise for the egg, even though no one knew it was missing and I don't have the egg, but it still might lead to whoever really killed Jaime, though I don't know how. Or why. Or who.

I counted houses until I found the one that backed to Mary-Louise's house, maybe six or seven down. A dog started to bark in the window. A red Irish Setter. Same as the dog who tried to jump the fence the last time I was here. And since he was inside, his owners probably weren't home. No cars in the drive, middle of the day, the street quiet.

The two single car garages backed up to each other with only a wood fence dividing them. I hurried up the drive and squeezed into the space between the side fence and the garage. I took another look around. A peaceful afternoon. Only the brackish smell of the marshlands and freshly cut grass.

I peeked over the fence on tiptoes. Mary-Louise's driveway was also empty, and her gate was closed, blocking any view to the street in front of her house.

The Irish Setter barked his head off and startled the crap out of me. His face took up the entire window space not twenty inches away. Man, that house was close to the fence. My heart hammered in my chest and I tried to wave him off. It didn't work. If possible, he barked louder.

I grabbed the top of the fence and hoisted myself over. It was easy enough, but I landed in a similar tight space and the damn dog kept barking. I hurried into Mary-Louise's backyard and grabbed the key from beneath the geranium pot.

Her house felt empty. Undisturbed dust and the scent of abandonment. The floor creaked, something I didn't remember. Maybe knowing the police were watching made me more observant.

Afternoon sunlight barely filtered through the heavy sheers of the front window. I approached the curio. The door opened with a tiny squeak. The sparkly ballet dancer was right where I remembered, between the gnome and the chicken. I lifted her out for a closer look. Delicately made with jewel-encrusted slippers and a tiara, most assuredly diamonds. She looked like she belonged in a royal music box. Or a multi-million dollar egg.

The floor board creaked. I turned to see a blur as Alex Whitaker rammed into me. I bounced off the curio, the sharp frame corner stabbed my back and I fell face first. The little dancer rolled under the sofa.

I scrambled across the floor, trying to gain traction on the thin carpet. My feet got tangled in my fluffy dress.

"Let me have her!" Alex Whitaker screamed. "Give her back!" His voice loud and hot and familiar. The man who attacked me in Jaime's closet, I thought.

He punched at my shoulders, finally grabbing one and wrenched me onto my back. He put his hands on my throat and squeezed.

I tried to scream, but no air or sound escaped from his grip. I couldn't breathe. I couldn't think.

"*Where is she?*" He yelled and squeezed.

I flailed at him, punching, kicking, scratching his hands around my throat.

"You killed him! I could've saved him!" He was nearly hysterical. He leaned down closer to me. "You killed my father!"

I grabbed his hair and pulled with everything I had. He

looked surprised. He loosened his grip. I punched him in the throat. Hard. He fell back, coughing. Sputtering.

I kicked him off me and scrambled up. I grabbed the edge of the curio cabinet and slammed it down on top of him.

He screamed. The glass crashed and broke. Thin shards scattered, the heavy wood frame knocked into his face.

I ran.

I slipped on the carpet, stumbling toward the door. It flung open and I ran straight into the arms of Officer Prickle.

Twenty minutes later, I sat on Mary-Louise's back porch in one of her dirty plastic Adirondack chairs, my hands handcuffed in my lap. A paramedic finished treating a cut near my eye. It stung like nobody's business.

A steady stream of police personnel, technicians and medical staff traveled between the gate and the house. Ransom and Parker were the last to arrive.

"Elliott," Ransom said. His face held no expression, but I saw worry in his eyes. He gently took my hands in his. He stroked my fingers. "You okay?"

Two medics wheeled Alex out of the house on a gurney, his hands handcuffed to the rail. I looked away. "I am now."

He touched my face. "How does this happen to you?"

I snort-laughed. "I was just thinking that. How come I keep getting beat up on cases, but you and Parker never do?"

"We carry guns," Parker said, then went in the house.

"Don't even think it," Ransom said.

"The director of the prestigious Ballantyne Foundation does not carry a gun. This isn't Texas, for shit's sake. Though a mace canister probably isn't a bad idea." I lifted the handcuffs. "Can you take these off now?"

"Hey, Prickle," Ransom called and stood. "Explain," he added when Prickle ambled out the back door.

"Surveillance saw her partner enter the fugitive's house and called for backup. When I arrived, these two were assaulting one another, probably a fight over splitting the loot. She was escaping when I came on scene."

Ransom looked at me and mouthed, "loot?"

"Alex Whitaker is not my partner. He assaulted *me* when *he* broke in. I had permission from the homeowner."

"Fugitive," Prickle said.

"Fugitive or not, she still owns the house. Alex must have followed me from the funeral home. Somehow he knew I'd figured it all out from the program in my hand. Or the look on my face. You'll have to ask him for the entire story, but my nutshell..." I looked down at my handcuffs, thinking how to word things while keeping Gilbert Goodsen in a positive light.

I left out the viaticals, both the legal and the maybe fraud kind, and told them my theory.

"Alex must have figured out the ballerina trinket his father sold actually belonged inside the missing Fabergé egg. Between him and his father and Gilbert, a lot of appraisers and Google searches were involved."

I could practically feel Officer Prickle's skepticism, but I chose to ignore it and spoke to Ransom instead.

"Alex Whitaker's been frantically searching for the figurine. He called the ballerina a 'her' and I thought he meant Jaime when he said he wanted her back that night in the closet. He didn't want Jaime back, he wanted the ballerina. He was desperate. He attacked me at Jaime's house searching for it, most likely killed her on Gilbert's boat searching for it. Almost killed me here for it. But he never got his hands on it."

"So you found the egg?" Ransom asked.

"Nope, but I found the ballerina. Inside, under the sofa."

"After all this, your egg hunt was unsuccessful," Ransom said.

"The hunt's not over until the little bunny sings, my friend."

I lifted my cuffed hands, ready to be set free.

TWENTY-FOUR

(Day #6: Wednesday Afternoon)

Luck finally shined her face upon me when Mary-Louise left me a voicemail, not only giving me permission to go inside her house, but stating she was heading to the station to turn herself in. Her Uncle Horace finally convinced her. I played the message for Ransom, Parker, and Officer Prickle shortly after they agreed not to arrest me. Or maybe it was shortly before.

Either way, I didn't stick around to press my precious newfound luck. Besides, I might be able to catch the end of the Wonderland Tea.

I climbed into the Mini and checked the rearview. A bruised cheek and a bandaged head. Well, that's that. I couldn't go to the Big House, I'd frighten the children. Plus, if Mr. Ballantyne saw my injuries, he might forbid me from investigating future inquiries. An obvious head wound wasn't quite as discreet as it sounded.

What I really needed to do was head to Bennett's Funeral Home. It would be awful to have a stranger tell Gilbert about Alex's arrest for Jaime's murder. Especially at her viewing, across the hall from the killer's father's funeral. I debated stopping at home to change, but I knew this news might make it to Bennett's faster than I did.

As I turned into the winding drive, a stream of cars pulled out onto Cabana, all with their lights on, following a sedate black hearse. Presumable Peter Whitaker's funeral procession on their way to a local cemetery.

I parked near the entrance and walked into the quiet lobby. Soft organ music drifted out the open door to Jaime's viewing room. I peeked inside. Alicia Birnbaum sat with three women, two of whom I recognized from mahj, and Gilbert sat alone.

Without looking at the casket, I tiptoed over and tugged his sleeve. When he turned, I put a finger to my lips and indicated to follow me to the lobby.

"Elli, what happened to your face?"

"Shhh, let's not disturb the others," I said, and walked over to a pair of parlor chairs in the far corner.

I scooted closer until our cushions were nearly touching. "The police made an arrest in Jaime's death. Alex Whitaker."

I expected him to shout or cry or something loud, but he gasped out, "What? Alex?"

"You knew him well?"

"Not well. Only with his father, Peter. His sister Kat's been asking me for the egg back. Why would he kill Jaime?"

"Was Kat the one harassing you?"

He dropped his head in his hands, slowly nodding up and down. "She really wanted it back, said if I couldn't give them the life insurance money back, then I had to give them the egg." He looked at me, tears fell onto his cheeks. "It's my fault. It's all my fault. I told her I didn't have it anymore, that Jaime did."

"It's not your fault, Gil. Alex killed her. His rage and grief consumed him." I lifted a torn flower applique on my dress. "He did this looking for the ballerina."

"Ballerina?"

"One of the figurines on the trinket tray Mr. Whitaker sold you. It was part of the egg, the surprise inside."

"But Kat never mentioned a ballerina."

"I'm not sure she knew, but either way, I doubt they would've told you. Makes the egg worth so much more."

"Jaime died for a trinket." Gilbert sat with his head low, softly crying.

I rubbed his back, then whispered, "I'm sorry, Gilbert."

*   *   *

Pulling into my cottage, I realized Ransom was spot on. I didn't find the egg. And if the Whitakers didn't have it, who did? I sighed. I turned off the car, sitting there, staring at my steering wheel. My suspect list was the same one I had the day before with Sid when we went to visit Judith.

I slapped my head. "Ouch!" I said aloud. "Judith said something about Jaime and how she had her way with words."

Like about not wanting the egg. Jaime told me she didn't want it, like she didn't want to keep it. She never said she didn't take it.

But where did she put it? And I almost slapped my head again. The slippery clue from earlier clinked into place. The one place Gil couldn't go.

I took ten minutes to wash up and put on my best tennis whites. As a non-athletic person who's never lifted a racket, I wore a white polo and crisp white shorts and clean white Vans. Once properly attired, I drove straight to Haverhill.

I called in a favor from Jake, the tennis pro at the club. He left me a gate pass, and I arrived at the clubhouse a few minutes later.

Walking across the pink marbled floors, I remembered being there with Ransom. It felt as if months had gone by instead of days. So much had happened. I passed an attendant on my way to the ladies' locker room and nodded as if I belonged.

It was quiet, mostly deserted. Fine wood lockers lined the walls, jutting out in short rows. Soft carpeting covered the floor, and marble tile led to a series of entries: the vanity area, the restrooms, the showers, then branched toward the steam room, plunge pool, and sauna. A lovely way to spend the afternoon. Except I wasn't there to spa, I was there to hunt.

Each locker had a brass nameplate on the front, which was a serious break for me. I did not want to test my theory three hundred times. As it was, I searched nearly half the lockers before I found the one I needed tucked in the last row. Two lockers, side by side. Birnbaum and Goodsen. I punched Gil's office alarm code into the tiny silver number pad and the Goodsen locker clicked open.

Alicia must not have had the heart to clean it out yet. A sharp white tennis skirt and performance top hung from the top bar. A variety of personal items sat on the shelf. Toiletries, socks, a bottle of perfume. But below, in the back corner, wrapped in club towel, was the Fabergé egg. It was more beautiful than Gilbert described, with gold trim and a stunning, deep orange fire opal for the clasp. I opened it. The perfect spot inside to fit a miniature ballerina. Gilbert was right. Jaime had it the whole time.

EPILOGUE

(Day #7: Thursday)

I spent part of the afternoon by the pool, sipping a glass of Carla's homemade lemonade iced tea. The ice settled into the glass as I settled into the sunshine.

"How's the eye?" Ransom asked.

"Blue. Black," I said. "Makes me look tough. That's what Zibby Archibald said, anyway."

"You came back to the Tea yesterday? I didn't think you would."

"Yeah, but after it was over. The committee was having their wrap-up meeting."

Ransom sat across from me and poured himself a glass from the pitcher. "Did she win the prize with the teapot you replaced?"

"You heard about that?"

"I hear about everything."

"I doubt that," I said with a half-laugh, half-snort. "But no, she didn't win. Nurse Elaine did."

"Nurse Elaine?"

I shrugged, not wanting to explain the moniker. Or the fact that she broke up with Matty and he and I had a date on Friday. I sipped my lemonade. "Zibby wasn't too disappointed. Gave her incentive for next year."

"Zibby with incentive, that should keep your hands full," Ransom said. He leaned back, crossed his legs at the ankle. "You ready to give up your discreet inquiry business yet?"

"Ha! I'm just getting started. Knocked another seventy-five hours off my PI requirements. Now only a smidge over five thousand to go." I poured a little more lemonade. "I'll tell you, like the cranky wicked smart tv Dr. House said, everybody lies. To protect themselves from embarrassment or jail or maybe out of compulsion, patients always lie. And for me, it's clients."

"You're just figuring that out?"

"I'm only a thousand hours in, so I think I'm pretty quick on uptake, considering. But seriously, had Gilbert Goodsen spilled his beans in the emergency room on Day One, most of this would've been avoided."

"Except for finding the egg," Ransom said. "Since Jaime had it all along."

"Just saying."

Even though I found the egg, neither Gilbert nor Kat Whitaker wanted it. Too many horrible things transpired for both families because of it. They let Jane auction it off through her gallery in Savannah. They donated the proceeds to two charities: one in Jaime's name and one in Peter Whitaker's.

Gilbert did accept the payout for his wife's life insurance policy. He convinced his attorney to accept actual money instead of the egg, and the Gil-animals fees were filed in a timely manner.

"How about saying yes. To a date. Since you said you're ready. This Saturday night?"

Tod appeared before I could reply. I tried not to look grateful.

"The Ballantyne Board short list is no longer needed." Tod slowly poured lemonade into a tall glass. "Mr. Ballantyne just appointed Matty Gannon to fill Leo's old spot. You're hosting a welcome lunch for him on Saturday." He tipped his glass at me and walked back into the Big House.

Ransom stood, finished his drink. Set the glass on the table. He took his sunglasses from his pocket and put them on. "So Saturday at seven, then?"

"We're still on?"

"Oh, it's on."

Kendel Lynn

Kendel Lynn is a Southern California native who now parks her flip-flops in Dallas, Texas. She read her first Alfred Hitchcock and the Three Investigators at the age of seven and has loved mysteries ever since. Her debut novel, *Board Stiff*, the first Elliott Lisbon mystery, is an Agatha Award nominee for Best First Novel. Along with writing and reading, Kendel spends her time editing, designing, and figuring out ways to avoid the gym but still eat cupcakes for dinner. Catch up with her at www.kendellynn.com.

Be sure to check out Elliott's prequel novella
SWITCH BACK featured in

OTHER PEOPLE'S BAGGAGE

Kendel Lynn, Gigi Pandian, Diane Vallere

Baggage claim can be terminal. These are the stories of what happened after three women with a knack for solving mysteries each grabbed the wrong bag.

MIDNIGHT ICE by Diane Vallere: When interior decorator Madison Night crosses the country to distance herself from a recent breakup, she learns it's harder to escape her past than she thought, and diamonds are rarely a girl's best friend.

SWITCH BACK by Kendel Lynn: Ballantyne Foundation director Elliott Lisbon travels to Texas after inheriting an entire town, but when she learns the benefactor was murdered, she must unlock the small town's big secrets or she'll never get out alive.

FOOL'S GOLD by Gigi Pandian: When a world-famous chess set is stolen from a locked room during the Edinburgh Fringe Festival, historian Jaya Jones and her magician best friend must outwit actresses and alchemists to solve the baffling crime.

Available at booksellers nationwide and online

Visit www.henerypress.com for details

Henery Press Mystery Books

And finally, before you go...
Here are a few other mysteries
you might enjoy:

PILLOW STALK

Diane Vallere

A Mad for Mod Mystery (#1)

Interior Decorator Madison Night has modeled her life after Doris Day's character in *Pillow Talk*, but when a killer targets women dressed like the bubbly actress, Madison's signature sixties style places her in the middle of a homicide investigation.

The local detective connects the new crimes to a twenty-year old cold case, and Madison's long-trusted contractor emerges as the leading suspect. As the body count piles up like a stack of plush pillows, Madison uncovers a Soviet spy, a campaign to destroy all Doris Day movies, and six minutes of film that will change her life forever.

Available at booksellers nationwide and online

Visit www.henerypress.com for details

LOWCOUNTRY BOIL

Susan M. Boyer

A Liz Talbot Mystery (#1)

Private Investigator Liz Talbot is a modern Southern belle: she blesses hearts and takes names. She carries her Sig 9 in her Kate Spade handbag, and her golden retriever, Rhett, rides shotgun in her hybrid Escape. When her grandmother is murdered, Liz high-tails it back to her South Carolina island home to find the killer.

She's fit to be tied when her police-chief brother shuts her out of the investigation, so she opens her own. Then her long-dead best friend pops in and things really get complicated. When more folks start turning up dead in this small seaside town, Liz must use more than just her wits and charm to keep her family safe, chase down clues from the hereafter, and catch a psychopath before he catches her.

Available at booksellers nationwide and online

Visit www.henerypress.com for details

DOUBLE WHAMMY

Gretchen Archer

A Davis Way Crime Caper (#1)

Davis Way thinks she's hit the jackpot when she lands a job as the fifth wheel on an elite security team at the fabulous Bellissimo Resort and Casino in Biloxi, Mississippi. But once there, she runs straight into her ex-ex husband, a rigged slot machine, her evil twin, and a trail of dead bodies. Davis learns the truth and it does not set her free—in fact, it lands her in the pokey.

Buried under a mistaken identity, unable to seek help from her family, her hot streak runs cold until her landlord Bradley Cole steps in. Make that her landlord, lawyer, and love interest. With his help, Davis must win this high stakes game before her luck runs out.

Available at booksellers nationwide and online

Visit www.henerypress.com for details

DINERS, DIVES & DEAD ENDS

Terri L. Austin

A Rose Strickland Mystery (#1)

As a struggling waitress and part-time college student, Rose Strickland's life is stalled in the slow lane. But when her close friend, Axton, disappears, Rose suddenly finds herself serving up more than hot coffee and flapjacks. Now she's hashing it out with sexy bad guys and scrambling to find clues in a race to save Axton before his time runs out.

With her anime-loving bestie, her septuagenarian boss, and a pair of IT wise men along for the ride, Rose discovers political corruption, illegal gambling, and shady corporations. She's gone from zero to sixty and quickly learns when you're speeding down the fast lane, it's easy to crash and burn.

Available at booksellers nationwide and online

Visit www.henerypress.com for details

ARTIFACT

Gigi Pandian

A Jaya Jones Treasure Hunt Mystery (#1)

Historian Jaya Jones discovers the secrets of a lost Indian treasure may be hidden in a Scottish legend from the days of the British Raj. But she's not the only one on the trail...

From San Francisco to London to the Highlands of Scotland, Jaya must evade a shadowy stalker as she follows hints from the hastily scrawled note of her dead lover to a remote archaeological dig. Helping her decipher the cryptic clues are her magician best friend, a devastatingly handsome art historian with something to hide, and a charming archaeologist running for his life.

Available at booksellers nationwide and online

Visit www.henerypress.com for details

THE AMBITIOUS CARD

John Gaspard

An Eli Marks Mystery (#1)

The life of a magician isn't all kiddie shows and card tricks. Sometimes it's murder. Especially when magician Eli Marks very publicly debunks a famed psychic, and said psychic ends up dead. The evidence, including a bloody King of Diamonds playing card (one from Eli's own Ambitious Card routine), directs the police right to Eli.

As more psychics are slain, and more King cards rise to the top, Eli can't escape suspicion. Things get really complicated when romance blooms with a beautiful psychic, and Eli discovers she's the next target for murder, and he's scheduled to die with her. Now Eli must use every trick he knows to keep them both alive and reveal the true killer.

Available at booksellers nationwide and online

Visit www.henerypress.com for details

PORTRAIT OF A DEAD GUY

Larissa Reinhart

A Cherry Tucker Mystery (#1)

In Halo, Georgia, folks know Cherry Tucker as big in mouth, small in stature, and able to sketch a portrait faster than buck-shot rips from a ten gauge -- but commissions are scarce. So when the well-heeled Branson family wants to memorialize their murdered son in a coffin portrait, Cherry scrambles to win their patronage from her small town rival.

As the clock ticks toward the deadline, Cherry faces more trouble than just a controversial subject. Between ex-boyfriends, her flaky family, an illegal gambling ring, and outwitting a killer on a spree, Cherry finds herself painted into a corner she'll be lucky to survive.

Available at booksellers nationwide and online

Visit www.henerypress.com for details

FRONT PAGE FATALITY

LynDee Walker

A Headlines in High Heels Mystery (#1)

Crime reporter Nichelle Clarke's days can flip from macabre to comical with a beep of her police scanner. Then an ordinary accident story turns extraordinary when evidence goes missing, a prosecutor vanishes, and a sexy Mafia boss shows up with the headline tip of a lifetime.

As Nichelle gets closer to the truth, her story gets more dangerous. Armed with a notebook, a hunch, and her favorite stilettos, Nichelle races to splash these shady dealings across the front page before this deadline becomes her last.

Available at booksellers nationwide and online

Visit www.henerypress.com for details

CIRCLE OF INFLUENCE

Annette Dashofy

A Zoe Chambers Mystery (#1)

Zoe Chambers, paramedic and deputy coroner in rural Pennsylvania's tight-knit Vance Township, has been privy to a number of local secrets over the years, some of them her own. But secrets become explosive when a dead body is found in the Township Board President's abandoned car.

As a January blizzard rages, Zoe and Police Chief Pete Adams launch a desperate search for the killer, even if it means uncovering secrets that could not only destroy Zoe and Pete, but also those closest to them.

Available at booksellers nationwide and online

Visit www.henerypress.com for details

In the mood for something fun?

Check out this lively chick lit romp
from the Henery Press Humor Collection

THE BREAKUP DOCTOR
Phoebe Fox

The Breakup Doctor Series (#1)

Call Brook Ogden a matchmaker-in-reverse. Let others bring
people together; Brook, licensed mental health counselor, picks up
the pieces after things come apart. When her own therapy practice
collapses, she maintains perfect control: landing on her feet with a
weekly advice-to-the-lovelorn column and a successful consulting
service as the Breakup Doctor: on call to help you shape up after
you breakup.

Then her relationship suddenly crumbles and Brook finds herself
engaging in almost every bad-breakup behavior she preaches
against. And worse, she starts a rebound relationship with the
most inappropriate of men: a dangerously sexy bartender with
anger-management issues—who also happens to be a former
patient.

As her increasingly out-of-control behavior lands her at rock-
bottom, Brook realizes you can't always handle a messy breakup
neatly—and that sometimes you can't pull yourself together until
you let yourself fall apart..

Available June 2014

Visit www.henerypress.com for details

11218957R00136

Made in the USA
San Bernardino, CA
10 May 2014